ABOUT THE AUTHOR

Dionne Haynes spent most of her childhood in Plymouth, England. She graduated from medical school in London and enjoyed a career as a doctor for over twenty years. After returning to Plymouth, she traded medicine for a career writing historical fiction. *The Second Mrs Thistlewood* is her second novel.

ALSO BY DIONNE HAYNES

Winds of Change
Running With The Wind
The Winter Years

For more information and updates:
www.dionnehaynes.com

THE SECOND MRS THISTLEWOOD

DIONNE HAYNES

Allium

Published by Allium Books 2020
22 Victoria Road, St Austell, Cornwall, PL25 4QD

First published by Allium Books in 2020
www.alliumbooks.com

A CIP catalogue record for this book is available from the British Library

ISBN: 978-1-9162109-1-2

Cover design by Robin Vuchnich, Mycustombookcover.com

For my mum

CONTENTS

PART I
1814

CHAPTER 1

SUGAR PLUMS. Bittersweet almonds surrounded by a smooth sugar coating. My favourite confections. I select a pale pink pebble from the top of the mound, then replace the lid on an elegant decorative bowl given to me by my mother. Arthur has never liked this bowl. He says the blue forget-me-nots are crudely painted and the very idea of a sugar bowl is extravagant and inappropriate while the poor starve in hovels they call home. I dread to think how he'd react if he knew I was hiding these little treasures within it.

I pop the comfit into my mouth and run my tongue over the smooth coating. The quality of the coloured shells varies between confectioners. This batch is perfect. The impulsive purchase forced me to settle for a cheap cut of meat for dinner, but with a decent gravy, I doubt Arthur will notice.

Arthur's right, of course. It's wrong to enjoy expensive treats while children run around in ragged clothes, their bellies hurting with hunger. Factory owners grow wealthy from the efficiency of machines, but the unfortunate souls who operate them live in squalor, barely able to put food on the table.

The sugar melts away and now it's a bitter almond's turn to assault my senses. I cannot help but crunch it before swallowing, savouring a flavour reminiscent of earthy wood. The truth of the matter is that if I stopped eating sugar plums, those men, women and children would continue to starve. They'd still lack warm clothing and suitable shoes, and their homes would remain unheated. And so, with a clear conscious, I swallow and digest the tasty morsel, reassuring myself that Arthur is doing everything he can to ease the plight of those who are suffering. His vigour and devotion to the cause is admirable, and he has my full support.

Arthur is reading the latest edition of the *London Gazette*. The lines in his furrowed brow appear deep because of shadows cast by the candles on a small table next to him. I'm mesmerised by orange flames flickering in the hearth and enjoying the soft ticking of burning coals. Now and then a downdraught strikes the coal basket and puffs pungent clouds of smoke into the room, causing us both to cough.

I draw my gaze away from the fire and drink in the vision that is my husband. Arthur is of slender build with eyes the colour of hazelnut shells and neatly cropped dark brown hair swept forward to frame his handsome face. His long sideburns are precisely trimmed, and he cuts a striking figure in a white shirt, blue pantaloons and a long blue coat. His image is still smart and his bearing commanding despite his military career ending several years ago. Arthur's only blemish is a slight scar beneath his chin. And don't let his Lincolnshire accent fool you. This gentleman is well educated. Although he appears sombre and brooding, he's simply preoccupied, processing information, thinking, seeking a way to overthrow the constitution and improve the lives of the many who are far less fortunate than ourselves.

Things haven't been easy for us. When Arthur sold his inheritance for an annual income bond, our new-found financial comfort evaporated eighteen months later when the purchaser of the estate went bankrupt. Reliant upon Arthur's savings and investments, I run the household on a tight budget and without the help of a maid. But I am one of the lucky ones.

It's a wonder Arthur was ever attracted to me. I'm plain and unremarkable with mousy brown hair, grey eyes, and lacking the elegant curves that most men desire. But I'm smart of mind and share Arthur's political views, and I do my best to encourage him in the fight against tyranny.

'I'll be out until late tomorrow evening.' Arthur folds his newspaper in half, then in half again. 'I'm meeting with Watson, Ings and Davidson, and expect a few others to join us. We're setting up a group called the Society of Spencean Philanthropists. Thomas Spence may have gone to the grave, but we will keep his ideas alive.'

I dip my head in acknowledgement. Mr Spence had been a revolutionary thinker, demanding annual parliaments, elected representatives and universal suffrage. He proposed the fair distribution of land between every man, woman and child.

Arthur slaps the newspaper against the arm of his chair. 'What gives the lords and their followers the right to partition common land and claim it as their own? It belongs to us all. They should tear down the walls and fences and give everyone their rightful share.'

The latter ideal is one I've always had trouble accepting. 'A noble principle, Arthur, but is it practical? What happens when more children are born? How will the land be redistributed? And what about when someone dies? It would become a legal nightmare and could lead to disputes and division within communities.'

Arthur clenches his fingers and I recognise the warning to press no more on this matter. Instead, I try to win back his favour. 'Complex it may be, but I have faith in you. You'll resolve this and other troublesome issues during your meetings. If only I could attend them too.'

'Perhaps one day, Susan. But for now, we plan to meet in public houses and I'd prefer you to stay out of those. They're not suitable for a respectable woman.'

I bristle at Arthur's condescending tone even though I realise he's protecting my reputation. I have no issue with the clientele of public houses, but meetings can become rowdy with the occasional outbreak of fist fights.

Arthur is quiet again. His chin tilts down, but his eyes are boring into me. When I meet his gaze, he smiles. I know what's on his mind. I'm not in the mood, but ever the dutiful wife, I throw him a coquettish smile.

'Come, Susan. It's getting late. Let us retire to bed.'

My stomach twists. Maybe I'll conceive a child. Julian's a delightful boy, a fine stepson, but not of my flesh. Arthur reaches for my hand. I yield to his warm grasp and he leads me along the corridor. I've not angered him this evening, so I'm hopeful he'll be gentle with me.

CHAPTER 2

SPICES TICKLE my lips while liquid chocolate coats my tongue in a veil of velvety luxury. Christmas is fast approaching, and Mother has arrived in London for a brief visit.

'Are you happy, Susan?'

A mouthful of chocolate sticks in my throat. 'Yes. Why do you ask?'

Mother reaches out to stroke my cheek. 'You're pale, your eyes are dull, and your smile no longer sparkles.'

My attention drifts to the windows coated with condensation. 'I'm very well,' I say, redirecting my eyes to meet my mother's penetrating gaze. 'In fact, I couldn't be better.'

Her eyebrows lift. 'Susan? Are you expecting?'

I grin, feeling a glow bloom in my cheeks.

'Why did you hold back such wonderful news? We must celebrate! Does Arthur know?'

'Not yet.' A shadow falls across the windows of the chocolate-house. The temperature drops and I stifle a shiver. 'It's too soon.'

'When did you last bleed?' She envelops my icy fingers

with her warm hands. The gesture is loving, reassuring, protective.

'Six or seven weeks.'

'Then say nothing until after Christmas. I'll tell your father and you tell Arthur. We'll write to each other and describe their reactions. What fine news to start the new year!'

The affection in her eyes causes tears to well up in mine. How I miss her! The snatched moments during brief visits to London are little compensation for the long months spent apart. She's more than a mother to me. She's my dearest friend.

'Look at you.' Mother laughs, then adds, 'Stone Cold Susan starting to melt and all because of a baby.'

Her comment surprises me. 'What do you mean, "Stone Cold Susan"? You make me sound uncaring.'

Mother draws her hands away from mine and lowers her voice. 'You've altered since marrying Arthur, and I worry for you. His passion for changing the state of the country is tipping towards something dangerous.'

'You think Arthur will turn violent?' I'm horrified by the thought. 'Mother, he only wants to encourage the common man to stand up for his rights. He'll campaign with rhetoric to urge the repressed members of society to take a stance against tyranny. He'll not promote bloodshed!'

Mother dabs her lips with a lace-edged square of linen. 'I fear his words will incite a mob and have them baying for the heads of political leaders.'

'Mother, you worry too much and overestimate Arthur's influence. The Spencean group meets only to share common ideals and a dream of equality across the nation. How could such a meeting ever tip the balance towards the massacre you speak of? Arthur's a gentleman. He'll find a peaceful way forward.'

'Arthur has a violent streak, Susan.'

I fidget on the padded chair, shifting my weight to relieve the pressure on my bruised flesh. 'He's a retired soldier. Violence is an inevitable part of his character. The important thing is that he keeps it for the battlefield.'

She fixes me with piercing eyes. 'And does he?'

I force myself to meet her gaze but say nothing. Mother shakes her head and drains the chocolate from her cup.

It saddened me to watch Mother board the stagecoach, but I put on a brave smile and waved goodbye. I can still smell her lily-of-the-valley fragrance while pretending she's beside me as I walk home.

Frigid air lingers indoors, the fires long since extinguished. There's an emptiness now Mother has gone. Arthur's at a meeting and I'm glad to have time alone. A mild cramp niggles at the bottom of my belly. I imagine a baby growing inside, pushing my innards aside to make way for lengthening limbs. I rest my hand above the ache and press with my palm to ease the pain a little, taking comfort from the knowledge that I'm to become a mother.

I set the fire and watch a flame reach towards the chimney flue. I hold out my hands to warm them, then struggle to my feet. The fire will take at least an hour to heat the parlour, so I need to fetch a pelisse.

Our bedroom is bitterly cold. Arthur will not allow a fire to burn in this room, insisting we have enough blankets to warm us while we sleep. I open the clothes press and remove my newest pelisse from the top shelf. As I close the door, something catches my eye. Nestled on a pile of shifts is a small parcel wrapped in coloured floral paper and tied with green ribbon. A gift from my mother. I unwrap the bottle of perfume and admire the pale amber liquid. A thin wax seal holds a smooth stopper in place, and after I've removed the seal and inhaled the scent of white rose, I notice the gift is from Floris. Arthur would never allow such an indulgence at an expensive parfumier. I dab a few drops on my neck and wrists, then stow the bottle in the press to save the precious liquid for special occasions.

I have an urge to empty my bladder. Squatting over a chamber pot, the pleasure of the unexpected gift recedes to nothing and I'm left with a void in my soul. I pull the chamber pot from beneath me and gaze at the contents. A pool of blood confirms my fears. God does not want me to bear a child.

Arthur returns home reeking of ale and sweat. He kisses me on the cheek and says he loves me. Tears trickle, and within moments I'm blubbing like an infant. His expression softens, and he hugs me to his chest.

'Susan, whatever has happened?'

I wipe my nose and work hard to calm myself. 'I was with child, Arthur. But it was not to be.'

Arthur holds me at arm's length, his face contorting as he processes the disappointing news. Then he turns his back towards me and storms out of the room.

PART II
1815

CHAPTER 3

THE AROMA of warm gingerbread draws a gurgle from my stomach. I inhale deeply and admire the little cakes fresh from the oven. I'm always a competent baker, but this is my finest batch to date.

A commotion at the front door announces Arthur's arrival. My limbs tense. He was not due home until later this afternoon.

'Susan?' His loud voice is laced with agitation.

'Here, Arthur.' I rush into the hallway to help him remove his overcoat. I shake out the wrinkles and hang the coat on the battered stand by the door.

His face is taut with concern, his eyes muddied by angst. He sniffs the air and his grimace slackens into a boyish smile. 'Gingerbread?'

Arthur always chides me for having cakes or pastries in the house, for it's insulting to indulge in such niceties while others dare not dream of them. But today is a special occasion. It's the start of a new year.

Arthur holds my hand and raises my fingers to his lips. 'This will be the year we overthrow the tyrants in government and give the common man the fair treatment he deserves.'

He smiles and pulls me closer.

'Do you have a plan?'

'A few ideas.' He grins and bends forward as if to kiss me when the front door flies open. He pulls away and stands erect as Julian, my stepson, stumbles into the house.

Arthur's smile fades. 'You're unsteady on your feet, Julian.'

The twelve-year-old grins. 'Tripped on the top step.'

Arthur grabs a fistful of Julian's wool coat and pushes him against the wall. 'Have you been drinking?'

I dislike the ominous tone.

'No, sir.' Julian pales. 'Just running about with my friends, that's all.'

Arthur clenches Julian's jaw and forces his mouth open, sniffing his breath. I avert my eyes and stare at the stained tiles on the floor. I know what's coming.

'What have you had?'

Arthur is too strong for the boy and Julian's feet hover an inch or two above the floor. No matter how often this happens, I cannot get used to it.

'I'm sorry, sir. Truly. It won't happen again.' The tremor in his voice tells me he's crying, but I dare not intervene.

'Well?'

'Gin, sir.' A sob. 'I had to. Everyone else was. John Martin found a bottle and shared it. I tried refusing, but they started on me and I had to take a few swigs to shut them up.'

'So you were weak-willed. You'll not grow into a fine gentleman if you're easily swayed by friends. I'm disappointed, Julian.'

I suppress a comment about Arthur's own gullibility. His migration towards radical politics coincided with the discovery of new friends at card tables. No doubt his poor investment choices were similarly misguided.

Arthur releases his grip and takes a step back. I clench my fingers and close my eyes, tight. A loud whack echoes around the hallway after Arthur's palm connects with Julian's face, then a dull thud as Julian's head strikes the wall. I look up. Julian's cheeks are shiny with tears and a livid red handprint lingers on his cheek. Blood seeps from his left nostril.

Arthur turns to face me and my legs quiver.

He beams at me. 'Time to eat that delicious-smelling gingerbread.'

Julian and I exchange fleeting glances. I want to embrace the boy, reassure him that all will be well, but I daren't. Instead, we troop towards the kitchen and settle at the table, pretending to enjoy the gingerbread that sticks in our throats.

'I need fresh air,' I say, preparing to push myself up from my chair.

'It's too late to be out by yourself and I'm expected at Watson's this evening. You'll stay indoors.'

I glance at the window. It's bright outside with dusk at least an hour away. Julian discreetly clears his throat.

'Julian can escort me,' I say. 'It'll be an opportunity to show his maturity.' I look at Julian and he gives a small grateful smile. 'Arthur? Will you let him go with me for one turn about the park?'

Arthur rises to his feet, the chair legs screeching across the flagstones. 'Stand up.' His left eyebrow twitches and his nostrils flare.

I catch my breath and do as he commands. My knees tremble and I bite down hard on my bottom lip.

'I said you will remain indoors.'

'But Arthur, it's still light.' I regret uttering the words the moment they fall from my lips.

Arthur steps towards me, his eyes narrowed and upper lip twitching. I should apologise, but the words remain buried in my throat. I lift my head and we lock gazes. Julian slips out of his chair and stands beside the table. I raise my hand to offer him reassurance when I'm struck by the full force of Arthur's palm against the left side of my jaw. The blow knocks me sideways. I stumble and fall, landing on my right side. My cheek stings and my hip throbs. I try to get up, but my legs have turned weak and I flounder helplessly.

Veins bulge in Arthur's neck. Saliva bubbles at the corners of his mouth. His staring eyes are flinty and there's a tight smile on his lips. He reaches for me with one hand and grasps my wrist, pulling me upright. As soon as I'm standing, he drives his knee deep into my belly. Doubled over, I fight for breath, but the air won't come. My vision greys and I sink to my knees, then collapse onto the unforgiving floor.

The cold flagstones revive me. No husband should treat his wife this way. I feel a rush of energy, and rage surges through my veins. I drag air into my lungs and take a moment to gather my senses. The strength returns to my muscles and I clamber up from the floor. Howling, I lunge at Arthur, pommel his chest and kick hard at his shins, eager to give him a fraction of the pain he so often inflicts upon me. Arthur's strong. He grasps my wrists and throws me against the kitchen table. I glance around, desperate for Julian to intervene, but he has left the room. Arthur pins me to the table top, then wraps his fingers tight around my neck.

He snarls like a vicious dog. 'You took a vow to obey. Do not disrespect me again.'

Arthur cocks his head to one side and watches me thrash about, fighting for air. There's a flicker of satisfaction in his eyes when I attempt to kick him away, but he presses his thighs against my shins, and I waste my effort. He relaxes the grip on my neck, and I take gulping breaths. Arthur smooths away invisible creases on his jacket, then turns to leave the kitchen.

I lie there on the table, gasping, staring at deep cracks in the ceiling. My heart pounds and my chest aches. Every day, from the moment I wake, I fear Arthur's violent tempers.

I have to end this marriage.

CHAPTER 4

WE HUDDLE TOGETHER in front of the fire, slices of bread skewered to the ends of our toasting forks. Usually I toast the bread alone and deliver it to the table, but the bite in the air and Arthur's good humour have brought the three of us together by the warmth of the hot coals. Julian is impatient and insists on removing his fork from the heat too soon, so his slice remains pale, limp and unable to draw the butter into its fabric.

Wisps of smoke rise from the bread, fragrant with the delicious aroma of breakfast. With our slices evenly coloured, Arthur and I make a dash for the table. After dabbing several small chunks of butter on to the toast, we watch the golden yellow puddles melt, then add a sparing layer of home-made apple jam. This March morning started with a frost and the fire is struggling to heat the kitchen, so we are all dressed in extra layers and relishing the warm sweet tea in our cups.

Arthur finishes his breakfast and blots his mouth with a corner of the tablecloth. 'The cost of bread will rise again soon,' he says, his expression turning serious. 'Time to be frugal with your spending.'

It's already a struggle to buy decent meat and undamaged vegetables on the pittance Arthur gives me each week. 'They intend to pass the Corn Bill?'

'They do. Fools! They'll inflict poverty, the scale of which this country has never seen.'

'Why would parliament pass such a bill? Do they not see those already starving on our streets?' Every time I step outdoors, I'm confronted by young children begging for scraps.

Arthur sighs. 'The country's governed by men who refuse to acknowledge the effects of their selfish actions. They'll forbid corn imports until the price at home rises above ten shillings a bushel.'

'Ten shillings! That's extortionate.'

'It is. Landowners and farmers won't complain. They'll make more money. With war in France likely to end soon, we should start importing corn again, but the rich whoresons are blocking the competition and dashing every hope of lower prices. With workers spending most of their wages on bread, they'll not be able to afford much else, so all prices will rise. Clothes, shoes, linen, coal, everything.'

The larder already holds little in reserve, and Arthur is unlikely to raise my housekeeping allowance so I'll have to make sacrifices like thousands of other women.

Arthur sniffs. 'We'll do what we can to protest but we can't stop the bill from passing.' He turns to Julian. 'I hope to have splendid news for you within the next few days.'

'What news, sir?' asks Julian, eyes bright with expectation.

'Thanks to a worthy contact or two, I expect confirmation of a place at Charterhouse.'

'What's Charterhouse?'

'A school. It's time you had a decent education. Your step-mother has performed well, but her breadth of knowledge is limited.'

I clamp my lips together and work hard to keep my expression impassive.

'If things were different, I'd oversee your lessons, but I'm occupied with affairs of my own and cannot commit the time required for a proper schoolroom, therefore you must go away to learn.'

Julian's face drops.

I place the tip of my index finger beneath his chin and force him to look at me. I want him to understand this change will be good for him. 'Charterhouse has an excellent reputation.'

Although we've heard tales of bullying at such institutions, Julian will fare better there, for neither of us is without bruises these days.

Arthur is oblivious to his son's disappointment. 'I see a glorious future for you, Julian. I hope you'll continue your studies at Oxford or Cambridge before embarking on a career that will improve the lives of our fellow countrymen.'

'What type of career, sir?' Julian asks, his voice cracking.

'Perhaps law, or politics?'

Julian hangs his head. 'I had hopes for an office apprenticeship. I'm competent with numbers and my handwriting is tidy.'

'You want to sit at a desk all day, hunched over a page of numbers? Has your stepmother turned you soft?'

Arthur pounds his clenched fist against the solid oak table top, causing us both to jump. I study scars left in the wood by the previous occupants of this house. There are deep gouges and black scorch marks, and I wonder if they appeared during happy family gatherings or volatile confrontations.

Julian clears his throat. 'Just a passing thought, sir. We must all do our bit to help those who are less fortunate and a career in politics would achieve that. My stepmother has often said I should use my knowledge for the greater good.'

The boy is a wonder. For several years, we have supported each other against Arthur's volatile moods. My heart will fracture when he goes away to school. But with Julian absent from the house, it will be easier to leave Arthur and not worry about the repercussions for my stepson.

'Thank you for securing this opportunity, sir. I promise to work hard at my studies and make you proud.'

Arthur's eyes are alight with pride and Julian forces a smile.

Arthur excuses himself from the table. Julian waits for creaking sounds to announce Arthur's ascent of the stairs. He rises from his chair and hesitates long enough for me to see tears in his eyes, then hurls himself at me and clings tightly.

'Will you be safe here without me?' he says.

Arthur flings open the kitchen door, creating a waft of chilly air. He staggers towards me, and I step back to avoid his flailing arms. I can't remember the last occasion Arthur was in such a state. He lowers himself onto a chair and tugs at his boots, removing one at a time and flinging them across the room. He rests his head on the kitchen table and closes his eyes. Cautiously, I approach. The flickering candlelight distorts the features of his face, making him ghoulish. His lips are parted and the cadence of his breathing suggests he has fallen asleep. I ease off his coat, praying I succeed without waking him. There's a long tear on one side which I must repair at first light because Arthur has no spare. Arthur stirs and heaves himself upright, groaning. I gasp and cover my mouth with my hands. There's a large bloodstain on his shirt.

Arthur opens one eye and peers at me from beneath a drooping lid. 'What?'

'Your shirt's covered with blood. Were you in a brawl?'

'Not exactly,' he murmurs.

'But you're injured.'

Arthur puts his elbows on the table and props his forehead on his hands. ''Tisn't my blood.'

He reeks of stale alcohol.

'Whoremongers did it.' He waggles a finger at me. 'Passed the Corn Law. I've had a... gruelling day.'

'At a Spenceans meeting?'

'No. Better. I stupported... supported a protest.' He belches and grins. 'Broken glass everywhere. From the rocks.'

'You threw rocks?' I can't imagine Arthur doing such a thing.

He stares into the distance. 'At Robinson's house. Asked for it. Pushed for the Born Kill... Corn Bill.' Arthur strokes the patch of dried blood. 'Troops fired.' He hiccoughs. 'Proper bullets.'

'Surely not!'

He laughs. 'Bullet killed a man. Brains blown out. Time for revloo... revolution. A proper war.'

Arthur's lids slide over his eyes and his breaths become slow and regular. As I watch the gentle rise and fall of his chest, hatred boils within me. I know he'd refuse to grant a divorce, and I'll not risk a beating by asking. I imagine plunging a knife deep into his chest and watching him draw his final gurgling breath. A butcher's daughter, I'm not squeamish and have slaughtered many chickens and lambs. But my liberty would be short-lived, and I'd hang for my crime.

I deserve a better life than this. No matter how long it takes, I'll find a way to set myself free.

CHAPTER 5

I FEEL SICK, but whether it's because of the smell of greasy juices oozing through the pastry casing of a mutton pie or the unseasonably chilly weather this April, I cannot tell. I angle my face towards the cloudless blue sky and take a deep breath before attempting another mouthful of fatty meat. Arthur is watching me, so I dare not leave this rare treat unfinished or I will suffer for wasting food and money. Bile rises to the back of my throat. I close my eyes and sink my teeth into something that should be pleasurable, fighting the urge to spew it over Arthur's shiny boots.

A carriage passes, kicking up a cloud of dust that coats my shoes. I give the fashionable female occupants my complete attention, envying their joyful faces and extravagant hats, while ignoring the nasty flavours assaulting my tongue. They make slow progress, these women parading through the park, exchanging secrets and giggling, no doubt discussing which eligible bachelors have taken their fancy now the London season is in full swing.

Julian is remarkably cheerful. After the initial disappointment of a confirmed place at Charterhouse, he now embraces the prospect of living anywhere but in the same house as Arthur. I cannot blame him. Arthur's fuse shortens by the day.

'Did you enjoy that?' Arthur watches me dab my lips with my fingertips.

I force a smile. 'Yes, thank you. It's rare for the three of us to venture out together as a family. We should do this more often.' Outside, in public, he cannot hurt us.

Arthur grunts. 'He'll do well at school,' he says, nodding towards Julian. 'He's a confident boy and should soon settle into the Charterhouse routine. The strict discipline won't shock him.'

No, it won't. Life will be easier at school. Julian is playing a game of marbles, his face beaming as he enjoys the companionship of new friends. I try to picture him sitting at a desk, absorbing information, scribbling notes with his quill, and immersing himself in the leisure activities permitted after lessons finish for the day. School will suit him.

'Right,' says Arthur, rising from the park bench, brushing flakes of pastry from his breeches. 'Now we've bought or ordered everything Julian needs, it's time to sort you, Susan.'

'Me?' I'm in my second-best dress, covered by a thick pelisse to prevent the breeze cutting through the muslin and chilling me to the bone.

Arthur's brow puckers and one corner of his mouth rises into a condescending leer. 'Can't have you looking like that when we deliver Julian to school. Your dresses are too plain, and your shoes... I've seen beggars walk in better footwear. We must invest in attire befitting of a Charterhouse parent.'

Nausea grips me. I dash behind a clump of bushes and empty the contents of my stomach. Light-headed and embarrassed, I hurry back to the bench. Arthur has disappeared. I study the group of boys, hoping to see Julian, but he too has gone. Then I rush towards the gate, fighting back tears, apologising to countless strangers as I press through a crowd of fashionable men and women. I fear Arthur has abandoned me and I must struggle with the long walk home.

At last, I spy Arthur and Julian laden with purchases, standing at the hackney coach stand on Hyde Park Corner. Arthur beckons to me. I quicken my pace and reach them in time to clamber into the last coach. It's a rickety affair with faded, peeling paintwork and straw spilling from holes in the tatty seats, but I prefer it to walking the stinking city streets.

I settle back and watch London slip past the windows. The winter smog has lifted. A pale mist hangs above the streets with skinny rays of sunshine poking through and reflecting off grimy window panes. The carriage stops at Cornhill near the Royal Exchange. Arthur jumps down from the carriage and holds out his hand, encouraging me to alight like a lady. He tosses coins to the coachman, then steers me towards Wood, a shoemaker's shop. I peer at Arthur, confused. This shop is notoriously expensive. He holds the door open and gestures for me to enter. Julian follows and makes straight for a chair where he sits and reads a chapbook. Ghost stories are his current tales of choice.

I am shown to a seat by a youthful man in smart attire with an apron tied at his waist. He kneels and places a wide strip of linen at my feet, then removes my tired old boots. I cringe as he handles my scuffed footwear, treating my boots with utmost care. Perhaps he fears they will disintegrate in his hands. Hiding my shame, I admire the merchandise displayed around the room. Exquisite shoes sit in neat pairs, in an array of colours, styles and decorations. They employ skilled craftsmen here.

An older man approaches. 'Mrs Thistlewood, it's a pleasure to welcome you today.'

I tilt my head in acknowledgement. Lost for words, I glance at Arthur. He smiles, then sits beside Julian and selects a newspaper from a selection laid out on a low rectangular table. Reassured by his demeanour, I relax and allow myself to enjoy this unexpected shopping experience.

'Do you have a preferred style?'

I survey the room until my gaze lands on a pair of lilac-coloured shoes. 'Something like those,' I say, pointing.

'Ah, yes. An excellent choice, madam. Similar styles have proven popular with several customers in recent weeks.'

'But not in that colour,' I add hastily.

'May I suggest a mix of slate and dove grey? The two shades together are a pleasing combination and flattering to most outfits.' He reaches for one of the lilac shoes. 'This lower section would be in slate leather which has a subtle blue tinge, and I recommend finishing the upper with a lighter dove silk inset which takes on a silver hue in soft lighting.'

'Silk! Oh, I don't know. Perhaps too fine for everyday wear?'

'There is an alternative. Excuse me for a moment.' He shuffles to the far side of the shop and disappears into what I presume is a workroom at the rear. He emerges bearing a fresh pair of shoes with sturdy heels and rounded toes. 'Do you prefer something like this? The top section of the shoe is a brocade woven with exquisite floral trails and the fabric is hard-wearing. With warmer months approaching, you'll find these easy to wear. The brocade will look elegant in the dove grey and, dare I say, fashionable?'

'Take his advice, Susan,' murmurs Arthur.

'Perfect, thank you.'

'For the fastening, I recommend narrow straps of leather

brought across from each side and secured in the middle with a small buckle.'

I nod my agreement. The junior assistant stands before me bearing a tray of buckles of various shapes and sizes.

'This one caught my eye.' I pick out a silver-coloured oval, sculpted into a chain of forget-me-nots.

'A perfect finishing touch.' The older man steps aside to make way for his younger colleague to take careful measurements of my feet.

Arthur glances up from his newspaper. 'When will the shoes be ready? My wife urgently needs them, as you can see.'

My cheeks flush.

'Average waiting time is three weeks but if you're willing to pay a small additional fee, we can have them ready by the end of this week.'

'We'll do that. I'll settle the account today as I won't be available to accompany my wife when she returns to collect them.'

The measuring finished, the junior assistant eases my feet back into my boots. I can't help but wonder what the young man is thinking as he ties the frayed ribbons. I lower my head to watch and stifle a giggle of surprise. The assistant grins. He has replaced my old ribbons with new ones.

It has been a tiring day. My leg muscles ache, my eyelids are heavy, but soon I'll have four extra dresses and a brand-new pair of shoes. Arthur has been generous, his behaviour reminiscent of before we married. I wonder why. The purchases for Julian need no explaining – the school administrator sent a lengthy list of items that Julian requires. But why buy clothes for me when we are cautious with every shilling of our expenditure? Arthur would not countenance laying out such sums on dresses if he could not match them pound for a pound to support his good cause. There can be only one explanation. He is gambling again.

I sit in front of the mirror and pull a brush through my hair, studying my reflection, wondering if I see what Arthur sees when he looks at me. The candlelight is sympathetic and softens thin creases at the corners of my eyes. Arthur is forty-one years old. I am thirty-four.

My thoughts drift to Arthur's first wife, Jane. She died in childbirth, the baby dying with her, not two full years before Arthur married me. Childbirth. I place my hairbrush on the table. When did I last bleed? Before or after the Corn Bill riots? Before, I think. I count the weeks on my fingers, then again to check.

I am two weeks overdue.

CHAPTER 6

I FANCY AN ORANGE. Concerned that I've been off my food and have lost a little weight, Arthur strides away in search of a street vendor.

The roads and parks are busy today, the first day of summer, with many families enjoying a few hours of fresh air and festivities. I exchange pleasantries with a young mother standing beside me. Her exuberant son is testing her patience, and she restrains him by his collar while we wait for the parade. Arthur returns with two oranges. He pulls a knife from his pocket and slices one into four. I take a quarter and bite into it. The sweet juice trickles down my chin. I draw a scrap of linen from my reticule and wipe away the wasted drops. Between us, we devour the oranges. Arthur teases me, laughing at the dribbles. I wish I was with anyone else but him.

'You look charming today,' he whispers.

I stiffen. There was a time when I tried my best to appeal to him, dressing carefully before my uncle's dinner parties, then delighting in Arthur's company while focusing on every one of his words. Renowned for generous donations to help the poor of Horncastle, Arthur was a widower and an excellent marriage prospect, desired by most of the single women in the town. Not any more. The London crowd changed him. So did losing his fortune. As funds dwindled, his violence escalated, the losses at gaming tables fuelling his rage. Before we wed, he confided tales of beatings by his father and expressed abhorrence of all such men. I pitied him. Believed him. Promised to cherish him. Now I'm trapped and bound to the man Arthur vowed he would never become.

His hand rests on my shoulder. The heat from his palm burns through the fabric of my new dress. He moves his fingers to the nape of my neck, then moves them up and down with gentle strokes. I hold my breath, sensing him lean closer. He sighs. I stare ahead, determined to do nothing to inflame his desire. Arthur will want his way with me later and I'm already dreading it.

'Here they come,' chortles the little boy, bouncing on his toes, straining against his mother's grasp. 'The sweeps and the Jack-in-the-Green.'

I hear them before I see them. A racket of flutes, fiddles, horns and drums creating a vibrant, cheery atmosphere. We watch the boisterous procession approach from beyond the curve in Regent Street. At the front of the group are two young chimney sweeps dressed in flamboyant costumes. Faces blackened, and wearing shrubbery crowns, they march along the street bashing brushes against shovels. They are followed by an extraordinary vison of an enormous tree, bedecked in flowers and ribbons, with two feet protruding from beneath and staggering from side to side. Men dressed as jesters, similarly unbalanced, try to steer the drunken tree by shoving one side, then the other. Next come a gaggle of jaunty dairymaids in summer dresses adorned with flowers, then a mix of men and women in fancy dress and members of the crowd who have joined the procession. The noise crescendoes as the joyful group passes with bawdy singing, cheers from onlookers and jumbled notes blaring from the haphazard orchestra. They pause before us and dance a merry jig, holding out hats for donations before continuing on their way. One cannot help but smile amid such revelry.

Arthur squeezes my elbow. 'I have a special treat in mind. It's a walk that will take almost an hour, but I'm confident you'll think it worth the effort.'

I nod and allow him to lead me away, avoiding the gutters where foul detritus bakes in the sunshine. I press my reticule to my chest to protect it from pickpockets and we dodge carriages and crowds. Emerging onto the Strand, we continue along its length until we pause outside the Golden Lyon, purveyor of fine teas. The shop has a handsome entrance with a statue of a gold lion above the doorway and a Chinaman seated on either side. The statues are magnificent, detailed and lifelike.

'Marvellous, aren't they?' I say, turning towards Arthur. 'The lion glows in the sunlight. Thank you for bringing me here.'

Arthur cocks his head. 'You think I brought you here to see the entrance to a tea shop?'

'Yes.' I force a smile.

Arthur laughs. 'Only a cruel husband would walk his wife so far to show her a shop doorway. We're here to buy tea.'

I frown. 'But Arthur, what about the funds for your campaign? Have we not spent too much on clothes and shoes, leaving less for your cause?'

Arthur shakes his head. 'I came into a sum of money. I've set aside a decent sum to pursue the ideals we covet, but should not every man and woman be permitted to drink tea?

Please, Susan, step inside and take your time to pick something we will both enjoy.'

The shop is a treasure trove with countless teas displayed on shelves. I struggle to make my choice. At last, I select a blend of Oolong, my decision swayed by the light floral fragrance of the rolled leaves and the thrill of never having tried it. Arthur is as delighted with the purchase as I am. We climb into a hackney carriage and head for home, both eager to sample the tea.

I pour the pale amber brew into a cup and pass it to Arthur. When he nods his approval of the taste, I settle into my chair with a cup of my own and we sit in silence, enjoying the refreshment.

Satisfied Arthur is still in an agreeable mood, I replace my cup on the tray and clear my throat. 'I have news to share.'

'Oh?' Arthur drains his cup and gestures that I should pour him another.

'I'm with child,' I say, scrutinising his face for a reaction.

Arthur says nothing. I swallow.

'Are you not pleased?'

Arthur frowns. 'Will it be like last time?'

I'm unsure to which last time he refers. The sad demise of his first wife or the loss I endured only five months ago? Either way, I hope for a wonderful outcome this time.

'I pray God will bless us with a healthy child, another son to continue your name.'

'We don't need another boy when we have Julian.' He scowls. 'And I've no estate to leave to an heir.'

My mood drops, and my heart rate quickens. 'But I'm not Julian's natural mother.'

'Yet you're fond of the boy?'

'Yes, but—'

'Then why crave another?'

I place my hand across my belly. I did not crave this baby, but I feel protective towards it. The pregnancy has made my future more uncertain, and already I fear for the safety of the child. Arthur must remain ignorant of my fears. 'I believe it's a gift from God, Arthur. A blessing on our union and a wonderful thing.'

A lengthy silence. He smiles. 'It is.'

I let out a slow steady breath, relieved he appears accepting of the news.

Arthur reaches into his jacket and withdraws a battered silver snuffbox. He places a small pinch on the back of his hand, holds it to a nostril and takes a quick sniff. He closes his eyes and grins as if congratulating himself on a job well done.

When night falls, Arthur proposes we retire to bed early. He undresses me while I close my eyes and distract myself by thinking about the Jack-in-the-Green parade, the tea-shopping excursion and the child in my belly.

I lie on the bed and brace myself for Arthur's attention. His lips brush against the corner of my mouth and his body joins with mine.

'I love you,' he whispers.

But when he finds his pleasure minutes later, it's not my name he cries, but Jane's.

CHAPTER 7

THE SMELL of cheese turns my stomach, but I persevere with preparing a plate for Arthur. He's due at a meeting within the hour and will not be home for dinner or supper. If I don't persuade Arthur to eat something now, he'll become distracted later and forego any opportunity to dine. An unfed Arthur is a volatile Arthur and not a man I wish to share a bed with.

I put the plate on the dinner table. Arthur glances up from his newspaper and grunts. He hands the paper to me and I take care to fold it with sharp creases before taking it to the parlour ready for when he returns home. When I walk back into the kitchen, he points to the chair at the opposite end of the table.

'Sit. I have something to tell you.'

His tone is unnerving. My hand flies to my belly to reassure my unborn child that all will be well.

Arthur scoops a spoonful of pickle and loads it on to a chunk of cheese before cramming the ensemble into his mouth. 'I have a surprise,' he says between mouthfuls. 'An opportunity has arisen, and I've taken it.'

I tense. 'Are we to move away from London?'

A flicker of confusion passes across Arthur's face. 'Move? Goodness, no! My work here is important, I can't leave. We're making headway with plans for a better England.' He drops his knife on to the plate and the harsh clatter sets my nerves on edge. The muscles in Arthur's face relax and he smiles. 'I've engaged a maid.'

'A maid?' I should show my delight but instead I say, 'Can we afford a maid?'

Arthur jumps to his feet, sending his chair reeling backwards, clattering against the flagstones. He pummels the table top with his fists and tiny beads of blood ooze through the skin of his knuckles. I bite my bottom lip.

Arthur glares, teeth bared, nostrils flaring, like a bull preparing to charge. 'You ungrateful goose,' he hisses, saliva spraying from his lips. 'I thought you'd be glad of help while in your condition.' He waves his hand dismissively, then retrieves the chair from the floor, slamming it into position with one hand.

'I am grateful! The news was a surprise, and a generous thought, Arthur, thank you. But won't a maid's wages deplete funds for your work with the Spenceans? And is it appropriate while you fight for those less fortunate than ourselves?'

Arthur has violet shadows under his eyes and his skin is sallow. He sits again and cups his face in his hands. After an uncomfortable silence, he looks at me. 'I respect your concern, Susan, but while we fight on behalf of other people, we must also take care of ourselves. We shouldn't feel guilty about our own circumstances as long as we remember the plight of others and do what we can to improve their lot. The child in your belly is mine and I won't risk losing it by having you do too much around the home. The maid will take over all heavy housework and anything else you instruct her to do. You'll have free time to enjoy activities befitting of a gentlewoman, but do nothing to compromise your health or that of my unborn son.'

'It might be a girl,' I say tentatively.

Arthur shakes his head. 'A son is preferable.'

How I would love a daughter! A little girl to dress in coloured ribbons, a companion to shop with when she's older. Now, I hope the child will be a lusty boy.

'When will the maid arrive?'

'Today.' Arthur pulls out his pocket watch to check the time. 'Soon, I hope. I must be on my way. I've engaged the maid for twelve months. We'll review the need for paid help when her contract expires.' He rises from his chair once more and strides to my side. He grasps my hand and plants a firm kiss on my fingers. 'I'm fond of you, Susan. You know that, don't you?'

If only that were true.

'I do.'

The knock is so gentle that I almost miss it.

'Good day, Mrs Thistlewood. I'm Nancy Loveday. I believe you're expecting me.'

A woman of nineteen or twenty years stands on the doorstep with a large bundle of clothes in her arms. I look her up and down. She's neatly presented in a plain dress and hair tucked under a cap. Her face is speckled with pockmarks and her eyes are as grey as rain clouds, but she has a sunny smile and I warm to her.

'Please, come in, Nancy.'

As she steps over the threshold, her eyes flit from side to

side, but her expression remains unchanged. She is neither overwhelmed nor underwhelmed and I presume she has come from a similar household to ours. If not, she is skilled at hiding her reactions.

'Let me take you to your room so you may settle in. I've cleaned the garret for you. The mattress is old but comfortable.'

Nancy's eyes widen. 'I would've cleaned the room meself, Mrs Thistlewood.'

This is my first experience of a maid and I'm uncomfortable with the formality. I'd prefer something more at ease. Not a friendship, but a companionship of sorts. 'Call me Susan whenever we're alone.'

'Very well, Susan,' says Nancy, grinning.

I return her smile and lead her up the stairs, wondering if Arthur will be less violent now another adult lives in the house.

We have new neighbours. While Nancy scrubbed floors, I washed windows so I could watch the goings-on next door. It has taken most of the afternoon and much of the evening to deliver their belongings with furniture arriving by many cartloads. They must have purchased the property outright and are filling it with their own possessions.

While making a show of buffing glass, I make eye contact with a middle-aged woman whom I presume to be the lady of the house. She adjusts her bonnet then waves at me. Embarrassed to be caught gawking, I wave back then withdraw from the window. My cheeks are aflame. What must she think of me?

Nancy barrels into the parlour. 'Did you see them, Susan? All those chairs? At least two dozen.'

So Nancy was watching too. I should chastise her for spying, but I'm guilty of the same crime.

'Come, Nancy. The light is fading. Let's have supper.'

'Aren't you going to call on your neighbours and welcome them to the street?'

'No, I don't think so.'

'You should. Me last mistress said it was important to welcome new neighbours. You never know what they might do for you or when you might need to call upon them for help. That's what she said, anyway.'

I'd like to make myself known to the lady in the bonnet and it's a chance to widen my social circle. London is far more enjoyable shared, and Julian's absence has left a hole that needs filling.

'Take something as a gift,' enthuses Nancy. 'I could make gingerbread.'

I'm swept along by her eagerness. 'Perhaps tomorrow. It would be inappropriate to knock at their door at this hour. It's getting dark.'

Nancy chuckles. 'I'll brew us a pot of tea instead then.'

I stay at the table and allow her to wait on me. So far, I'm enjoying having a maid.

CHAPTER 8

Mrs Rebecca Wilkinson's kitchen maid has baked scrumptious biscuits. Dry, they make a tantalising crunch against my teeth, but dipped in tea they soften and melt on my tongue, releasing a warm spicy after-note. It's odd to eat biscuits this way and such a contrast to dipping them in wine as part of a dessert course. But Mrs Wilkinson prefers them like this. When asked how the unusual practice started, she laughed and said it was an accident. One morning, her kitchen maid produced a batch of delicious-smelling biscuits. Eager to taste one, and with no wine to hand, Mrs Wilkinson dipped a biscuit in tea despite risking fearful indigestion. The flavour and texture were so delightful that she's been having biscuits with tea every morning since that day.

Beckey, as she likes to be known, has been my neighbour for three weeks. Her husband is a physician and seems to be rather successful. I suspect he serves a wealthy clientele because Beckey hinted at this being a larger house than their last home; and her furniture is of excellent quality. I confess I'm relieved to have a physician as a neighbour, but I hope we'll not need to call upon him in his professional capacity.

'Susan, I'm hosting a musical gathering tomorrow. Do you play an instrument?'

I shake my head. 'No. I had a few lessons for the harpsichord but didn't practise. I preferred reading.'

'But you enjoy listening to music?'

I take a sip of tea before answering. 'Yes, but I've had few opportunities in recent years.'

'Then join us tomorrow,' she says, clasping my hands. 'Many of my friends are talented musicians. You'll recognise a tune or two, and if you know the words, sing along.'

Shyness creeps up on me. My brothers used to tease me for my flat tones when singing hymns in church. 'I don't know.'

Beckey refills my teacup. 'I insist you come, if only to listen. This will be my first soirée in this house and I'm eager for the other ladies to meet my new dear friend and neighbour.'

I'm flattered she thinks of me so. We've grown fond of one another after spending time in each other's homes every Tuesday and Thursday morning since she moved to the neighbourhood. 'Very well. I'll join you tomorrow evening.'

Beckey claps her hands. 'Come and see the music room.' She rises gracefully from her chair and bustles out of the room.

I follow her across the hallway, and she opens a door with a flourish. Now I know why two dozen chairs arrived at the house. Most of them are in a large semi-circle with a modern pianoforte just off-centre and a large harpsichord next to it. Music stands are situated for sharing between musicians, and armchairs linger at the sides of the room for the comfort of observing guests. Paintings adorn the walls, each with a musical theme – angels playing flutes and violins; still-life studies of pipes and drums; and a youthful woman sitting with a harp, eyes closed, absorbed in a sweet melody.

'It's magnificent,' I say. 'How I would love something similar.'

Our home is narrower than Beckey's, with fewer rooms. I have neither the space nor social standing to need a dedicated music room.

Beckey places her hand on my arm. 'Come to every recital! You'll always find a welcome here. May I teach you how to play the violin?'

'Perhaps one day. For now, I prefer to listen.'

It takes over an hour to decide what to wear, even though I have only four suitable dresses. I want to make a good impression when I meet Beckey's friends this evening. I was nervous about what Arthur would say, but he was glad I accepted the invitation. He said that one day we might have to canvas their financial support for his cause, and their husbands will be at least as wealthy as Dr Wilkinson with consciences to match. No doubt he's right, but my priority is to make friends.

Eventually, it's Nancy who decides for me. 'You want to appear fashionable, but not overdressed,' she says. 'Wear a dress that looks expensive but won't put every other lady to shame.'

I don't own an expensive dress. 'This is the one I keep for best,' I say, lifting a sky-blue cotton piece from the bed.

Nancy pouts and points at the frills surrounding the bottom of the skirt. 'Too fussy. This one's better.' She holds up a blossom-pink dress, embroidered with sprigs of rose-pink flowers around the hem. 'Not only is it elegant, but it sits well with your pale complexion and you'll feel comfortable in it.'

'I like that one too. It's my favourite.'

'So it's the obvious choice.'

Nancy gives a reassuring smile and helps me change. She ties the laces at the back of the bodice and turns me to face her.

'You look divine,' she says. 'The ladies will love you. Now, let me see to your hair.'

The evening passed swiftly, and I revelled in the company of Beckey's delightful companions. There were no prying questions, only straightforward queries about my musical tastes and other interests. I sat to one side listening to violins accompanied by the pianoforte, and a harp interlude. Then I found the courage to join in with a trio of ladies singing a familiar song. My voice faltered on the high notes, but I persevered.

'You made a fine impression tonight,' says Beckey, flushed with the success of the evening.

'I can't think of a better way to spend a couple of hours,' I say, beaming. 'I don't believe I've ever enjoyed an evening as much as this.'

Beckey tilts her head. 'You know, I think we should train that voice of yours. What do you say? Shall we work on a solo for next time?'

'Are you sure? I'm not known for my singing.'

'It's a game of confidence, my dear. With practice, you'll be able to sing like a nightingale. Among friends, you'll lose your fears, and if you enjoy the music and relate to the words of the song, you'll sing as well as anyone. Remember, we do this for pleasure, sharing a passion for music and song. We're not competing and we're not judging. Away from the menfolk, we are who we should be – cheerful, confident individuals.'

Beckey's truth rings in my ears. I'm a butterfly spreading its wings for the first time, realising its true potential and venturing towards its destiny. But two thoughts niggle. Will Arthur notice the fully fledged version of me? And if he does, will he punish me for it?

CHAPTER 9

A THICK SLICE of lean ham glistens on my plate. I haven't felt this hungry for weeks. I load my fork with meat and a chunk of pickled onion, then raise it to my lips while inhaling the scent of vinegar and spices.

'They say Bonaparte's readying troops again.' Arthur rips off a wedge of bread.

'Dear God, no!' I shudder at the thought of bodies on a battlefield, bloodied and lifeless. 'Too many lives have been lost already. Do we have an army capable of ending his domination of Europe?'

Arthur shrugs. 'Our army is but one of many. The allies will taste victory soon, I'm sure.'

I think of the countless soldiers begging on London's streets. So many young men maimed by war, reduced to a life of poverty, disregarded by society and surviving on scraps. No doubt they dreamed of a hero's welcome, not another living nightmare after the one they left behind.

'Pregnancy suits you,' says Arthur, taking me by surprise.

I stop munching to study his face. He appears sincere, and

I cannot help but smile. I rest my fingers on my lower abdomen, revelling in the slight thickening of my waist.

We finish supper in silence. When Nancy clears away the plates, she drops Arthur's knife. The loud clatter of metal on stone makes me tense. I close my eyes, waiting for a tirade to burst from Arthur's lips, but nothing is forthcoming. Apprehensive, I open my eyes and look towards him. He's leaning from his chair, retrieving the knife from the floor and passing it to Nancy.

Nancy's face is scarlet from brow to neck. She accepts the knife from Arthur and mumbles an apology. Arthur glances at me, then lowers his gaze to his pocket watch. He rises from the table and strides to my side.

'I'll be home early tonight.' He takes my hand and presses my knuckles to his lips. When he releases me, I wait for him to turn away, then wipe my knuckles on the tablecloth.

Beckey has a remarkable skill for training voices. I had an extra lesson with her this evening to prepare for the next soirée two weeks hence. The melody repeats in my mind and I'm singing the enchanting verses of 'Greensleeves' when I walk into the parlour. Nancy jumps up from my armchair, but I'm in no mood to chastise her for snatching a few minutes of comfort. She worked hard today. Not only did she beat the dirt from every carpet, but she also scrubbed the walls and floor of the small bedroom that will become the nursery.

Nancy apologises and I raise my index finger to silence her. I place my palm on her arm as a gesture of reassurance. She gives a thin smile then slinks from the room.

Weary from the excitements of the day, I flop onto the

well-worn cushioned seat, settle my head against the back of the chair and lower my eyelids. I ease my swollen feet from my shoes and wiggle my toes. Once again, I cannot stop myself from singing. As the pitch rises with a lilting melody, I know my voice is in tune. My confidence enhanced, I sing louder and continue to the end.

'Bravo!' announces Arthur, stepping away from the window, clapping. 'You sang well, Susan.'

'Arthur! How long have you been home?' I stumble over my words. 'I didn't hear you come through the front door.'

Arthur opens his snuffbox. 'About an hour ago.' He grins and deposits a small pinch of snuff at the base of his left thumb. 'Your entertainment was exquisite.' He presses against his right nostril and inhales the snuff through the other.

A hot flush spreads from my neck to my face and I smile meekly. How did I not notice him? Then a sensation overwhelms me, one I'm less familiar with. Suspicion. It's so unlike Arthur to allow a maid to sit in the parlour. I think of Julian, the bastard son of a maidservant, passed off as Arthur's legitimate heir. I watch Arthur for a minute or two. He's relaxed, unruffled, his attention absorbed by today's newspaper.

I can't believe Arthur would risk making the same mistake twice. But what if he did? Thoughts tumble and collide, and it's difficult to make sense of them. I am bound to Arthur by law and unable to leave him without his permission – unless he commits adultery.

CHAPTER 10

I GLARE at a bowl of broth with globules of grease glistening on the surface. I wish it would disappear. The broth is like me – pale, cold and weak. I push the tray towards the edge of Arthur's side of the bed and sigh as liquid slops over the rim of the bowl. The bowl is no better than me at clinging to its precious contents.

My mind is numb, my heart aches, and I plead with God to release me from misery. I cannot sleep, nor can I drag myself from beneath the covers. My hair hangs limp in tangled tresses and my shift reeks of stale sweat. But what of it? Life continues outside this room. I can hear the hustle and bustle of the street outside – carriages clattering past; street vendors hawking their wares; children calling to each other as they hurry to school. Children. My eyes mist with tears and I lower my eyelids, but then I see blood and lots of it. God must think me a dreadful sinner, because I'm trapped in purgatory now.

The bedroom door opens, and footsteps cross the room. They're not Arthur's footsteps, for they have a woman's light tread. I should turn to look but cannot. Someone holds my hand, their touch warm and comforting. My vision is blurred, but I know who it is.

'Mother.' My voice cracks and tears slide across my cheeks. I convulse with sobs, consumed by grief.

My mother cradles me in her arms and coos with soothing sounds, reminding me of childhood and an easier life untainted by fear. How times have changed. The fragrance of Mother's perfume is a balm to my aching heart and I nestle against her, relishing the contact and her outpouring of love. The long-case clock in the parlour strikes the eleventh hour, the sounds muffled by the bedroom floorboards. Mother strokes my brow, and I drift into a troubled sleep. When the clock announces midday, I open my eyes again.

'Who asked you to come?' I whisper.

'Your friend.'

'Beckey?'

'Yes.'

'Not Arthur?'

'No. Not Arthur.'

'He's busy with meetings.'

'No doubt.'

'Mother, there's something I must tell you.'

She tilts her head, waiting for me to continue.

'I can't... don't want...' Words desert me. My parents enjoy a marriage of mutual love and respect. How can I tell her I long to end mine?

'My dear, you need say nothing. When the day comes, Father and I will gladly have you live with us.'

'How did you know?'

'When a mother and daughter share a bond as close as ours, such things are obvious.'

'I wish I could leave now.'

'As do I. But our home would be the first place where Arthur would search for you, and no doubt he'd beat you for your trouble.'

More tears while I grieve for everything I have lost.

Mother allows me several minutes of self-pity. She reaches for my hand and squeezes my fingers. I turn to face her and see that she too is grieving for me. 'Susan, you've been in this room for three days. It's too long.' She releases my hand and stands. 'It's time you started looking after yourself again. I'm going to the kitchen for a fresh pot of broth. Will you take it this time?'

I nod. 'I'll try. But I've no appetite.'

Mother kisses my brow, then glides from the room.

I gaze at the window while I wait for her return. Thick bands of sunshine stream through the glass, striking a bright puddle of light on the oak floorboards. If only I could step into that bright circle and disappear to a life where loss and grief do not exist.

The door creaks. This time I turn towards it, but it's not my mother who comes bearing the broth. It's Beckey. Tears fall again.

Beckey places the tray on a side table placed by the bed. 'Dearest Susan,' she wraps me in an embrace. 'I've been so worried about you.'

I cling to her as if my life depends on it. She is the best of friends. I try to speak but cannot get the words out. When she releases me, she plumps the pillows and eases me back against them.

'Was I right to send for your mother? I wasn't sure. Arthur thought it unnecessary, expecting you to be up and about the next day. I explained that sometimes it's hard to recover from an ordeal like this, so he left the decision to me.'

'Thank you.' My face creases. Another onslaught of overwhelming grief.

Beckey strokes the back of my hand and waits for my sobs to settle.

'Try a few mouthfuls of broth, Susan.'

Holding the bowl in one hand and a spoon in the other, she feeds me a small sip of the warm liquid. I'm surprised by how much I savour the taste. It's bland but I detect a hint of thyme, my favourite herb. The gentle aroma reaches into my nostrils and awakens my appetite. Beckey places a cushion on my lap, then balances the tray on top. I manage a thin smile and take the spoon from her. There's a hunk of bread on the tray, and I break off a small corner. It has a stale texture, but soaked in broth it's palatable and almost enjoyable.

I feel a little better after eating, but the days spent languishing in bed have weakened me. 'I think I'll fall asleep again in a moment,' I murmur.

Beckey pats my hand. 'I'll pop back later, if you're up to it.'

I nod and close my eyes.

When I wake, the daylight has faded, confirming I've slept for several hours.

Mother hurries to my side. 'How are you?'

'Better, thank you. Is Arthur home?'

She shakes her head.

'Will you help me downstairs to the parlour?'

'Not now. You're still weak. Perhaps in another day or two when you've eaten more food and regained some strength.'

I look around the room and sigh. I feel the need to do

something. 'Will you bring the newspaper to me? I'm sure Arthur will have bought one this morning. If not, yesterday's will do.'

Mother hesitates.

'What is it?'

'Perhaps a book, dear?'

'I lack concentration for a book. I'd prefer the newspaper.'

Nancy hollers from the foot of the stairs. 'Mrs Wilson's here!'

Mother rolls her eyes at the maid's lack of propriety. 'I'll welcome her and send her up with some reading material.'

When Beckey enters my bedroom, I greet her with a warm smile.

'That's better,' she says, sitting beside me on the bed. She has a book in her hand and a newspaper tucked under her arm. 'Shall we read poetry together?'

I like the idea of reading together. I'll study the newspaper after Beckey leaves.

We spend a delightful part of the evening indulging ourselves in poems by Wordsworth, Keats and Blake. Beckey chooses carefully to avoid returning me to a pit of despair. When it's time for her to leave, she places the poetry book on Arthur's pillow.

'And the newspaper?' I ask.

Her face drops. 'Please, Susan, not today. Perhaps tomorrow.'

'Why not today?' I ask, confused.

Beckey grimaces.

'Beckey? What is it?' Even to me, my voice is bordering on hysterical.

'Very well.' She unfurls the newspaper. 'There's good news and bad news,' she announces. 'The good news is that

Napoleon was defeated at a village called Waterloo, near Brussels.'

'Thank goodness,' I say, my panic subsiding. 'And the bad news?'

Beckey's face drops. 'The victory came at a substantial cost with many lives lost.'

I turn the page and my gaze falls upon a list of officers killed and wounded. The list is extensive but excludes regular soldiers. Images flash through my mind, bodies hacked apart and strewn across grassy fields stained heavily with blood. While I lost my child, thousands of men lost their lives.

I close the paper and pass it back to Beckey. 'You couldn't have hidden that news from me forever. With so many mothers grieving for their sons, I've no right to indulge in self-pity.'

'You have every right, Susan. It's painful to lose a child regardless of circumstance. I understand the agony you endure. I too have visited that dark place.'

'You have?'

Beckey nods. 'Grace is not my daughter.'

I've seen Grace only once. Her beauty is striking, her demeanour sunny and warm.

'But she addresses you with such affection!'

'And I love her as if she were my own. She's a delight, and it has been my honour to watch her grow into the adorable young woman she is now.'

'How old was she when you first met her?'

Beckey chuckles. 'Three. Dressed in rags and streaming from both nostrils. A proper little ragamuffin.' She laughs at my horrified expression. 'Grace isn't Samuel's daughter either. Her mother died trying to bring a second child into the world. Samuel was summoned by a neighbour but arrived too late. There was nothing he could do. Grace's mother passed away with the babe still in her womb. Samuel knew the neighbours from earlier visits to Vauxhall and couldn't bring himself to leave Grace there.'

My eyes widen.

'Not that type of visit,' she says, laughing. 'The ladies of Vauxhall are like many others – in need of guidance and medical expertise, and we do our best to help them. They may be society's fallen women, but they're human beings and deserve compassion. I digress. Samuel could not bear to abandon Grace in the state she was in, so brought her home, and it was love at first sight.'

'Does Grace know?'

'She does. We didn't want it to be a secret. Believe me, Susan, a child is a wonder of the world, even when not of our flesh.'

Beckey's right. 'I have Julian,' I say. The thought of him makes me smile. 'That boy brings so much pleasure and I'm counting the days to his return home for the summer holiday.'

'There, you see? You've not lost everything. Now try to sleep.'

A rap at the door. It startles us both. Beckey says farewell, promising to return tomorrow, making way for Arthur to come to my side. He sits on the bedroom chair and stares at me.

'I'm told you're better now. That's good. And I wanted to tell you I'm sorry for your loss.'

I roll onto my side, turning my back towards him. 'Our loss, Arthur. *Our* loss.'

CHAPTER 11

BECKEY RUMMAGES in her basket and withdraws a small wooden box. She prises open the lid and reaches inside with finger and thumb.

'Here, this will help,' she says, dropping a hard, transparent drop onto my palm.

The smell of mint with a hint of lemon sets my mouth watering. 'Thank you,' I say, before popping the confectionary treat into my mouth.

'Try not to crunch it, Susan. You'll want to savour the mint for several minutes while your senses adjust.'

It can't be worse than the stink of the street. Stale effluent festers where it landed after being tipped from a chamber pot from an upstairs window. Rotten food decays in the warm summer sun, too far gone to tempt the scavengers that prowl the streets. We pause outside a ramshackle building, part of a terrace of tall houses all in a similar state of disrepair. Beckey appears to be preparing for some kind of horror indoors.

'Time to go in.' Beckey takes a deep breath and nudges the

door with her shoulder, using the full force of her weight to prise it open.

The air indoors is dank despite the warmth outside. We climb a rickety staircase flanked by faded ancient wallpaper peeling in strips. Several doors lead off from the first-floor landing, most soiled by countless dirty hands. I wonder which door we will pass through and breathe a sigh of relief when Beckey reaches for the handle of the cleanest one.

I roll the sweet across my tongue, moving it from the inside of one cheek to the other. The peppermint essence warms my throat, and the aroma fills my nostrils. It tastes almost as delightful as my beloved sugar plums. A flush of guilt warms my face – I ate three before leaving home.

I follow Beckey into a dim room. 'Dear God!'

My cheeks burn and my ears flame.

Beckey pats my arm. 'It's fine, Susan. I had a similar reaction when Samuel first brought me to a place similar to this.'

I've heard others speak of poor housing conditions and I've read many articles about those struggling with poverty, but never imagined that real people live like this. The stench of a stagnant chamber pot makes me gag. Beckey slips me another peppermint drop before moving forward a few paces. It's only then that I realise someone else is in the room. Through the gloom I make out the shape of a woman curled on a bed, her dark hair matted and trailing across a filthy pillow. I head for the window and try to release the catch, but it's stuck fast. The stifling air is heavy with odours of stale food, disease and sweat. I want to smash the window to let fresh air gush in, but the stricken woman would not thank me for it, especially come winter. Frustrated, I turn my back to the daylight. My eyes adjust to the gloom and reveal what a hovel the room has become. The walls are wet, blackened with damp, and the amenities are basic – two chamber pots, both in need of emptying; a washstand with a chipped jug; two cooking pots on a narrow hearth; two cracked bowls; a line strung across the room adorned with a stained shift and scraps of stained linen; a table covered with folded clothes; and a box filled with sheets at the foot of the bed.

'Susan?' Beckey beckons me towards her. 'Help me change the bedlinen. I'll support Anna while you start with the pillow.'

I wrinkle my nose in disgust. Beckey ignores my indiscretion.

'Quick as you can. I can't hold Anna for long.'

If Beckey can hold the woman against her, I can change the cover on a pillow. I work fast, taking care with the threadbare fabric, replacing it with a soft white cotton cover from the top of Beckey's basket. I plump the pillow, then Beckey lowers the woman towards it. Together, we roll her emaciated body one way, then the other, changing the sheet beneath her. Beckey shows no sign of disgust at the soiled cloth. Following her lead, I conceal my revulsion.

A mewling sound floats through the air.

'A cat must have followed us into the building.'

Beckey shakes her head but stays focused on Anna.

I notice a flicker of movement among the box of sheets. I approach with caution in case the animal leaps out and scratches me. But there is no cat. A young baby shakes a feeble fist and the sight of him makes me cry. My distress coincides with his and our volume escalates.

'Poor little lamb,' says Beckey. 'Anna's milk dried up and the other nursing mothers in this building refused to help. Samuel suggested diluted cow's milk mixed with a large spoonful of sugar but so far it has caused the most dreadful diarrhoea.'

Beckey lifts the baby from the box and paces the room,

muttering soothing words in his ear. He settles and nuzzles against her, but the respite is brief and soon he is wailing again.

'How old is he?' I ask.

'Eight weeks.' She eyes me strangely as if waiting for a reaction.

Then I realise. 'To the day?'

Beckey's lips stretch into a thin smile. Anna's child was born on the same day I lost mine.

'He looks younger. Little more than a newborn.'

'He's starving. Anna's stopped producing milk.'

She lays the baby on the bed then peels away his soiled linens, exposing a large patch of angry skin speckled with weeping sores. A pungent odour of stale urine rises from him. His mother weeps.

'We need water, Susan.' Beckey nods towards the cooking pots.

I reach for one and lift the lid. 'It's empty.'

'There's a water pump at the end of the road. We passed it on our way here. Do you mind?'

'Of course not.'

I'm driven by an overwhelming urge to help these wretched souls. I hurry about my errand and return to find a fire burning in the grate. Beckey gestures for me to put the water on to boil.

'Exposing the skin to the air will help and I have a pot of soothing balm. Samuel said to bathe the sore patch of skin before applying it. I must ask him to send someone to fix that window. It's doing them no good being shut up in here in the summer heat.' She strokes the baby's face. 'Poor little mite.'

Anna has not uttered a word since we arrived, although her eyes are open and follow me as I move around the room. I bend to whisper in Beckey's ear. 'Does she speak?'

Beckey chuckles and smiles at Anna. 'She's the most garrulous person I know, aren't you, dear?' Turning back to me, she adds, 'But now she's less inclined to speak and not only because she's unwell.'

'Then why?'

Beckey sighs. 'Because Anna's French. Many residents in this tenement block became penniless widows when their husbands were left strewn across battlefields in France. They associate Anna with their loss and hold her, and others like her, responsible.'

'But it's not her fault!'

'I agree. None of us choose our country of birth. But so many women here are grieving. They're angry and need to vent their rage. Anna's too convenient for them. Mind you, they were eager enough to treat her as one of their own when she repaired dresses for free and helped look after their children – until their husbands lost their lives at Waterloo.'

'How did you meet Anna?'

'An old client of hers expressed concern to Samuel. My husband's done the best he can for now and asked me to keep a watchful eye. He's unsure what has stricken her thus but expects her to recover.'

Anna reaches out a skeletal arm towards Beckey. 'I feel a leetle better.' Her words fracture into soft croaks.

'That's excellent news,' says Beckey. 'I brought soup. Susan will warm it while I attend to little George.'

I lift a china bowl from the basket. The contents have turned to jelly but will soon revert to liquid when heated. I scrape the soup into the other cooking pot and set it in front of the fire. I'm sweating. The heat from the flames is intolerable, but my suffering is insignificant compared with Anna's. I pour boiling water into the cracked china bowl. Beckey tops it up with a glug of cool water from the jug, then sets about bathing George's skin.

Anna stares at me with large brown eyes. Her gaunt face bears the scars of recent flea bites, but I can see a natural beauty will return when she's back to good health. She takes the bowl of soup from my hand, nods her thanks, then concentrates on taking small sips. I take the empty bowl from her, swill it with hot water and tip it over the coals. It will not matter if the fire dies now.

Then I surprise myself. 'Shall I help you wash and change into a clean shift?'

Anna smiles. 'Oui. I'd like that very much.'

When we step into the street, a woman pelts us with rotten vegetables.

'Mrs King!' Beckey glares. 'I expect better behaviour from you.'

'What do you think you're doing coming here to help that French whore?' The same woman hurls a fistful of stinking peelings. A toddler clings to the back of her skirt and peers out from behind her mother's legs.

'A Waterloo widow?' I whisper.

'She is,' comes the muttered reply.

'If I see you coming out of her place again, I'll chuck stones next time.'

'You punish me for offering kindness to a woman who was once your dearest friend?'

'Was. Until they Frenchies took me husband from me.'

'I don't believe it was a personal thing,' says Beckey.

'Mrs King,' I say, taking a tentative step towards her. 'I'm sure if things were different, and you were alone with your child in France, Anna would help you. I hear she's looked after you before now. You and several others.'

Mrs King frowns. 'She has. But things have changed.'

'How so? Anna's the same charming woman who became a widow herself only six months ago. Her life is as much a daily struggle as yours. She wishes you no harm and is as saddened by your loss as she is by her own.'

'Where's your compassion, Mrs King?' says Beckey, in a kind but firm tone. 'If you want free advice from my husband again, you must prove yourself worthy of his time. Be as charitable towards others as he is to you.'

Mrs King's face works through a range of expressions.

Beckey presses on. 'That's right. Think about the kindness shown to you. Who cared for little Nelly when you took to your bed? Who used her savings to pay the apothecary when you needed medicine? And who promised to care for your daughter if you died? It was Anna, wasn't it?'

Mrs King lowers her head and clears her throat. 'I'm sorry for losing me temper and I hope you can find it in yerselves to forgive me. I've let the opinions of others sway me. Won't happen again, I assure you. Now, if you'll excuse me, I have a friend who needs me help.' She strides towards the door to the house, her daughter trotting to keep pace.

Beckey and I exchange smiles. We blot vegetable juice from our dresses and head for home.

'Arthur?' I close the front door behind me, listening for a response.

I make straight for the kitchen expecting Nancy to be there, but I'm alone. Dirty dishes sit in piles on the table. I wash them and tidy them away, grateful for the time to myself. While Arthur champions his political campaign for change, I will do what little I can to help some of those who suffer so near to our home. Beckey was delighted when I volunteered to go with her again – Samuel often asks her to visit those he has treated and, as she said, two pairs of hands are better than one. Their kindness knows no bounds. I am determined to become more like them.

An unpleasant odour wafts up from the stains on my dress, so I hurry upstairs to change before Arthur sees me. As I reach the landing, I spy Arthur making his way down from the garret.

'You're home,' he says, tucking his shirt into his breeches, then fiddling with the cravat that dangles loose at his neck.

'What were you doing up there?'

'Nancy's window was jammed,' he says. 'I fixed it. It's stifling up there in this hot weather.'

Nancy appears behind him, cheeks flushed. 'Mrs Thistle-wood,' she says, bobbing a minimal curtsey before scurrying down the stairs.

'Is the window open now?' I ask.

Arthur leans against the wall and puffs out his chest. 'It is.'

'Excellent. I know of another one requiring your attention.'

His brow puckers and I suppress a smile. I turn away and glide towards our bedroom, hoping Arthur's attention was on more than the window while he was with Nancy in the garret.

CHAPTER 12

NANCY'S MUTTON stew is delightful. The red wine gravy is a little extravagant, but Arthur does not seem to notice. The sharp tang of rosemary is warming on such a cold autumnal day, and the onions add a surprising sweetness. I wipe my plate clean with a crust of bread and then watch Arthur do the same.

I take small sips of ale, waiting for Arthur to drain his cup, and then I say what's on my mind. 'Arthur, we have a serious issue to discuss.'

Arthur raises his eyebrows. 'And what might that be?'

'Nancy.'

He places his knife and fork on his plate and sits back in his chair.

I lean forward and lower my voice. 'Arthur, I think she's pregnant.'

The colour fades from his cheeks. 'That's quite an allegation. Are you sure?'

'Quite sure. Have you noticed how her face is radiant, her figure full? You can't ignore the swelling of her breasts. I swear they'll soon burst from her bodice!'

Arthur splutters. He rises from his chair and paces the room. This revelation has set him on edge, and I'm heartened by his reaction. At last, freedom is possible.

'Have you spoken to her?'

'Not yet. I wanted to discuss it with you first. Lord knows how she got herself into such a state, for she's rarely out of the house. But then, a few stolen moments of passion can leave a lifetime of consequences. Could have happened on a day off, I suppose, although I'm not aware of a young man in her life.'

'She… she's not mentioned anyone to you? I thought you were close.'

'Don't be daft, Arthur. I'm no more friendly with her than you are.'

Arthur runs his hands through his hair. 'How did this happen?'

'Girls dream, Arthur. They have a natural urge to find a husband and bear children.'

His face reddens, and he bangs both fists hard against the kitchen table. I brace, expecting him to turn on me.

'What was she thinking?' His face is pale, his brow crinkled with concern.

'Shall I dismiss her?'

'No. I'll talk to her. She should have taken steps to avoid getting a babe in her belly.'

'Either she's had a lapse of judgement or she's planning a future with the child's father.'

Arthur shakes his head. 'No,' he murmurs. He lifts his head and meets my gaze. 'Where is she? I'll speak to her at once.'

'On an errand. I sent her out as soon as dinner was ready, to guarantee privacy while we discussed the issue.'

'Send her to my office the moment she returns. I'll give

this matter the urgent attention it deserves.'

I pray Nancy is with child. If I can persuade her to confirm the child is Arthur's, my freedom is as good as guaranteed. This delicious idea overwhelms me. I choke back tears of hope and start clearing the table.

Ten minutes pass before I hear Nancy at the front door. I rush out to relieve her of packages of linen and ribbons and instruct her to go upstairs to Arthur's office.

Her face contorts. 'Did I do something wrong?'

'Mr Thistlewood will explain. He has questions for you.'

Nancy hangs her cloak on the coat stand before climbing the stairs. Her footsteps cross the hall and a door closes. I resist the temptation to listen outside – I cannot risk Arthur finding me lurking there. Instead, I tear myself away from their muffled voices and seek refuge in the parlour. I treat myself to a sugar plum and open a book of poetry.

When the clock strikes the hour, I realise Nancy has been in Arthur's office for over twenty minutes. Unable to contain my curiosity, I climb the stairs. Before I reach the landing, a door opens releasing the sound of Nancy's delighted giggles followed by a deep throaty chuckle from Arthur.

'Oh! I didn't expect to see you there, Mrs Thistlewood.' Her cheeks glow, framed by unruly locks escaping from beneath her cap. Arthur loiters behind her, smiling.

'What's going on?' I ask. 'Why the laughter?'

It is Arthur who replies. 'There's been a huge misunderstanding.'

Nancy clasps her hands across her belly. 'Master said you thought I might be pregnant.'

My eyes drift to the pale mounds of flesh bulging through the opening in her dress.

'I'm just a well-nourished maidservant,' she says, interlocking her fingers and lowering her head. 'My master and mistress are generous employers.'

'And you're not with child?'

Nancy frowns. 'No, mistress.'

'I've reassured her she'll stay here at least until the twelve months are up,' states Arthur.

It takes all my effort to avoid crumpling to the floor. I'm destined to spend the rest of my life suffering at the hands of Arthur.

PART III
1816

CHAPTER 13

OYSTERS GLISTEN ON A PLATE, fanned around half a lemon. I'm eager to pick one but know I must wait. My stomach gurgles. Beckey insisted on an early start this morning to be sure we'd have the pick of the freshest fish at Billingsgate market. Now, with our packages stowed on a chair, we can enjoy an unusual breakfast at a reputable inn. A serving girl brings another half of lemon, two more plates and a tray of bread. Beckey slips the girl a coin, then squeezes a little lemon juice over the oysters. She gestures for me to take the first pick.

I hold the wide end of a shell against my lips and take a sip of oyster liquor, relishing the mild briny flavour of the sea before tipping in the oyster itself. As I bite into it, the taste of the ocean gives way to a subtle sweetness with a delicate mineral finish. It's not unusual to eat oysters, but to eat them fresh from the sea is to enjoy them at their best.

Our appetites sated, we order tea to warm ourselves before the journey home. It's the first time I've visited Billingsgate – these days I rely on Nancy to source our provisions. But Beckey invited me to accompany her this morning.

She likes to visit the market now and then, and I confess she might persuade me to join her again because the market is a feast for the eyes! Rows of stalls stretch into the distance with traders calling out to customers and drawing attention to the fish displayed before them. Crowds of merchants and members of the public scrutinise the goods on offer, picking fault and haggling over prices. Hawkers rub shoulders with customers and elbow their way through the packed market-place, offering shellfish, knives and loaves, and trinkets crafted from discarded shells. My favourite section is a jumble of permanent shops selling tableware and leather goods in a less raucous area, flanking a steep slope towards the fast-flowing Thames.

The door to the inn flies open, admitting a blast of arctic chill.

'We should leave,' says Beckey. 'The weather's turning.'

It's been a bleak winter so far, although not cold enough for the annual frost fair on the Thames. The mornings are so dry and chilly that speech lingers in little mists. But before a waiter slams the door to seal the warmth indoors, I glimpse little white flecks dancing in the air. We drain our cups, then wrap ourselves in scarves, wool coats and thick hooded capes. Bracing ourselves for the icy chill, we clutch our purchases in mittened hands.

The sky is heavy with snow.

'This will get worse,' I say.

Beckey's face drops. 'We'd better find a cab before everyone else has the same idea.'

We retrace our steps through the market. The crowds have dissipated and traders are packing up their stalls. Discarded fish guts litter the cobbles, the slippery surface making our path treacherous. When we emerge from the opposite side, we see a hackney carriage offloading passengers. The coachman is eager for us to board, declaring us his last job for the day even though it is not yet mid-morning. We raise our eyebrows at his laziness and settle on a shabby seat.

As we clatter through the city, our view through the windows diminishes. Smog hangs in a low cloud, the by-product of thousands of home fires burning in grates from morning until night. Snow falls in thick clumps, further obscuring the view, and the wind strengthens, blowing gusty draughts through gaps in the carriage doors.

'The carriage is slowing,' observes Beckey, slipping her arm through mine and snuggling against me so we may share the heat from our well-clad bodies.

'Listen,' I say.

Beckey cocks her head to one side. 'I can't hear anything.'

'That's my point. Not even hoofbeats on cobbles.'

The carriage rolls to a stop. The coachman opens the door on my side and we both gasp. He's covered in a thick layer of snow.

'Is there a problem?' asks Beckey.

'Sorry, ladies. Can't go no further.' He shivers. 'It's been snowing 'ard for some time now.'

A gust of wind tips him forward. He steadies himself, each hand clutching the side of the doorframe. Snow slides from the roof, coating him in another layer, while large clods fall inside the carriage and land in a pile at my feet.

When the wind drops, he steps aside. 'Ladies.' He holds out his hand and helps me step down before doing the same for Beckey. Then he reaches for our parcels and retrieves them from his seat. 'These'll still be as fresh as when you bought them, 'specially in this chilly air.'

We take the parcels from him and watch him trudge away, leading the horse by the reins.

'Now what do we do?' Beckey's eyes are wide, her teeth clenched.

'I suppose we walk.'

I study our surroundings, trying to recognise landmarks smothered by snow. The dome of St Paul's Cathedral looms through the murk. White lumps tumble from the sky, clinging to our capes and melting on my boots, the icy water spreading too easily through the fabric.

'This way,' I say.

We press forward, our boots crunching in unison. The wind is more persistent now, blowing us to the side, forcing us through thick drifts. Each laborious step carries us closer to our homes. A few other stragglers pass us, but we exchange no words of greeting because it takes all our concentration to keep moving, dragging our feet one slow step at a time. My toes are numb and my fingers hurt. I need thicker mittens. We pause in a shop doorway to recover our breath, disappointed the shopkeeper chose not to open today. Our rest is brief. It's too cold to linger. We need to get home.

Nancy flings open the door. 'Master, come quickly,' she yells.

I heave myself over the threshold, warm air wrapping around me like a soft woollen blanket. My chest aches, and I can't feel my toes. Nancy relieves me of my packages. I mutter my thanks and shrug off my cape, creating a puddle of snow.

'Susan?' Arthur hurries along the hallway towards me. I watch his approach, but his image fades as he draws closer. Everything is silent around me, and my vision greys. Then I buckle and drop towards the floor. When I come to, I am in Arthur's arms being carried up the stairs like a child. He huffs and puffs, struggling with my weight, then drops me awkwardly on to the bed.

'I'll send Nancy to help you change into dry clothes.' Each word freezes for a second, then vanishes.

'Perhaps she can light the fire, too?'

Arthur makes a show of removing his pocket watch and checking the time. He shakes his head. 'It's not yet midday.'

'I fainted, Arthur. I need to rest awhile, and it's freezing in here.'

Arthur glances at the window. Snow has gathered on the ledge outside, obscuring the lowest row of panes.

'Make do with an extra blanket. There's no sense in wasting coal while there's a fire burning in the parlour. Join me there when you've had enough rest.'

I glare at his back as he walks away, wondering how long it will take to leave this frosty, loveless marriage.

CHAPTER 14

ONE CAN ALWAYS RELY on a royal wedding to lift the spirits of the nation. Princess Charlotte is to marry her prince today, and their happy union is being celebrated across the country. Even Arthur is in a cheerful mood.

An atmosphere of excitement bubbles in Beckey's music room. Three ladies settle in a corner to practise an ensemble with harp, violin and cello, while I join a sizeable group of women to rehearse a choral song that we have practised countless times in recent days. Samuel and his two brothers are expected to arrive soon to add their tenor and baritone voices. Beckey flits about the room, checking us over, ensuring not a hair is out of place nor a dress soiled.

There's a fluttering inside my chest and it takes great effort to control my breathing, but I refuse to allow my nerves to get the better of me. How fortunate I am to have Beckey as a neighbour and the greatest of friends. She has offered me kindness, educated me about true suffering, given me the gift of music and song, and now opened a door to an opportunity of a lifetime. My life is so much richer for knowing Beckey. My heart swells with love for her, and that's all I need to overcome any small anxiety I may have about my voice remaining confident and in tune.

The door opens and Beckey calls for silence. We gravitate to the edges of the room and turn our expectant attention towards her.

'Dear friends,' she says, 'today is a merry day. With the Prince Regent's permission, his daughter, Princess Charlotte, will wed Prince Leopold. And what a fine day for a wedding! Twenty-five years ago today, I wed a prince of my own – my dear husband, Samuel.' She gestures towards the door as Samuel strides into the music room, flanked by his younger brothers. 'In honour of our anniversary, I made an unusual request of my cook. She has made a bride cake for us to share.'

The cook enters the room to hearty applause, carrying a large iced cake on a glass plate. She sets it on a table and retreats from the room. Samuel follows her out, and returns with a trolley clinking with champagne bottles and glasses.

'Let us raise a toast to Princess Charlotte,' he says, 'followed by a second toast to Beckey, my dear wife. She has shown unwavering faith and devotion towards me over the years and I want her to know how much I appreciate her.'

The gesture brings a tear to my eye. Arthur has never said kind words about me.

'But you're not to drink too much,' laughs Beckey. 'Keep your wits about you and don't spoil your voices.'

Samuel pours champagne while his brothers hand out heavy crystal flutes two-thirds filled. We raise our glasses to the imminent royal newlyweds, with a louder toast for our beloved friends. It is my first experience of champagne and oh, how I love it! The aroma is divine, and bubbles tingle in my mouth, releasing hints of apricot and honey.

The bride cake is a delight to behold with pure white

icing and tiny sugar-paste rosebuds around the edge. Beckey cuts the cake into small slices, and we take turns to help ourselves to a piece. I take a bite and close my eyes, relishing the cocktail of flavours – plump juicy fruits, brandy and spice.

Beckey claps her hands. 'Come now, ladies. A last run through everything before we leave.'

We take our places in a neat semi-circle, the musicians off to one side. Following Beckey's lead, the rehearsal runs from beginning to end without a hitch.

'Well done, everyone, that was perfect. Our transportation's ready, so let us depart.'

We file out of the music room with a hum of excited chatter. As I step outside, I catch my breath. We live in a respectable neighbourhood, but never have I seen such elegant coaches and carriages lined up along the side of the street.

A footman helps me into a massive town coach and three other ladies join me. I'm dying to say something about how luxurious it is, and so befitting of the occasion, but I don't wish to embarrass myself. For all I know, my companions always travel in such style and assume I do too. Arthur is standing at our parlour window. I wonder what he's thinking.

I'm fizzing with excitement as the coach lurches forward. The horses pick up their pace to a slow trot and their metal shoes clatter over cobbles in a mesmerising rhythm. We fall silent inside the carriage, each one of us lost in our thoughts.

The horses slow to a walk.

My neighbour leans forward to peer through the window. 'Oh, my!'

An enormous crowd has gathered in Pall Mall. I have never seen so many people gathered in one place. Men, women and children cheer as we pass, no doubt assuming we are something to do with the royals. We smile and wave back, enjoying every moment until we trundle into the courtyard of Carlton House, home of the Prince Regent. A footman lowers the steps so we may disembark. I step into the sunshine, in awe of my surroundings. A grand portico looms in front of me, the high roof supported by tall columns. We wait until we're all assembled and then file through the entrance into the Grand Hall. The hall takes my breath away. An ornate high ceiling floats above archways supported by marble pillars, and statues stand in arched recesses presiding over activities on the white and black tiled floor. I pinch my arm to remind myself this moment is real and I'm standing inside a royal palace.

A footman informs us the Prince Regent is dining with guests and instructs us to keep our noise to a minimum. We follow him along a corridor, down two small flights of stairs and into a large storeroom where chairs are set out for us. I'm disappointed by this turn of events, for I would very much have liked to watch the comings and goings through the Grand Hall of the palace. The footman says we must stay hidden in this room for two hours, before he will return to escort us to our performance location. Two hours! How will we pass the time?

I needn't have worried. The minutes soon pass. We share stories of our own wedding days and try to guess the style of Princess Charlotte's dress. We stand and sing to the distant music of 'God Save The King' and then hurry back to the Grand Hall. During our absence, the hall has become congested with royal attendants in state costumes, and every wall is aglow with hundreds of candles. We arrange ourselves in our practised semi-circle and wait for our cue to sing. A butler gives a discreet wave to Beckey, then she leads us into our medley of songs, accompanied by our talented musicians.

Thank goodness Beckey insisted on so many rehearsals. While my eyes follow members of the royal family passing by, the song floats from my lips. The atmosphere lifts when the Prince of Saxe-Coburg approaches in full British uniform, and he pauses to listen, nodding his approval of our performance. His sword and belt are peppered with diamonds and coloured gemstones which twinkle in the light, adding a hint of magic to the occasion.

Beckey gives the signal to begin our grand finale. Our voices meld like a choir of angels and we sing 'Ave Maria' in perfect pitch. Then we see her, the bride, emerging from an anteroom, leaning on the arm of her uncle, the Duke of Clarence. I have not seen many brides, and my wedding was a simple affair, but I know Princess Charlotte is the loveliest bride I will ever see. Her dress is exquisite – a fine silk net laid over a delicate silver slip, embroidered at the bottom with flowers and shells, and trimmed on the sleeves with fine lace. The manteau glistens with silver laid over white silk, the edging trimmed to match the dress. She wears a crown of glittering diamond rosebuds, and large diamonds sparkle from her earlobes and around her neck. The silver threads of her dress catch the candlelight, shimmering as she walks. It's like watching a fairy-tale princess.

Our performance finishes and the doors close behind the bridal party. While the marriage service takes place, we prepare to leave.

Beckey bustles towards me. 'Susan, Mrs Ashbrook offered to take us home.' She links her arm through mine, and we step outside into the courtyard where we board our coach and wait for the ceremony to finish before we're allowed to leave.

A gunfire salute from nearby St James's Park announces the end of the formal ceremony. A footman signals to the coachman of the front carriage, and we begin a slow rumble across the courtyard.

The gentle sway of the carriage sends Mrs Ashbrook to sleep. Her head tips forward and she snores softly. I gaze through the window and watch trees slip by, wishing the magic of the day could have continued a little longer.

'Susan? What is it?' Beckey's voice is gentle.

I shift on the seat and turn to face Beckey.

Her brow puckers, and her smile fades. 'Susan?'

I bite the inside of my cheek and shake my head, desperate to keep a torrent of tears at bay. I glance at Mrs Ashbrook. Still asleep. By the time I turn my gaze to Beckey, my cheeks are soaked.

Beckey pats my forearm. 'My dear, tell me what troubles you. Perhaps I can help?'

'Arthur.' It's a struggle to say his name. 'I can't bear to be around him any more.'

'I sensed something might be wrong between the two of you. Is he really so bad?'

I clench my lips in a thin line and nod.

Beckey sighs. 'It's common for a husband and wife to have periods when the relationship is difficult. Samuel and I went through something similar many years ago.'

I want to tell her more, confide in her, but fear it will fracture our friendship if I say too much. As my husband, Arthur may treat me as he pleases, and it would be inappropriate to discuss intimate details with Beckey. I wipe away tears with the back of my hand and return my attention to the passing view.

Beckey grasps my hand in hers and gives it a reassuring squeeze. 'It's a phase, Susan, nothing more, and it will pass.

Have patience and keep working at it. Do whatever it takes to keep Arthur happy, and he'll treat you well. Every marriage demands tolerance and compromise, including my own. I'm sure Arthur cares deeply for you, beneath that haughty exterior of his.'

I'm sure he does not. How I envy Beckey, returning home to a man she loves.

CHAPTER 15

A LEMON DROP snags against the inner surface of my cheek, ripping the delicate flesh. The metallic taste of blood mixes with the sharp acidic tang of the sweet. Irritated, I crunch the drop into tiny shards, then curse myself for doing so. Fragments stick to the surfaces of my teeth and I don't want to be seen picking at them with my fingernails.

Shadows fall across the street as a thick mass of grey cloud swallows the autumn sun. I quicken my pace and hurry to Paternoster Row, bursting through the door to my favourite bookshop before the first heavy drops of water strike the filthy cobbles.

'Good day, Mrs Thistlewood.' Dear old Mr Brown emerges from behind the counter. 'Your arrival is well-timed because we're about to have yet another heavy downpour.'

Seconds later, his prediction comes true. Rain splatters against the window, running down the glass panes in thick rivulets. A gentleman, encumbered by a large, heavy umbrella, barges into the shop. Mr Brown takes the dripping umbrella and props it beside the door, creating a small puddle. The gentleman doffs his hat to acknowledge my presence.

'Mr Westcott, I didn't expect to see you this week.'

The gentleman unbuttons his frock coat. It gapes open, revealing a set of handcuffs dangling from his waistcoat.

'An investigation brought me to the neighbourhood, Mr Brown. Thought I'd call in on the off-chance before reporting back to Bow Street.'

His voice is deep, mellow and comforting.

'The first edition you requested has arrived,' says Mr Brown, retrieving a package from beneath the counter and handing it to the delightful gentleman. 'The quality is superb. I'm confident you'll be pleased.'

I cannot tear my gaze away, curious to know the title of the book this gentleman is purchasing. He unfolds the paper wrapper to reveal an exquisite leather-bound volume with pristine gold lettering along the spine.

'*Mansfield Park*,' I exclaim, daring to look into his pale grey eyes. 'Written by the lady who wrote *Sense and Sensibility*. You enjoy her novels?'

He shakes his head and smiles. 'Not me. This book is a surprise for my mother.'

'Your mother is a fortunate woman to receive such a lovely gift.'

His eyes lift at the outer corners and his lips twitch as if trying not to laugh. Then I realise I'm contorting my face while struggling to dislodge a sticky clump of confectionery with the tip of my tongue. My cheeks burn and I turn away from his scrutiny.

'Do you enjoy reading this lady's novels?' he asks.

I summon the courage to face him again. 'Very much. As a matter of fact, I've read them all.'

'Perhaps not all,' interjects Mr Brown. 'The publisher released another just a few weeks ago. *Emma*.'

I frown. 'No, I haven't read that one. Is it in stock?'

Mr Brown bows his head. 'Four arrived last week, but there's only one remaining.'

'Then I'll buy it today. May I browse while you serve this gentleman first?'

'Browse at will, Mrs Thistlewood,' says Mr Brown, gesturing that the shop is mine to wander about as I please.

'Mrs Thistlewood?' The other customer has an amused expression.

'Yes. Have we met before?'

'No. Forgive my impertinence. Thistlewood is an uncommon surname, and I should not have reacted so.' A discreet bow accompanies his apology, followed by an engaging smile.

I move to the furthest aisle, giving the gentleman privacy to make his purchase. A collection of travel journals provides adequate distraction, and I take my time to admire an atlas filled with maps coloured by a careful hand. The tinkle of a bell and the roaring of windswept heavy rain announce Mr Westcott's departure. I hope the foul weather eases soon because Arthur is expecting me home to greet a guest for dinner and I mustn't have my clothes looking as though I dragged them straight from the laundry tub.

'Does anything else appeal today, Mrs Thistlewood?'

'I'll just take *Emma* please.'

Mr Brown slides a package towards me. It's wrapped in pale blue paper and tied with a dark blue ribbon.

'You've already prepared it?'

'While you were browsing.'

I rummage in my reticule for coins. 'The price please, Mr Brown?'

'There's nothing to pay.'

'I don't understand.'

'Mr Westcott paid for this book when settling the account for his other purchases.'

'That's unacceptable. I must pay, and you will reimburse Mr Westcott when he visits next.'

Mr Brown raises his hand. 'No, madam. Mr Westcott is a loyal customer. It would offend him to refuse his kindness.'

'Then I must thank him. May I have a piece of paper to write a note for you to give to him?'

'With pleasure.'

He disappears into his office, then beckons me to enter.

'I thought you'd be more comfortable writing at my desk, so I've cleared a space.'

After settling on Mr Brown's well-worn chair, I spend a few moments considering my words. I settle on a simple statement of gratitude and regret that I could not thank Mr Westcott in person. After folding the paper twice, I write his name on the outer surface, then return to the shop counter and hand the note to Mr Brown. As I prepare to step outside, I'm relieved to see the rain has eased. I pull my cloak around me, cover my hair with the hood and bid farewell to Mr Brown before scurrying along the sodden streets with the book pressed to my chest.

'Where've you been?' Arthur's face is pinched and pale.

'I went to the bookshop at Paternoster Row.' I keep the tone of my voice light and submissive to avoid further aggravating Arthur's mood. 'I mentioned it at breakfast and offered to buy a book for you.'

He grunts and scowls. 'Our guest arrived an hour ago. It's time we ate dinner.'

I place my parcel on a side table, then remove my rain-soaked cape and drape it over the banister to dry. The air in the hallway is cold and there's a draught around my ankles. With a guest in the house, Arthur will have a crackling fire in the parlour, and I crave the heat of the flames. I hurry to the kitchen, where the air is warm and welcoming, thick with the aroma of roasted meat and rich gravy. My stomach grumbles. I ask Nancy to serve dinner in the parlour, then retreat from the kitchen to join Arthur.

Arthur's guest has settled in my armchair and does not introduce himself. I sit at the dining table and wait for the men to join me.

'This is my wife, Susan,' says Arthur, glaring at me, as if I were the ill-mannered one.

I look at the guest. He says nothing.

'And you are…?' I ask, forcing a smile.

'John Castle.'

His tone is gruff, and I take a dislike to him. 'A pleasure to make your acquaintance, Mr Castle.'

Arthur seems satisfied with the introductions. 'Castle's a recent recruit to the Spenceans and we've asked him to serve on the committee.'

'You must have made a good impression,' I say to Mr Castle. 'My husband likes his committee members to be articulate men with excellent planning skills.'

'I try my best.'

I study his clothes. His shirt is of rough linen and his jacket is threadbare at the elbows. 'Do you work, Mr Castle?'

He exchanges glances with my husband. 'Yes.'

'What line of work?'

'Well… I—'

'He was a whitesmith,' interrupts my husband, coming to the aid of his guest.

'Was?'

'He's committed to taking action along with the rest of us. His tin-polishing skill is no longer a priority. A revolution is coming, Susan. Castle has contacts that will help us gather soldiers for a new style of army.'

The room seems to tilt and I'm light-headed. Arthur has spoken of a revolution for many months. I thought he was using rhetoric to glorify a vocal campaign against the government, but Mr Castle's presence casts doubt over that and has put me on edge. Something about the man reeks of cruelty and I fear he will draw out Arthur's darker side.

'Do you plan protest marches?' I ask, struggling to steady my voice.

Mr Castle leans towards me and I recoil at his sour breath. He sees my reaction and smirks.

'It'll take more than a parade,' he says, sneering. 'The country's collapsing. We were victorious at Waterloo, but now we're taxed to the hilt to pay for it. Bread's a luxury, and thousands live in poverty while the Prince Regent primps himself and throws lavish parties. Let's hope something happens to him so he never becomes king.'

'We're planning a big rally,' says Arthur. 'Castle thinks Henry Hunt will speak for us.'

I've read detailed reports in Arthur's newspapers about Mr Hunt's great orations. 'He's an acclaimed speaker. Do you think he'll oblige?'

'Nothing to lose by asking,' growls Mr Castle, watching Nancy approach with plates of food.

'I'll write to him,' says Arthur. 'Tell him what we want him to say. He has radical views of his own, so a well-penned letter is certain to persuade him to support our cause.'

Mr Castle leers at Nancy as she pours extra gravy over his dinner. He raises his eyebrows and licks his lips. Nancy giggles and stifles a smile as if a familiarity exists between them.

Arthur frowns and clears his throat with a loud cough. 'Fetch dessert,' he snaps. 'We must leave soon to attend a meeting.'

I take a mouthful of potato and chew as if it were a chunk of tough meat. I struggle to swallow, worrying that Arthur wants an English version of the bloody French Revolution. And Mr Castle is providing ammunition.

I'm at the foot of the staircase on my way to prepare for bed when Arthur stumbles through the front door. His gaze softens when he sees me, and he runs his tongue across his upper lip. My instinct is to turn and withdraw to the kitchen, but Arthur is too quick for me. He lurches forward, wraps his arms around me and kisses me hard on the lips. The tang of sour wine turns my stomach.

'Today was a splendid day,' he slurs. 'At last, we have a plan. Action this time. Not words.'

My heart is pounding. I try to wriggle out of his embrace.

'Don't be difficult,' he says, pulling me closer, nuzzling against my neck.

I press my palms against his chest and try to push him away. Arthur grasps my shoulders and presses my back to the wall. His body is heavy against mine and I can't take a full breath. He fumbles with the bodice of my dress.

'Arthur, stop.' My voice cracks as I plead with him.

Suddenly, his hands clamp around my neck and propel

me downwards, pinning me to the lower steps. My ribs collide with the edge of a stair, and I cry out.

'Be quiet,' he growls.

He wrenches on my skirt and shift, ripping them both, raising them to expose my thighs. Pinning me down with one hand squeezing my neck and a knee on one of my thighs, he releases himself from his pantaloons and rams into me. Again and again, he lunges, struggling to find the release he seeks. At last, he judders, draws away and runs up the stairs, taking them two at a time. Through my tears I see Nancy and her expression confirms she witnessed the whole sordid event. She helps me to my feet and dabs at my cheeks with the corner of her apron before leaving me alone with my shame.

My heart aches. My body trembles. It's not the first time Arthur has forced himself on me with such violence. It will not be the last. The law permits a husband to use his wife's body in any way he chooses. But I refuse to believe that all gentlemen behave like Arthur.

CHAPTER 16

Sips of hot sweet tea improve my mood. A few weeks have passed since the humiliating incident at the foot of the staircase, but Arthur's rage persists. Each day, from the moment I wake, I dread bedtime. Our bedroom has become a war zone, and I am defenceless.

Fresh bruises encircle my neck and colour my arms. It's winter so I can hide my arms beneath sleeves, but my neck bruises rise above the collar of my dress and I have no wish for others to see the scars of my marriage. I press lightly on a livid green thumbprint at my throat. It's tender to touch and a reminder I must try harder to avoid angering Arthur again.

How long must I tolerate this life? As Arthur's campaign plans become more violent, so too does his treatment of me. I cannot bear to look at him and shudder at his slightest touch. The marriage vows that were once so dear to me are a gaol sentence now. God has forsaken me.

'Susan, I have an idea.'

Nancy's cheerful voice interrupts my troubled mind. I turn to face her, conscious that my hand is shielding evidence of Arthur's most recent assault.

'You could wear this around your neck.'

'A sash? It belongs at my waist, Nancy. My friends will think me mad if I tie a giant bow at my collar.'

Undeterred, Nancy chuckles. 'I thought you could drape it like a scarf.'

'A scarf? Indoors?'

'It's as light as air and compliments your dress.'

I take the pale blue length of muslin from Nancy and hold it against me. She's right. It picks out the light blue spots woven into my midnight blue dress. I glimpse her smile reflected in the mirror. She takes the sash from me and wraps it around my neck, not too tight, then ties it at the front.

'There. Now only you and I know what lies hidden beneath.'

'But what excuse can I give for wearing it indoors?'

'Say you've had a stiff neck. Tell them the warmth from the scarf has helped ease the discomfort.'

I nod. 'Thank you, Nancy. Is Arthur home?'

'No. Someone called by in a cab an hour ago and he left. Took all those handbills too.'

'Good.'

'There were so many. What were they for?'

'A campaign. The handbills are for members of the public, to encourage them to join the crusade.'

Arthur and his fellow Spenceans want a reduction in the price of bread and the return of common land to the people. They demand that ministers resign and make way for a new enlightened government. I'm relieved Nancy couldn't read the handbills for herself. The message was a call to arms with a promise of violence, and I fear that if they achieve the desired effect, we will move towards something like the revolution that massacred so many soldiers in France. Thank goodness Julian is at school and out of harm's way.

I pass a pleasant afternoon with Beckey, aiding the sick and delivering food to the poor. Arthur has restricted my house-keeping allowance and I cannot contribute much to our impoverished neighbours and friends. But Beckey appreci-ates my company and my shared dedication to improving the lives of others. Anna's English has improved, and with baby George now a sturdy toddler, she has found her calling, helping other widowed mothers with childcare while they seek honest ways of earning money. From the looks of them, some women still trade with their flesh, but others commit to tasks such as stitching, hawking and housemaid work. Alas, it will take more than our tiny contribution to stamp out poverty and suffering, but we've helped improve circum-stances for a few. They no longer spit or hurl abuse, but welcome us as visitors to this deprived neighbourhood. The greatest pleasure for me is spending time with the children. I grieve for those I've lost, but the sweet smiles and cheeky faces of the youngsters under Anna's care are enough to warm any heart.

It's a chilly day to be riding in a carriage and I'm relieved to reach the door to my home. As I step inside, I hear voices from the parlour. Arthur sounds cheery, but I'd prefer not to endure his company, so I continue towards the kitchen.

Nancy looks harassed.

'Do we have an unexpected guest for dinner?'

She nods. 'Don't know who he is, but he looks important. Talks loud, too.'

'But what will we serve him? We didn't plan on feeding an extra mouth today.'

'It's no bother, the mutton will stretch to one more. I've thinned out the gravy, so you'll have to mop it up with bread, but that should do to fill the gent's belly.'

'Clever of you. Well, I suppose I'd better join them.'

This time our guest stands for an introduction.

'Mrs Thistlewood. It's a pleasure to meet you. Henry Hunt, at your service.'

I gasp. 'Oh, Mr Hunt! Welcome to our home. Forgive me for not being here to greet you when you arrived.'

'Please, don't worry. It was a last-minute thing. Your husband wrote to ask me here once before and I was remiss in not replying. So today when he invited me for dinner, it was my pleasure to accept.'

'We would have prepared something more palatable had we known you were coming.' I'm gabbling, I know, but Henry Hunt is a familiar name across the land. I turn towards Arthur. 'I trust your day went well?'

Arthur nods, beaming. 'Mr Hunt agreed to speak at the meeting at Spa Fields on Friday. He'll draw a crowd and set hearts racing. They'll be clamouring to join us in battle by the time he finishes his speech.'

Mr Hunt clears his throat. 'Indeed, sir, but I don't believe in promoting violence. We want supporters to show mental resilience, not brute force. An intelligent approach is more likely to convince the hierarchy of the requirement for parliamentary reform, not a marauding pack of rabble raisers.'

Arthur dips his head in acquiescence. There's something about his expression that tells me violence is precisely what he desires. I excuse myself and ask them to take their seats at the table while I help Nancy serve the dinner.

Nancy has worked wonders with the food. With limited funds for purchasing groceries, she could not afford a decent cut of meat, but by simmering a mutton stew, she has produced a tender, delicious dish. The gravy is thinner than we are used to, but wonderfully seasoned and flavoured with rosemary. Oblivious to our frugality, Mr Hunt is bent over his dinner plate, mopping up every drop of juice. His grey hair glistens with silvery streaks, his neck is thick and his clothes strain at their seams. He is the most unlikely person to be campaigning for those who endure deprivation and squalor.

'During my speech, I'll refer to the demand for secret ballots and universal suffrage,' he says, wiping grease from his lips with the back of his sleeve.

'For women too?' I ask, for I believe universal suffrage should include everyone.

'Women?' Arthur guffaws. 'One step at a time, Susan. Let us win votes for men first, for they are the decision makers.'

'Women make decisions too,' I say, keeping my voice level.

'About dresses and groceries.' Arthur sneers and looks to Mr Hunt for his agreement, but Mr Hunt remains silent, his face impassive.

'Women run businesses,' I say, bravado getting the better of me, 'and they make decisions about staff members, stock and wages.'

'Widows,' Arthur replies, fixing me with a haughty stare. 'Widows, continuing businesses established by their husbands and using existing knowledgeable employees to keep things operating.'

I dare not press my point. Anna is the only woman I can think of who runs a business she set up herself, and I doubt Arthur would accept a French woman, paid for childcare, as a suitable example.

'It is men who must make important political decisions.' He chuckles and smiles at Mr Hunt. 'She'll be advocating a vote for children next.'

Mr Hunt gives me a weak smile, then says, 'Annual parliaments. That's something else we should demand. If an elected government can't fulfil its promises to the nation, the people should be able to choose a new one. If a government fulfils its promises, then it can be confident of re-election. A universal vote today would end Liverpool's run as leader. He's allowed machines to replace artisans so workers are losing their skills and doing menial tasks with no pride in their work, enduring longer hours for meagre pay. Meanwhile, the capitalists accumulate yet more wealth. We live in an unfair society.'

'Hence the demand for revolution,' mutters Arthur.

'The entire system is wrong,' declares Mr Hunt, his voice gaining volume as he rehearses for Friday. 'With fences enclosing what was common land, the poor can't trap wild animals to feed their hungry children. The middle classes can't vote because they don't own enough land to meet the eligibility criteria, and the rich grow richer and abuse their position by making inappropriate decisions for the running of our country. How is that fair? And how will things improve if the wealthy members of our society continue supporting each other's ambitions while depriving those who would take them on in a fair fight?'

'How do you propose to bring about change, Mr Hunt?'

Words are all very well. I want to know what action he proposes.

'After attending rallies and hearing about the need for change, men and women will unify into one loud voice, petition the government, and make themselves heard. Such mass cohesion will instil a fear of riots and that fear will be enough to provoke Lord Liverpool and his men to change.'

Arthur sucks in his cheeks and stares at me, unblinking. 'Leave us, Susan. We have things to discuss in private.'

'As you wish. Farewell, Mr Hunt.'

I stack the emptied plates and carry them to the kitchen, irritated by Arthur's dismissive attitude.

'The political tide will soon turn.' Arthur's black mood has lifted. He smiles, watching me undress and prepare for bed.

'That's marvellous news,' I say, discomforted by his scrutiny. 'Mr Hunt has a captivating presence about him. No wonder he attracts a crowd.'

'That's why we want him at our rally,' says Arthur, clambering into bed beside me and dragging chilly air beneath the sheets. 'As he said, we must instil fear into the government if we want change. When words fail, and they will, we'll use weapons to frighten those who are ruining this country.'

As Arthur rants about a need for revolution, I realise his lust for bloodshed could give me the freedom I yearn for.

Especially if he's caught doing something illegal.

CHAPTER 17

Arthur's pensive when he arrives home. It's not until Nancy serves the most delicious poached pears that he relaxes and starts talking about his day.

'Hunt was as popular as we hoped with the crowd. We definitely have more supporters now.'

Juice drips from my spoon to my dress, narrowly missing the white lace trim of my bodice. I dab at my skirt, regretting the wastage. 'I'm not surprised. He's a rousing speaker and has an aura about him.'

Arthur grunts and slurps red wine syrup from his bowl. 'I think interest will continue to grow. There were a few thousand disgruntled citizens present today. They'll spread the word and swell the crowd even more for our next meeting.' He leans forward and waggles a finger at me. 'The political tide is turning, Susan.'

I study the lines and creases of his face and the cold glint in his eyes. This man is a monster.

'What will happen when you get the level of support you seek?'

A flicker of a smile ripples across his lips. 'Go to war.'

Images of maimed bodies rush into my mind. I shudder.

Arthur narrows his eyes. 'You sympathise with Liverpool and his cronies now, do you, Susan?'

'No. Far from it.' I soften my voice. 'I dream of better lives for everyone. Something must be done, and soon. Mr Hunt's advice to use intelligence in preference to force is all very well, but...'

'But what?'

I breathe in and out, steadying my nerve. What I'm about to do relies on grown men having the strength to defend themselves against Arthur. I'm putting other people in danger, but it's for my own safety, and I'm relying on Arthur being arrested before anything serious occurs.

'Words are easy to forget, but actions are memorable. Do something that will cost the Cabinet members personally, and by any means necessary.'

Arthur's expression softens. 'Good to know I have your support. Can I trust you?'

'Trust me with what?'

I stare towards the measly fire dying in the grate. Arthur insisted I was frugal with coal.

He sniffs. 'Now and again you might hear things. I don't intend to hold many meetings at home, but if I do, you must speak of them to no one.'

'Your campaign's no secret.'

'No, but successful battles rely on the precise sharing of information, telling only those who need to know and when they need to know it. Timing is crucial.'

'I'll not divulge anything, Arthur, I swear.'

Arthur considers me for a moment, then grins. 'We plan to seize the Tower of London.'

The man's a fool! I stifle a laugh. 'The Tower?'

His face is aglow, his eyes gleaming. 'The Bank of England too. And, Susan, we'll destroy the bridges over the Thames and take control of the city.'

'How?'

Arthur sits up straight and fiddles with his cravat. 'I have visited barracks and guardrooms where discontent is rife. Many soldiers have pledged allegiance to us. The hungry, ill-treated workers will see we're building a proper army, and we'll rise together. It will be a perfect storm.'

Arthur's insane. I smile. He interprets my smile as admiration of the plan and we sit in silence for several minutes, each lost in our own thoughts.

Arthur takes out his snuffbox and flips open the lid. 'I regret to share disappointing news now.' He selects a pinch of snuff as if it were a precious jewel. 'We're running out of money. Nancy has to go.'

'Oh.' I lower my gaze to my lap and pick at a caught thread. If Nancy leaves, Arthur will expect me to stay at home to cook and clean. I'll have less time to spend with Beckey and Anna. My happiest hours are those I spend outside the house. 'Shouldn't we honour the agreed twelve-month term?'

Arthur snorts. 'Under normal circumstances, yes, but I've found an alternative position for her. Mr Castle has agreed to take her on.'

'In what capacity? He didn't strike me as a gentleman in need of a housemaid.'

Arthur ignores my question. 'Julian will leave Charter-house, too.'

'No!' I won't let Arthur's madness ruin Julian's future. 'He has a scholarship. You don't pay fees.'

'But I have to clothe him, buy books and dress you to a standard befitting of a Charterhouse parent.'

'But, Arthur, my clothes are in fine condition and I handle them with care. Julian has plenty of room to grow into his uniform. Bringing him home will add another hungry mouth to feed, so isn't it more cost-effective to leave him where he is?'

Arthur sighs. 'I suppose so. We don't have to visit the school so he can stay for now. And there's one more thing,' says Arthur, fiddling with his spoon. 'We can't stay in this house. We'll move to cheaper lodgings.'

'Dear God!' My hand flies to my mouth as I struggle to resist a torrent of sobs. 'Where will we go?'

Arthur shrugs. 'We've no need of this grandeur. I'll find somewhere with fewer rooms. Something easy for you to manage alone.'

I'm speechless. Arthur has enjoyed opulent surroundings in the past – as have I. My father's butchery business provides a large income and a spacious comfortable home for my mother, but Arthur and I have only two bedrooms and the garret. Thousands of families cope with properties smaller than this and I should not be ungrateful, but must we live like paupers?

Arthur takes my silence as acceptance.

'That's settled then. I'll be out until late tonight, so don't wait up.' He rises from his chair and strides out of the room.

When the front door closes behind him, I flee from the parlour and scamper up the stairs, eager to avoid Nancy. As I enter the bedroom, I glimpse the blue wrapping paper of Mr Westcott's gift and fall to my knees, distraught. If our funds are as low as Arthur suggests, my trips to Paternoster Row are over. I reach out and caress the ribbon, vowing to keep the package wrapped as a promise of a happier future while I pursue a campaign to rid myself of Arthur.

~

A creaking on the stairs announces Arthur's return. He creeps to my side of the bed. I keep my eyelids closed, feigning deep sleep, and resist the urge to wrinkle my nose at the revolting concoction of odours emanating from his body. The bittersweet fragrance of burnt tobacco and the stale tang of sweat mingle with fumes of gin and cheap wine.

Arthur's fingertips brush against my cheek. I hold my nerve and do not flinch, keeping my breaths slow and regular. At last he shuffles away. I'm alone in the room, and the tension evaporates from my muscles.

Arthur's footsteps retreat along the hallway, heading towards the staircase. There's a moment of silent hesitation, then the groaning of stairs. My heartbeat quickens and I sit up in bed wondering if my ears deceive me. Footsteps creak above the ceiling, confirming Arthur is in the garret. Curious, I wrap myself in a blanket and slip out of bed. I make my way to the bottom of the staircase, avoiding the squeaky floorboards, straining to detect noises from above. Several minutes pass. Nothing. But then my patience is rewarded. A muffled conversation with no distinct words. I mount the lower stairs, placing my feet to the sides where I know they'll make no sound.

Halfway up, I pause and listen. Silence. Arthur and Nancy must be sleeping. Fatigue engulfs me and I turn to head back down to the bedroom. As I lower one foot to the step below, a noise stops me. Hands gripping the banister, I stand still. There it is again. A soft smacking sound of lips joining and separating in passionate kisses.

A giggle tumbles down the stairs followed by the creaking of a bedframe. Muted moans ricochet off the walls.

'Shh!' says Nancy.

There's a volley of panting, then a loud, satisfied sigh.

I perch on a stair, cocooned in darkness, brimming with optimism. If I can prove Arthur's adultery and violent mistreatment, I will have legitimate grounds to petition for divorce.

CHAPTER 18

THE BREAD TILTS and flops from the fork, landing between flames and settling on dusty coals. It doesn't matter. I have no appetite for breakfast – a small blessing as Arthur has finished the rest of the loaf. With a busy schedule today, he won't have time for another meal until this evening.

Our new routine suits me well. Arthur stays out late most days, and when he comes home, it's not my sleep he disturbs but Nancy's. My bruises are fading, the tenderness gone, and I am almost whole again. This is a mixed blessing because if my life is not in danger, I cannot petition for divorce. But I'm willing to bide my time. It won't be long before Arthur crosses to the wrong side of the law.

My relationship with Nancy has altered. While my husband favours her with his attention, we cannot pretend to be friends, so I've insisted she respect me as her mistress. She may no longer call me by my given name and will attend to her chores without my help.

Arthur has enjoyed a winning streak at the gaming tables, so much so that he has given me a large wad of notes from which there will be enough to pay Nancy and the rent for a few months yet. As delighted as I am with this windfall, I dread to think what state we'd be in now if he had played and lost. I've stowed the money in a hiding place known only to me, ready for when Arthur's luck changes.

And so Nancy continues working for us. Her fulsome breasts attract Arthur's gaze as she leans forward to remove dishes from the table. It's a welcome sight. While she keeps Arthur's attention, I need not fear what he'll do to me.

Flames curl at the edges of the stricken slice of bread. It blackens and releases acrid smoke that makes me cough. As I wave a newspaper to clear the air, a piece of coal spits onto the rug, releasing the stench of burning wool. I grasp a pair of tongs and fling the coal back into the grate, then stamp on the charred carpet. This little drama unsettles me. Now I have an unpleasant feeling about the day ahead.

Dear Anna is poorly. The cool damp summer followed by a sodden autumn has encouraged mould growth on the wet walls of her home. The harvests were poor, and food prices have risen so high that Anna cannot spare money to buy coal. To think we could have been neighbours, and I might have shared her plight. This sobering thought makes me more sensitive to her suffering.

As Beckey unloads a basket of food, I perch on Anna's bed and rub her back. It's heart-breaking to watch her fight for breath while her chest rattles, clogged with infection.

'Here, take this.' I press a shilling into her hand.

Anna widens her eyes and tightens her fingers around the coin. 'Thank you,' she says, before a fit of coughing steals her strength and colours her lips blue. How desperate she must be to accept my charity without protest. I rearrange her pillows and cushions, propping her up to make it easier for her to breathe, then Beckey feeds her several sips of a thick syrup.

'What are you giving her?'

'White horehound. Samuel suggested hemlock, but I'm wary of giving Anna something that might poison her while she's weak. The horehound will improve her appetite and help clear her lungs.'

George sits in the corner, eyes wide with fear, watching his mother suffer.

'Come here, little man,' I say, scooping him up with my hands and hugging him close.

George touches my face with pudgy fingers and my heart swells with affection. Tears prick as my yearning for a baby returns, even though it seems unlikely I'll have a son or daughter of my own. I inhale the childish scent of George's skin and nuzzle his neck, eliciting a torrent of giggles.

'Who's looking after the little ones while you're unwell?' I ask, for Anna is in no fit state to care for her neighbours' children.

'Mary King,' replies Anna, between gasps.

'Mrs King?' I exclaim. 'The same Mrs King we had the pleasure of meeting not long after you had George?'

Anna manages a weak smile and nods.

'Just goes to show how terrible times bring out the best in people,' says Beckey.

'Shall I ask her to look after George so you can rest, Anna? I'm sure sleep will help you recover.'

Anna reaches for my hand. 'Mary offered... but George screamed... He might... settle with her... now.'

'Upstairs, two flights up, directly above,' says Beckey.

'Shan't be long.' I capture George's attention by bouncing him in my arms and pulling funny faces.

I hear the noise from Mrs King's home long before I reach the top of the stairs. There's a brief lull in the shrieks and laughter of happy children, and I take the opportunity to knock three times.

A girl who looks about eight years old pulls the door open. 'You're not George's mother.'

'His mother is sick, and I was hoping Mrs King might take George for an hour or two.'

'Ma, George's 'ere,' shouts the girl, keeping her eyes fixed on me.

Mrs King looms behind her. 'At last, Anna has come to her senses and accepted me offer,' she says, taking George from my arms.

I glance inside the room and count six children excluding George.

Mrs King smiles. 'Seeing me differently now, aren't you? I'm not a wicked person, you know.'

'Can you cope with so many children?'

I expect a sharp retort, but her tone remains amicable. 'I'm the eldest of eight, so Ma always relied on me. I'll be fine, but you're welcome to stay awhile.'

Her offer is genuine and unexpected. With regret, I decline. 'We have to make more house calls. Perhaps another time.'

I blow a kiss to George and hurry back downstairs. As I bustle through Anna's door, Beckey puts a finger to her lips and we creep around gathering our things. Anna has fallen asleep.

~

I sit in my armchair, wiggling my toes in front of the fire. I'm tired. Heavy rain has dampened everyone's spirits, and together with the ever-increasing cost of buying food, it has left the poor hungry and vulnerable to illness. Coughs and sneezes reverberate in every building and it's a wonder I haven't succumbed. Most of those we tended to today were children, their widowed mothers almost penniless and unable to pay for medicine. Beckey and I did as much as we could, drawing on Samuel's generosity and a few coins from my secret hoard.

I close my eyes and rest my head against the back of the chair, but the moment I drift off to sleep, I'm disturbed by a visitor pummelling at the door.

'On me way,' yells Nancy as she hurries from the kitchen.

I sit bolt upright in the chair, straining to hear a muffled conversation and learn what brings a caller so late in the evening.

Nancy taps on the door to the parlour, then steps inside without waiting for my invitation. 'Sorry to bother you, mistress, but there's a youth here to see you. I tried to shoo him away, but he's having none of it. Says he won't leave until he's spoken to you in person.'

A skinny boy follows Nancy into the room. He's panting and his cheeks are crimson. 'Sorry to barge in, missus, but you'll be wanting to hear this.'

The boy wears shabby clothes and his skin is grey with grime. He looks about twelve or thirteen years of age, and it would not surprise me to learn he works long hours in a factory. The tension in his facial muscles suggests now is not the time for casual conversation.

'Well? What do you wish to tell me with such urgency?'

The boy squirms. 'There was chaos.'

'Where?' My mouth has gone dry. Let him be the bearer

of the news I've been waiting for. 'Is Mr Thistlewood injured?'

'Started during the meet at Spa Fields, missus. The talk of taking up arms set tempers flaring and 'undreds went on the rampage, smashing shop windows, stealing weapons, doing what they thought was wanted of 'em. They were furious Prince Regent won't give much money to feed them poor mariners, and about the corruption in government. They were angry. Troops came to disperse 'em and even read The Riot Act.'

'How does this concern me?' I hope he's about to tell me Arthur was arrested for inciting the riot. Perhaps he followed through on his promise to seize the Tower and burn London's bridges.

'Mr Thistlewood was trying to rally support for an attack on the Tower of London, but the people who turned up to hear 'im thought it was a bad idea so turned tail and fled. And then your 'usband didn't get the support 'e expected from the troops and instead of joining with 'im, they was hunting 'im. 'E 'ad to run for 'is life!'

'How do you know this?'

'From me stepfather, missus. 'E's acquainted with your 'usband, and they 'ave the same opinions on many things to do with the government. Me stepfather was with yer 'usband when the trouble started.'

'And where is my husband now?' Please God, let him be languishing in gaol.

'Gone into 'iding. Said 'e'll get word to you when 'tis safe to do so, but to warn you it might be a long wait.'

My heart flutters. 'What's your name, boy?'

'John, missus. John Davidson.'

I retrieve my reticule from beside my chair and take out a sixpence.

'Thank you, missus.' He flips his cap onto his head and follows Nancy out of the room.

I press my palms together and thank God for the wonderful news.

Arthur is a wanted man.

PART IV
1817

CHAPTER 19

ARTHUR IS PALE AND GAUNT, his eyes rimmed with violet shadows. The basement room is airless, and a chamber pot festers in a corner, giving off pungent fumes of human waste. There are stains on the tangled bedsheets and Arthur's clothes are filthy.

This is my first visit to his hiding place.

'Why didn't you come sooner?'

I cower on the edge of his bed, elbows pressed to my sides.

'Well?' He waves his arm, dismissing the brute who led me here at knifepoint.

I wait for his henchman to climb the stairs and step outside before answering.

'Every time you have a visitor, you risk being discovered.' My voice is reedy, barely recognisable as my own.

Arthur steps towards me and raises his hand. I shrink away, but instead of striking my face again, he reaches into the basket beside me and pulls out a cloth containing bread and cheese.

'Eat with me.'

I shake my head.

Arthur tears off a small hunk of bread and holds it out. 'I said eat with me.'

'I had something earlier.'

'Then eat again. For all I know, you've poisoned the food.'

The thought crossed my mind. I blame Beckey for mentioning hemlock when Anna was unwell. An apothecary agreed to sell it to me, but I lost my nerve and asked for a small bottle of aniseed oil instead.

I accept the piece of bread and chew slowly. It clings to my tongue and the roof of my mouth and I cannot swallow. Arthur passes me the flagon of ale. I take a sip and it almost chokes me. Arthur pulls a knife from under his pillow and cuts off a wedge of cheese. My stomach turns and I taste bile, but I know what I must do. I take a small bite and force myself to swallow, helped by another sip of ale. Satisfied the food poses no risk, Arthur rips into the bread and crams it into his mouth.

My legs ache from trying to suppress trembling. My shoulders twitch, and a pressure builds in my bladder.

Arthur wipes his mouth with the back of his sleeve. 'Thought you didn't want to see me, Susan. Assumed you'd abandoned me.'

'No, Arthur. The only reason I didn't come was to protect you.'

He stares at me, eyes flinty, lips twitching. At last he looks away, and the tension eases in my limbs.

'I've worried about you. You can't stay here forever. What will you do?'

'What do you want me to do? Give myself up to accusations of treason? They'd march me to the gallows saying I incited the murder of Cabinet ministers and the Prince Regent.'

'Isn't that what you wanted? A violent uprising?'

'It was rhetoric!'

He had me fooled.

'Can you persuade the authorities your intent was only to stir up feelings?'

Arthur paces the room, banging his temples with his fists. 'Doubt it. No one will listen. Nothing I say will convince them.'

A glimmer of hope for me then.

He stands over me and grips my shoulder. 'I have form, Susan.'

A shiver passes through me. 'What form?'

'There are people who will say I've shown unreasonable levels of violence in the past.' He resumes pacing.

'Have you?'

'I did what any other fellow would have done in certain situations. There's one man out there, blind in his right eye and walks with crutches. For a few shillings, he'd accuse me of attempting to murder him.'

'And did you?'

Arthur's mouth lifts at the corners. He says nothing. Doesn't need to. He drags a rickety old chair across the room, places it in front of me then sits and takes my hands in his.

'I've been unkind, and I'm sorry.' He looks around the room, then fixes his eyes on mine. 'Cooped up in here, I've had time to reflect. I may have mistreated you and had an indiscretion or two, but I want a second chance, Susan. We've misjudged each other. Let's move away from London, start again somewhere else and enjoy one another's company like we did in the early days of our marriage.'

Memories dance before me. My imagination peels away layers of time and I find the Arthur I fell in love with. Smart, handsome and opinionated, but with laughter in his eyes and a gentle manner. From somewhere deep in my heart, a sliver of affection resurfaces.

'Do you mean it, Arthur? Your henchman brought me here with a knife held to my back.'

'Captivity's sending me mad, Susan. I wasn't thinking straight and was desperate to see you.'

'And if I'd refused to come, would your man have killed me?'

Arthur shakes his head. 'No, he was only instructed to frighten you, to make sure you came. Believe me, Susan, I want to give you the life you deserve. Help me. Get me away from here.'

I slip my fingers from his grasp, wondering if I'm capable of loving him again. I've no choice but to try, otherwise I'll risk having another of his thugs hold a knife to my side.

'It won't be easy, Arthur. I'll end Nancy's contract. She's an unnecessary expense.'

'Agreed.' His face is lined with determination. He slides off the chair and kneels before me. 'Forgive me, Susan.' He peppers my hand with kisses. 'I know I've not always been a kind husband, but from this day forward, I'll love and respect you.'

For the first time in our marriage, Arthur's offering something that resembles a genuine apology. His expression is sincere, his eyes full of adoration. What choice do I have other than to believe him?

～

I invite Nancy to join me at the kitchen table.

'With things as they are, I regret I must release you from our employ.'

Her face drops. 'I wondered if this day was coming. Where's Arthur?'

I stiffen at her lack of respect. 'Mr Thistlewood is in lodgings elsewhere for the time being. I'm not at liberty to tell you where.'

She raises her eyes to the ceiling. 'How much notice?'

'One week. That should suffice for seeking alternative employment.'

'Very gracious,' she says, her tone loaded with sarcasm. 'I've got options. Seeing as I'm no longer wanted here, I'll leave as soon as I can.'

'Would you like a letter of reference?'

Nancy stands and puffs out her chest. 'That won't be necessary, but thanks anyway. Now, excuse me while I pack up me things.'

'Of course.'

Nancy sucks in her cheeks. 'I only did what I did 'cos your husband threatened to hurt me. You know what he's like. He means trouble.'

'He's changed.'

Nancy shakes her head. 'Men of his type never change.'

'I have his word.'

'Then there's no point disputing it. Good luck, Mrs Thistlewood.'

A shadow of doubt engulfs me.

As evening draws in, I crave company. I call at Beckey's and ask if I may sit with her for a while.

Samuel's out attending to an emergency, and Beckey's glad of my visit. She has proven herself a genuine friend since learning of the warrant for Arthur's arrest. I've enjoyed several delicious dinners with her and Samuel, and Beckey gave me three fashionable winter dresses which she claims do not fit any more although there's no evidence to suggest she has gained weight.

I share the news of Arthur's dreadful lodgings and the decision to end Nancy's employment.

'What does he plan to do next?' she asks.

A breath catches in my throat. 'The only viable option is to leave the country.'

Beckey cocks her head to one side. 'A perfect opportunity for a fresh start. Are you open-minded about where you go? And is Arthur willing to work?'

'Yes, I'm sure he is. Do you have an idea?'

'It'll break my heart to have you so far away, but there is something I can do.'

'Oh, Beckey, please tell me more.' I sound desperate, but my dear friend may be about to solve the biggest dilemma I've ever encountered.

'I have a brother in America. Matthew borrowed money from Samuel to set up a business and has yet to repay the debt. I could write and ask him to take on Arthur. Matthew owns a large printworks. He can provide a position for Arthur and an apprenticeship for Julian.'

'You'd do that for us?'

Beckey's face softens. 'It's a pleasure to help.'

Snuggled in bed, I try to imagine a life in America. I'm excited. Beckey let me read her brother's letters describing the sights and sounds of New York. It's so different to London. More exotic. Eagerness gets the better of me and I slip out from beneath the covers. The remnant of a candle burns in its holder, the flames casting an enticing glow over the blue paper enclosing *Emma*. I stroke the ribbon, still taken aback by the generosity of the gentleman who bought it for me.

I decide to retrieve my money from its hiding place to check there's sufficient to pay for three passages to America. As I push a hefty wooden trunk along the exposed floorboards, I cringe at the loud scraping noise and hope it didn't wake Nancy. I press on one end of a short floorboard and grasp the opposite end with my fingers when it tilts upward a few degrees. A large splinter slides under my fingernail. I squeal but persevere with raising the board. After considerable effort, it pulls free. I reach for the candle and hold it above the gaping hole. Something is wrong. I reach into the darkness and grope around for the old scarf in which I wrapped Arthur's winnings. It must have slipped deeper when I made the last withdrawal. I tilt the candle, lowering it towards the hole. Hot wax drips into the void and the small flame illuminates the gap beneath the floorboards. I sit back on my haunches, and the room sways. A heavy feeling settles in the pit of my stomach. The money has disappeared.

Did I hide it somewhere else? I wrack my brains, recalling every action from when I retrieved the bundle a week ago. There's no doubt I replaced it here. I remember snagging my skirt on the same splinter that drew blood from my finger tonight. No one else knew the money was there, unless...

I run up to the garret, stumbling on the stairs, holding my breath in case it extinguishes the candle. I burst through the door and the flickering light confirms my fears. The room is empty.

Nancy has gone.

CHAPTER 20

MOTHER LAYS thin slices of bacon side by side in a hot pan. The sizzle is comforting, the aroma mouth-watering. Two days at home with my beloved parents have restored my sanity. But they are not yet aware of the reason for my visit.

We sit together at the oak table in the centre of the kitchen. My youngest brother departed earlier on an errand and the two older ones left late yesterday evening to return to their own families. I'm relieved to have my parents to myself. We settle down to a breakfast feast and eat in companionable silence. I wipe my plate clean, mopping up every glisten of grease and a slick of yolk with a generous hunk of fresh bread. It is the most delicious meal I've eaten for many weeks.

'Tell me, Susan, how much money do you need?'

My cheeks burn. 'Father?'

'It's been years since you came to Horncastle. I read the newspapers and have seen reports of riots that also mentioned Arthur's name. Things must be difficult for you with him in gaol.'

'He's not in gaol.'

Father raises his bushy silver eyebrows. 'Then where is he?'

'I can't say.' I'm wringing my hands beneath the table, uncomfortable withholding the truth from my parents. My mother's homely face is full of pity. I'm determined not to cry.

'We plan to leave England and put this dreadful time behind us,' I say, with forced levity. 'We'll start afresh, re-establish ourselves away from all this trouble. My dear friend Beckey has written to her brother calling in a favour, advising him a debt will be repaid if he takes Arthur on at his print works and Julian as an apprentice. Her brother has a thriving business in New York.'

Mother catches her breath. 'Must you go so far away? We might never see you again.'

I stare at my lap. I've chosen to forgive Arthur and must not waver. 'Mother, it's six weeks by packet ship. My brothers can manage the business while you and Father spend time with us after we're settled.'

Mother grimaces. 'Such a visit is unlikely, as you well know. Arthur deserves his fate but I can't believe you're allowing him to drag you into his mess.'

I reach across the table for her hand. 'It took something as drastic as this to show Arthur how unreasonable he's been. We've talked it through, and he acknowledged he was disre-spectful. He apologised and assured me he's a changed man.'

Father frowns.

Mother rolls her eyes. 'A leopard does not change its spots, Susan. Arthur's the same man he's always been, and always will be.'

'No, Mother, not this time.'

'Is it what you want?' Father's eyes bore into me, watching for every tiny twitch of reaction.

'Yes, Father.'

Mother rises from her chair and glides out of the kitchen. I know her heart is breaking. Mine is too.

Father lets out an exasperated sigh. 'Very well. I'll provide sufficient money to pay for three passages to America. There will be a little left over to cover basic expenses and tide you over until Arthur receives his first wages.'

'Thank you, Father.' I hesitate. 'We'll repay you one day, I promise.'

Father rolls his eyes. 'Perhaps, Susan, but never make a promise unless you can keep it. I'd prefer you to consider the money as a gift from a father to his daughter.'

Mother's eyes are red. She clings to me, and I wrap my arms around her, whispering reassuring words. I wonder if we'll ever see each other again. With a heavy heart, I board the coach and begin the long uncomfortable journey back to London.

The stagecoach rumbles and jolts, bouncing along rutted roads and throwing me from side to side. It's a wonder the horses do not lose their footing and tip the coach on its side. I'm certain that by the time I arrive home, I'll have multiple bruises from knocking against the side and the bony elbow of the elderly lady next to me. Thank goodness Father paid extra for my comfort, otherwise I'd be riding headlong into a storm along with the poor wretches outside.

Hailstones beat against the carriage windows and draughts seep through the edges of the doors. With one hand, I pull a coarse blanket across my legs and over the lap of my neighbour. My other hand grips the box given to me by my father. I still don't know what's inside.

At last I stumble through my front door. The house is cold and unwelcoming. No fires burn in the grate. No candles flicker in the sconces. The pantry is almost empty, and all I can find to eat is pickled onions and plum chutney. I'll go out early tomorrow morning for provisions.

Fatigue catches up with me and I struggle up the staircase, clutching my travelling bag in one hand and Father's wooden box in the other. I sit on the edge of the bed and place the box on my lap. After closing my eyes and counting to ten, I prise open the lid.

Tears drop to my dress and spread into a dull pink stain. Father has saved us. I flatten the bundle of notes and count them twice. Two hundred pounds.

CHAPTER 21

TIRED AND HUNGRY, I sit next to Julian on the edge of a narrow bed. I open a package that Beckey pressed into my hand moments before the carriage rolled away from our home. Monkey biscuits. I offer them to Julian. He hesitates, then helps himself to three before pushing my forearm away. My stomach is churning, my heart racing, but I force myself to nibble on a biscuit. I can't shut out the image of Beckey's tear-stained face when we said farewell to each other. There was a finality about it, and the enormity of what we are doing settles heavily on my mind.

Our cabin is small with two beds separated by a battered chest of drawers, and the cramped space smells of weak stomachs from previous voyages. A crewman said the *Perseus* transported convicts to New South Wales. How apt that Arthur should join the same ship. I glance at the door. He should be here by now.

My eyes ache from lack of sleep, and I'm on edge. I worry about forgetting to call myself Mrs Wilkinson and blowing Arthur's cover. Thankfully, Arthur's contact, Mr Moggridge, booked the berths, because if it had been left to me, I'm

122

certain I'd have used the name Thistlewood. I'm nervous about this clandestine behaviour, but Julian's taking it in his stride. He follows my instructions without question and sticks by my side like a limpet clinging to a rock. Or am I clinging to him? It's hard to tell.

A scuffle outside in the corridor. I tense, and Julian stiffens beside me. There's a mumble of words, a slight rattle of the door handle, then the patter of several pairs of footsteps moving away. A simple case of mistaken cabin. I let out a slow breath.

'Ma?'

My skin tingles at Julian's decision to address me thus.

'Should we go up on deck? Father won't know which cabin to come to.'

I chew my top lip. 'The instruction was to wait inside so as not to draw attention.'

'Other passengers are on deck, waving to family and friends. What we're doing is unusual.'

Julian has a point, and it throws me into turmoil. I mustn't annoy Arthur and jeopardise our fragile relationship by going against his word, but our absence on deck is unlikely to cause a stir because no one else here knows us. We can't hide in a cabin for the duration of the six-week voyage.

'Give it a few more minutes,' I say.

Julian shrugs, then asks, 'Will he be glad to see me?'

I put my arm across his shoulders. 'Your father has mellowed, Julian, and realises his behaviour was intimidating. He doesn't want us to fear him any more.'

Julian lowers his head. 'It won't be easy.'

Twenty minutes pass with no sign of Arthur. My mouth is dry, my palms clammy. What if Arthur arrives too late? I can't go to America without him.

'Come, Julian. Let us wait on deck, after all.'

Julian's face is pale, jaw muscles taut. He forces a smile, then opens the door.

The fresh air is a welcome respite from the stale air of the cabin. A sizeable crowd has gathered on Gravesend dockside to wave off the ship and the hubbub of noise is reassuring. A glance at other passengers reveals travellers with varied emotions, some eager to be under way, others mourning the severing of family ties.

'There! Look, Ma! There's Pa.'

Julian waves to attract Arthur's attention, but Arthur ignores him. I frown. Something's wrong. Arthur is with three other men. One resembles Mr Moggridge – he didn't mention accompanying us when I paid for the tickets. I clutch my reticule with Father's beneficence inside. Most of the money remains intact because Mr Moggridge charged only twenty guineas for the cabin and ten guineas for his trouble.

'Ma?' Julian's voice trembles. 'What's happening?'

Two official-looking gentlemen approach Arthur. A debate takes place, and I pray that Arthur remains calm.

'Come. We should go to your father.'

'Are you sure?'

It's a struggle to hide my concern from Julian. I lack the confidence to sail without Arthur and so I push Julian ahead of me towards the gangplank.

'We cast off in two hours, missus.'

I nod at the deckhand, afraid to use my voice in case it betrays our subterfuge.

'Wife,' says Arthur, reaching for my hand. He squeezes my fingers then releases his grip. 'We need permission from the Alien Office inspector to sail on the *Perseus*.'

'Why? We're leaving the country, not arriving from some-where else.'

'Mrs Wilkinson, I presume?' says a portly gentleman with an authoritative air.

I nod, relieved to have remembered my assumed name.

'There's no cause for alarm.' His voice is soothing. 'We carry out routine checks on passengers leaving and arriving, particularly when there are persons of interest who want to leave England.'

'Persons of interest?' asks Arthur, raising an eyebrow.

'Yes, sir. You know, criminals, spies and the like.'

Arthur chuckles. 'I guarantee you, sir, we're not spies. We're embarking on a family adventure to seek opportunities England cannot provide. I've accepted an offer of work from a family friend in America.'

'Very good, sir. That simplifies things. After the inspector has seen your papers, he will record your details in a ledger and you will be free to go. This way, if you please.' The inspector leads us to a small boat.

I hesitate at the quayside. 'A wherry? Where are we going?'

He points to a moderate-sized craft anchored nearby. 'Just there, Mrs Wilkinson. No further, I assure you.'

A few strokes of the oars and we reach our destination. My legs shake as I'm helped aboard the Alien Office inspector's ship.

'Right then. This way to the office. Follow me.'

We traipse along behind him, passing a row of doors. He opens one at the very end and instructs us to enter. Inside is a single table and two chairs. Arthur flicks his hand towards a chair, and I sit.

'The inspector will be here soon.'

The official closes the door and I hear the creak of metal

as a key turns in the lock. I catch Arthur's eye and can tell he heard it too. He gives a tiny nod and I know to hold my tongue in case someone is listening on the other side.

Minutes tick by and I worry the *Perseus* will leave without us. The sound of heavy footsteps announces the inspector's arrival. At last.

The cabin door flies open and my heart skips several beats. Casting his shadow into the cabin is a Bow Street principal officer. His cheeks are red, his eyes hawkish.

'Arthur Thistlewood, it's my duty to arrest you—'

'On what charge?' blusters Arthur.

'High treason.'

'No!' I jump from the chair and rush to Arthur's side. 'You're mistaken.'

A second officer enters the cabin. 'Alas, we are not, Mrs Thistlewood.'

'You?' My cheeks flame.

A ripple of thunder passes across Arthur's face. 'You know this man?'

'Not well. We were patrons at the same bookshop in Paternoster Row.' Thank goodness Arthur has never asked about the little blue package that now almost fills my reticule.

The scowl on Arthur's face says he thinks I betrayed him.

'Arthur, it wasn't me. Beckey, Samuel and my parents knew our plans, and Mr Moggridge whom you trusted to pay for our cabin. But I swear, I told no other person.'

Mr Moggridge wears a hint of smugness. Did he betray us?

'Please come this way.' Mr Westcott makes eye contact with me and I try to read his thoughts. What low opinion must he have of me now? I lower my gaze to the well-worn deck boards. Arthur is handcuffed and bundled out of the cabin. Julian shuffles out after him.

'What about our travelling trunks on the *Perseus?*' I ask Mr Westcott.

'They must stay where they are. Our instructions are simple – none of you may leave the country.'

'But it won't take long to retrieve them. Our clothes are there. And jewellery. How will we get it all back?' I have only a few of my own possessions, but their sentimental value is huge.

Mr Westcott shakes his head. 'I'm sorry.'

I follow Arthur and watch in horror as he falls into the wherry, unable to steady himself with restrained hands. He sits on the furthest bench seat, blood trickling from the corner of his left eye. I try to move forward to join him but Mr Westcott grasps my arm to stop me. I sit and stare at my lap, picking at a loose thread, wondering what will become of us.

Arthur is bundled onto a cart and driven away at speed. Julian and I climb into a small carriage, followed by Mr Westcott. Once again, he sits beside me.

'Where are you taking us?' I ask.

'Bow Street. You'll both have to answer a few questions and after that, I expect they'll let you go.'

I nod. The three of us fall silent as the coach rumbles over cobbles. The uncomfortable rattling and shaking are the least of our troubles now.

'You should have come to me,' whispers my temporary gaoler.

'I beg your pardon?'

'Why didn't you seek my advice? I could have stopped you getting mixed up with this.'

'Why would I visit you to discuss our troubles?'

'The note.'

'What note?'

'I wrote a brief note and asked Mr Brown to place it inside the cover of *Emma*, so you'd find it.'

I hug my reticule. It's straining at the clasp because the book only just fits inside with the bundle of cash nestled beneath the lining. 'I didn't unwrap it. It was inappropriate to accept a gift from an unfamiliar gentleman.'

He nods as if he understands. I wonder what he wrote.

We arrive at Bow Street faster than I would have liked. A constable takes Julian and me to a plush room where a magistrate bombards us with questions. I'm reprimanded for supporting Arthur's subversive behaviour and travelling under a false name, then dismissed with an informal warning.

Mr Westcott escorts us to the exit, where a hackney carriage awaits. I have given Beckey's address to the coachman, for she and Samuel are sure to take us in until we find new lodgings of our own.

I'm about to step inside when Arthur comes to mind. 'Where's Mr Thistlewood?'

Mr Westcott puffs out his cheeks before answering. 'They've taken him away.'

'To where?'

He gives me a pitying look. 'The Tower of London.'

CHAPTER 22

SETTLED at the back of the courtroom, I chew a dried apricot.

'How can you eat at a time like this?' says Beckey, her eyes glistening with sympathy.

I shrug. 'Food's comforting. Concentrating on the flavour helps take my mind off Arthur.' The memory of his prison cell slides into my consciousness. It was horrific. Dark. Damp. Cramped, with insufficient headroom to stand. I'm surprised Arthur held on to his sanity, bent double from morning until night and guarded as if he were one of the Crown Jewels. I take time to select my next apricot. As I bite into it, someone gives the order to rise and everyone stands while Mr Justice Bayley glides behind his bench. An officer of the court gives a signal for us to sit and then the jurors are sworn in.

Mr Justice Bayley clears his throat before his voice booms across the courtroom. 'Gentlemen of the grand jury. You are assembled as grand jurors for this county, to discharge the duty of that service.' His voice is deep and captivating. I'm mesmerised by the tone until he utters words that capture my full attention. 'There is likely to be brought under your consideration a charge different from those which ordinarily occupy the attention of the grand jurors in this place – a charge of the highest crime that can be committed – the crime of high treason.'

A murmur ripples through the public gallery. Observers exchange whispers. Even I want to comment to Beckey but stop myself. It is Arthur who stands accused. Only the jury's opinion stands between Arthur's life and execution. Sobs catch in my throat and heads turn to look at me. Beckey hugs me until I calm myself.

Mr Justice Bayley is still speaking. His voice is irritating, monotonous and threatening.

'The charge of which I have spoken as likely to be brought before you will consist, I believe, of four different descriptions of treason. There will be – the first, compassing and imagining the king's death; second, compassing and imagining to depose the king; the third, levying war against the king; and the fourth, not actually levying war against the king, but conspiring to levy war, to force the Crown to change its measures and counsels.'

I have endured Arthur's tirades against the Establishment and his proclamations of fighting the government. I encouraged talk of violence, endured beatings, and dreamed of his arrest. But Arthur promised to change. This trial is happening before we had the chance to start again. I fix my gaze on Arthur, willing him to look in my direction. But Arthur does not turn his eyes towards me. His haggard face glares at the judge, hating every miserable word.

The directive rumbles on until, at last, the judge's tone changes. 'I am sure you will give this high and heavy charge the fullest and fairest investigation; and you will not return a bill against all or any of these persons unless it is proved, to the satisfaction of your minds, that they are guilty of all or some of the charges.' He gives one more instruction before the jurors rise from their wooden bench seats and file out of the courtroom.

'Where are they going?' I ask Beckey.

'To another room. They'll read the bill of indictment, then come back for the witness statements and decide whether there's a case for Arthur and the others to answer.'

'Oh.' My stomach makes a loud grumbling noise and I try to silence it with another apricot. I will have to sit on this uncomfortable wooden bench for many hours yet.

The jurors return and Arthur sits up straight, chin jutting forward, face rigid with concentration. I wonder what thoughts pass through his mind and worry for him. His face shows no fear and I take reassurance from that.

The day drags on, one witness after another, until half-past five when we are told the case will continue tomorrow.

～

The foreman of the jury stands. 'We find true bills against Arthur Thistlewood, James Watson the elder, Thomas Preston and John Hooper, for high treason.'

The Attorney General addresses the court, but I'm deaf to his words. Arthur is one step closer to the scaffold. I sit there, numb, unable to make sense of what's happening around me. It's like trying to hear the softest whisper against the incessant banging of a loud drum. My head hurts. My chest aches. How am I to endure this?

～

Arthur enters the court escorted by two yeomen and my heart lurches. How he has wasted away in the past two weeks. He's wearing a sailor's jacket and trousers that sag from his skinny frame. I wonder who loaned him the clothes for they are not his own. A light-coloured waistcoat makes a feeble attempt to present him as the gentleman he is, and a red neckerchief stands out as a token of rebellion against his current predicament. His eyes appear sunken, his face grey, but his resilient spirit fights on. He perks up when he sees his friends. They bow and greet each other and the solicitor for whose services Samuel contributed generously.

The court is quieter than usual because the arraignment date was not made public. For this, I give thanks. Formalities begin, and the accused men line up before the bench.

Lord Ellenborough, Lord Chief Justice of the King's Bench, addresses them. 'Would all, or any of you, wish to have counsel assigned? Thistlewood, would you?'

Arthur's back is towards me, but his words are loud and distinct. 'Certainly, my lord.'

'Would you name him now, or would you wish to have until Monday or Tuesday to name him?'

'My lord, I will wait, for I have not decided yet.'

I wonder how we will pay for Arthur's counsel. I cannot concentrate on what follows thereafter for worrying about securing funds for Arthur's legal fees. What if I can't? Will they execute Arthur without a trial? I shuffle and fidget in my seat. Beckey strokes my arm, but the gesture does little to calm me.

Words float across the room, partial sentences referring to destruction of the government, assembling weapons and making war. Even the accused cannot focus and talk among themselves while passing notes back and forth.

My ears prick up when someone calls Arthur's name.

'Arthur Thistlewood, are you guilty of the premises charged in the indictment, or not guilty?'

Arthur's voice rings out across the court. 'Not guilty.'

The Lord Chief Justice asks each accused man the same question. Each man gives the same answer.

'How will you be tried?'

'By God and our country,' they reply in unison.

The accused men confirm they have received copies of the bill of indictment and lists of the jury and witnesses. A trial date is set for three weeks hence. Arthur makes a point of looking for me this time. He smiles and my heart lifts.

But then the Attorney General kills the moment with his proclamation. 'My Lord, I have now to move that the prisoners be remanded to the Tower.'

CHAPTER 23

A SMALL MOUTHFUL of jellied eel hits the back of my throat and it's a struggle not to gag. I have never understood the fascination for this East End dish, nor Beckey's desire for her cook to recreate it in her kitchen, but I don't wish to offend her by declaring my distaste for it.

Arthur devours his as if he hasn't eaten for weeks. Beckey closes her eyes and savours every mouthful. Samuel, however, pushes his food around with a spoon, lost in contemplation. I think of a sugar plum, imagining the taste of the sweet, hard shell while wet vinegary jelly slithers towards my stomach.

My spoon taunts me with an enormous piece of chopped eel and I shudder. It's too big to swallow whole, so I hold my breath, force the mouthful of punishment between my lips, and chew.

'I'm sorry, but there's something I need to say.' Samuel's spoon clatters against the delicate rim of his china bowl. 'Arthur, it's time you moved out.'

'Samuel?' Beckey looks as shocked as I feel.

Samuel raises his hands in a gesture of despair. 'I didn't want it to come to this, but I can't tolerate it any longer.'

'Samuel, I'm sorry. I'm trying to...' My voice trembles and my fingernails dig into my palms.

'It's not you, Susan.'

We all look towards Arthur.

He draws himself to full height and glares at Samuel. 'And what have I done to offend your delicate sensibilities?'

Samuel remains calm. 'That's it there, Arthur. Your tone, your manner, your complete disrespect for anyone other than yourself. After the judge directed a 'not guilty' verdict, we welcomed you here. But as each day passes, your mood blackens and your language becomes more aggressive. No doubt it's only a matter of time before you engage in violence, and I've no wish to associate with such a man. I'm disappointed because I hoped we would become the closest of friends.'

Samuel's right. Arthur has slipped back into his old ways. For two days, he was a kind, attentive husband, complimenting me on my appearance and making promises about a contented life. On the third day, he dropped the pretence. He pummelled me for knocking his snuff tin off the nightstand and spilling the contents across Beckey's thick pile carpet. He has resumed weekly sessions at the Spenceans and, judging by his frequent absences during the evenings, several clandestine meetings elsewhere. The jingle in his pocket speaks of gaming tables and there's an odour of debauchery clinging to his skin.

Eel sticks in my throat. What a fool I've been! Tiny cracks form in my heart. I can't imagine resuming a life with only Arthur for company. I'm safer here.

'We'll move out tomorrow,' declares Arthur.

'Tomorrow?' My heart skips a beat and my vision blurs. 'So soon?'

'We mustn't inconvenience the wonderful doctor and his wife. You still have most of your father's money, which will pay for modest lodgings.'

Beckey's pity envelops me like a shroud. Our eyes meet. There's no need for words.

Fetid city air seeps through gaps in the window frames. I consider blocking them with strips of old linen and paper, but any draught is welcome in the stifling heat of our living room. I try to convince myself that our home is not so awful. The aged building is shabby from the outside but the neighbours are quiet and clean. We have only basic furniture – two armchairs by the fire; a battered old table with two rickety chairs; a bed; and a cupboard for clothes. Beckey donated a few pots and pans for the narrow kitchen, and several plates and cups.

I'm struggling to accept such reduced circumstances. Mother wrote with news that Father has paralysis on his right side and cannot speak after an attack of apoplexy, so I cannot seek their help. I must take responsibility for myself and the choices I have made.

Arthur has written to the Home Secretary, demanding compensation for the items we abandoned aboard the *Perseus* at the time of his arrest. Aside from the sugar bowl given to me by my mother, I no longer miss any of them. My only remaining treasured possession remains wrapped in blue paper and stowed in my reticule. I'm never without it because I cling to the hope of a story with a happy ending. I wonder about the note tucked inside the book but resist the urge to tear at the blue paper to retrieve it. While the note remains unread, it offers a spark of hope to guide me through the dark gloom of my future.

A knock at the door.

'Ready?' Anna beams at me from the dirt-strewn pavement.

'I am.'

I close the door and smile as Anna links her arm through mine. We are as good as neighbours now.

'How is Mrs King faring?' I ask.

Because of a frailty of her lungs since her last illness, Anna can no longer cope with caring for her neighbours' children. Mrs King surprised us by volunteering to take over the task.

'She's doing well. Her nature has softened, and she's become a friend.'

Anna has lost most of her French accent by modelling her speech on the well-to-do ladies who frequent the shop where she now works as a dressmaker. I doubt anyone could guess at her heritage.

She squeezes my arm. 'You'll enjoy it, Susan. Just you wait and see.'

Butterflies tickle my insides as a small brass bell announces our arrival. An immaculately dressed woman rushes forward. She looks to be in her mid-forties with grey hair bundled at the nape rather than sculpted on top of her head as is the trend. This simple act of fashion rebellion radiates confidence and charm.

'You must be Mrs Thistlewood,' she says taking my hands in hers and smiling. 'Anna has told me all about you. I'm Nelly Hooper.' She gestures towards a door at the rear of the shop. 'Ellen and Martha are in the workroom. Anna will introduce you later.'

'A pleasure to meet you, Mrs Hooper.'

She looks me up and down, causing my cheeks to burn, for I know my clothes appear tired.

'You have an eye for fabrics that complement your complexion,' she says. 'A sign you're suited to this trade, my dear.'

My days of helping the sick and the poor with Beckey have ended. With Father's gift dwindling and Arthur unable to secure enough money to meet our needs, I persuaded him I should earn a wage. Julian has settled as an apprentice clerk – we couldn't return him to school after his father's arrest. He's older than most new apprentices, but content with his career choice and comfortable in his small rented room at his master's house. Julian's a bright boy and I'm confident he'll do well.

'Your role is to greet customers and make them comfortable. Most of the ladies bring fabrics purchased from drapers, although recently I've bought a range of cottons and silks to keep in stock. The customers enjoy browsing the samples, so offer them if you think it appropriate. While Anna and I measure, pin and tuck, you will tidy up behind us. The amount of dust created is surprising. Handling and cutting fabric is not as clean a job as you might imagine.' Mrs Hooper's voice is gentle but I detect an air of authority hidden within her warm tone. 'Some customers are with us for over an hour, so offer those ladies refreshment. And finally, you will manage the appointment diary. We run a strict booking system, but walk-ins must believe there is no better place than here to have dresses created. If the diary is full, make the customers feel privileged to wait for attention. I will handle all bills and payments. Questions?'

'No, Mrs Hooper. Not at the moment.'

'Ask if there's something you're unsure about, but I believe you'll soon settle into your role.'

The little brass bell snatches our attention and I step forward to welcome two ladies into the shop. As my greeting floats across the room, Anna grins. I invite the ladies to take a seat, then return Anna's smile.

CHAPTER 24

I TIDY AWAY the breakfast dishes and lick marmalade from a spoon. The tangy syrup coats my tongue with delicious sticky residue, and my taste buds tingle beneath the intense flavour of orange.

I reach for Arthur's empty cup, taking care to avoid brushing against him. He's engrossed in writing a letter. Curious, I glance over his shoulder. I can only make out a few words, and they spell out a chilling message:

Should you deem this unworthy of your attention, I will have to take drastic action. Ignore this at your peril.

My pulse quickens and I stifle a gasp. Several letters preceded this one and I wonder if Arthur wrote them in similar tones.

'Who are you writing to, Arthur?'

He glances at me and snarls. 'Sidmouth's Under Secretary. The whoreson refused to compensate us for the items left on the *Perseus*, choosing to overlook the 'not guilty' verdict. They had no right to force us to abandon our possessions in such a humiliating manner and there's no justification to withhold recompense.'

Arthur reloads his quill with ink and glares. His eyes are muddy like the River Thames in a storm. I look away and am relieved when he resumes scratching ink across the paper.

An October breeze rattles the window, inviting me to peer through the glass. Leaves drift along the street, rising and falling on unseen waves, sticking to cloaks and tickling horses' hooves. I'm mesmerised by figures appearing through the mist as if stepping through a doorway from one mystical world to another.

With silent footsteps, I creep up behind Arthur and peer at the letter in his hand. As he reads it through, I strain to make out the words on the paper. There's a list of demands and insistence upon the return of our belongings. I spy the calls for a mix of items including shirts, pantaloons, waistcoat and hat, inkstand, writing books, music books and goose-quills.

'Trousers for a little boy! At fourteen years of age, he's almost a man.'

I regret my outburst. Arthur rises from his chair. His jaw muscles tense. I swallow hard and take a step back to increase the distance between us. He stands facing me and tilts his head.

'What did you say?'

I shrink away from him, but he steps closer, clenching and unclenching his fingers. I reach behind my back for something to cling to, finding nothing but air.

'They won't take kindly to a lie,' I say, stammering. 'It may get you into more trouble.'

Arthur snorts. 'They're more likely to be sympathetic if they believe they robbed a child of waistcoat and trousers.'

I know better than to push him further.

Arthur folds the letter ready for delivery. As he scrawls the name 'John Cam Hobhouse' across the front, I realise that only one thing of mine was on the list, and something of no importance. An umbrella.

It takes several minutes to conceal the bruise above my left eye – a reminder of Arthur's temper after I tried to refuse his amorous advances last night. With judicial use of powder, I have reduced it to nothing more than a faint shadow, but it does not fool Anna.

'Susan, I fear for you. If your husband strikes you like this, you are in danger. Please stay with me. My home is small and George will pester for attention, but you'll be safe.'

Her kindness is overwhelming, and I smile at her with tear-filled eyes. 'That's generous, Anna, thank you.'

'Has he done this before?'

I nod.

'I should have offered sooner.'

I'm relieved she knows nothing of my other injuries, although she will notice my discomfort when I try to sit down.

'Come home with me this evening.'

'I'll need to fetch some clothes.'

'A spare dress and shift is all you need to start with, and perhaps one or two personal items. We'll collect them later, together, after work.'

'But if Arthur sees…'

Anna looks at me through large, pitying eyes. 'If he's at home, tell him I've offered to alter one of your dresses with embroidery on the bodice or something like that. Wrap any other items inside the dress and I'll take them, then you can slip away later when the moment is right.'

We complete our walk to work in silence. I'm nervous

about moving in with Anna, but grateful Arthur does not know her address.

My hands shake as I open the front door.

'Arthur, I'm home.'

I stand still in the hallway. Silence. Anna taps me on the arm, urging me to hurry. I nod and walk towards the parlour door. I peer into the room. Arthur's chair is empty and no fire burns in the grate. I check the kitchen. No sign of him there. Finally, I step into the bedroom. Arthur's coat is missing and I'm reassured that he's attending a meeting.

I spread my favourite dress on the bed and lay two shifts on top. Then I add a little pot of face powder and my hairbrush. It amounts to so little, but with time I'll rebuild my wardrobe and collect new little trinkets. As I'm about to walk through the door, I remember the package concealed beneath the mattress. The ribbon has frayed at the ends and the paper worn thin on the folds. I doubt it will hold together much longer. I push it into my reticule and hurry to join Anna.

CHAPTER 25

THE DAY DRAGS at Mrs Hooper's shop and I can't resist the temptation to eat the last three lemon jam tartlets provided for the customers. The girls are busy in the back room adding finishing touches to garments while Anna and Mrs Hooper cut pieces of silk for new dresses. I accept two deliveries from home-workers who've added exquisite embroidery to evening dresses, but the appointment book remains empty. Dreary weather keeps genteel ladies at home. I have buffed and polished every surface, swept every inch of the shop floor, and tidied shelves and storage boxes. Even the windows endured a scrubbing. Mrs Hooper permits me to finish early, providing an opportunity for a special treat. A visit to Paternoster Row.

Keeping a brisk pace, I reach Mr Brown's shop in less than an hour. Mr Brown opens the door, welcoming me with his friendly face and smiling eyes. The fragrance of books wafts through the air and my eager eyes scan the shelves. I fancy a poetry book today, something to dip into whenever I need to escape to a better world.

As I turn the pages of an illustrated anthology, I stumble

across a poem by William Wordsworth, a modern romantic poet. The opening line tugs at my heart because it encapsulates the way I have been feeling for many months.

'I wandered lonely as a cloud,' I murmur, reading the poem aloud. By the time I reach the end, I'm absorbed in Mr Wordsworth's image of yellow daffodils dipping their heads in gentle winds, casting light to kill darkness and lifting the bleakest of moods. When I raise my head, I'm surprised to see Mr Brown beside me.

'Months have passed since your last visit,' he says.

'I wish I could visit more often, Mr Brown.'

'Do you want to buy that one?' he asks, nodding towards the little book clasped in my hands.

I shouldn't. It would be an insult to Anna's kindness. I need every spare coin to contribute towards the food we will eat tonight. 'Another time, perhaps.'

Mr Brown squints at me. 'I don't suggest this to many customers, but if you'd like to take it today, you can have it on account and pay another time.'

My skin tingles and I feel queasy. Has he guessed at my reduced circumstances? If I save the odd coin here and there, I'll have enough to settle the account in six to eight weeks. Pride stops me refusing the offer.

'Thank you, Mr Brown.'

'I'll wrap it. We don't want the damp air to ruin the pages.'

His talk of wrapping compels me to reach inside my reticule and run my fingertips over the precious blue package. It's reassuring beneath my touch, promising happier times. I remove enough coins to pay a small deposit for the poetry book, then close the reticule to shut out the memory of Mr Westcott's generosity. Mr Brown hands over my parcel wrapped in cream paper and tied with a length of purple ribbon. He holds the door open and as I step outside into the miserable autumn air, I realise I've been harbouring a foolish fancy that I might see Mr Westcott today. I glance along the street in both directions, willing him to emerge from the shadows.

Disappointment settles like snow. He's nowhere to be seen.

There's a break in the thick grey clouds and the sunlight beyond creates an alluring silver shimmer. The vision is ethereal, hypnotising, and for a few brief moments, I believe I have found contentment.

A powerful arm wraps around my body, pinning my elbows to my sides. A hand clamps across my mouth and I'm pulled backwards into a narrow alleyway. My heart beats so fast I fear it will burst. I try to wriggle free, but the arm tightens. I breathe through my nose but cannot get air to my lungs. My vision greys, the alleyway ripples and fades. And then, nothing.

When I come to, I'm lying across a seat inside a scruffy coach, bumping and jerking over cobbles. A man sits opposite, his legs clad in dark trousers. My head throbs and it hurts to move my eyes, but I lift my gaze to see who has rescued me.

'Susan.'

My stomach lurches. There's a roaring in my ears. This man is no rescuer.

'Two nights away from home but no message to tell me where you are. What were you thinking by leaving without telling me?'

'How did you find me?' My voice is a ragged croak.

Arthur laughs. 'You made a poor job of hiding. Your employer has a memorable name, and it wasn't difficult to find a dress shop near Oxford Street run by a woman called Nelly. I had someone watch the store and when he sent word that you'd finished early today and gone to Paternoster Row, I came straight away.'

I touch the top of my head to discover a sizeable tender lump and my fingertips come away sticky with blood.

Arthur leans forward, lips stretched in a tight smile, his gaze intense. 'As my wife, you belong at home with me. You took vows to serve and obey me for as long as we both live, and you will honour those vows. Otherwise, I'll kill you.'

CHAPTER 26

CRISP, firm chocolate biscuits fail to lighten my mood. Nevertheless, I help myself to a third, seeking comfort from the rich taste of quality cocoa. Mrs Hooper sent out for them this morning – Lord knows we needed cheering up after learning Princess Charlotte gave birth to a stillborn son last night. We're all tearful at the news, as is most of London. Every time I think of our gentle princess, tears prick at my eyes. Singing before her wedding made me feel closer to her. It's as if I'm mourning a dear friend.

'To work, ladies, if you please.' Mrs Hooper gathers empty plates and cups while the rest of us resume our tasks.

A steady stream of bookings keeps us busy. By mid-afternoon, there's a shift in atmosphere. The mood darkens further and Lady Tylney, known for her punctuality, is already running twenty minutes late for her appointment. When the clock strikes three, we predict something is very wrong. We gather by the doorway and windows and peer into the empty street.

'What on earth has happened? Where is everyone?' Mrs Hooper's brow is furrowed.

I point across the street. 'The drapers are as bewildered as us.'

'Martha, be a dear,' says Mrs Hooper. 'Hurry to Oxford Street and find out what the devil has happened. Everyone else, back to work.'

The counter tops are gleaming, the floorboards clear of threads and scraps. Scissors slicing through cotton make an eerie sound against the background silence. We are all lost for words. Something terrible has happened.

Martha flings the door wide open. Her face is ashen, glistening with tears, and strands of hair cling to her wet cheeks. A newspaper trembles in her hand.

Mrs Hooper flies to her side. 'Martha, whatever has happened?'

We all stand still, watching Martha, waiting.

'She's… she's…'

'Who, dear? And what is she? Take a breath. Tell us what upsets you.'

My legs tremble. The deserted street tells of momentous bad news.

'It's the princess,' Martha blurts out between sobs. 'She's dead!'

I cannot breathe. My chest aches. 'Dead? How?'

'I don't know.' Martha thrusts the newspaper into Mrs Hooper's hand.

I lower myself to a chair. My brain turns to bubbles, each one bursting as I try to make sense of this news. Princess Charlotte was adored by everyone.

Mrs Hooper wipes her eyes with the back of her hand, then flattens an extraordinary edition of the *London Gazette* on a countertop. She takes a deep breath, then reads aloud. 'Her Royal Highness, the Princess Charlotte Augusta, daughter of His Royal Highness the Prince Regent and consort of his Serene Highness Prince Leopold of Saxe-Coburg was delivered of a stillborn male child at nine o'clock last night.' Mrs Hooper pauses for a few long seconds. This news we know already. There must be worse to come. 'About half-past twelve, Her Royal Highness was seized with great difficulty of breathing, restlessness and exhaustion, which alarming symptoms increased till half-past two this morning, when Her Royal Highness expired.'

I bury my face in my hands. Dear, sweet Princess Charlotte. Dead.

With puffy faces and quivering lips, we console one another. No wonder the streets are empty. A period of national grief and mourning has already begun. We gaze from one sad face to another, dumbstruck.

Mrs Hooper interrupts the silence. 'Ladies, finish what you were doing and go to church to pray for her soul. Then find comfort at home with your families. Do whatever helps you move forward from this sad moment because tomorrow we will be busy. London will want to wear black.'

Anna and I take quiet steps towards the church. When we turn a corner, we see a crowd before us, a silent swarm of mourners. We join the back of the throng and await our turn to enter the church. As each sad face leaves its god behind, a new one steps through the large arched doorway, seeking answers to questions and comfort for grief. We find space on a crowded pew near the front of the church where the altar is swathed in black silk. Weak strands of November sunlight filter through the stained-glass windows, casting a sad grey-blue light on dipped heads. We sink to our knees and pray as if our lives depend upon it.

~

A feeble fire burns in the grate, dwindling from lack of attention. Arthur's in his armchair, fingertips pressed together, head lowered. He lifts his head and glowers at me when I enter the room.

'You're home early.'

A small flame rises among the coals. It flickers and fades.

'Isn't it the saddest news?'

'What is?'

'Princess Charlotte.'

'What of her?'

'You haven't heard? Her son was stillborn last night and then...' I take a moment to suppress my grief. 'Arthur, she died.'

'Oh, that.'

'Is it not heartbreaking?'

He snorts. 'Worse things have happened.'

'Like what?' I struggle to control my exasperation.

He leans forward with menace in his eyes. 'Susan, have you forgotten already? The death of an overindulged privileged woman has taken attention away from the plight of our people! While the wealthy hurry to outdo one another with expensive black silks, the poor go without food and watch their children die of hunger.'

'I feel as if I've lost a friend.'

Arthur roars with laughter. 'No member of the royal family would ever be friends with you, a commoner with nothing to offer except home-made preserves and biscuits. You need money to mix in those circles, and plenty of it.'

I keep my voice calm. 'I was at her wedding, Arthur.'

'Did she speak to you? Did she say, "Good evening, dearest Susan. What a pleasure to see you"? I wager she didn't even glance at you. Did you attend the ceremony, or were you lurking in a service corridor?'

I recall the shimmering apparition that passed by as we sang like a choir of angels. Her gaze did not flick towards me because her eyes sought her husband-to-be beyond the door to the room where the marriage service was about to take place. I shake my head.

'You were a nobody to her, Susan, like every other commoner. Anyhow, it leaves one less member of the family to grieve for the regent when he dies.'

'What do you mean?' I have images of our bereaved Prince Regent so stricken by grief that he has taken to his bed.

'Peaceful protest didn't put our country right so now we need drastic action. Hunt and his reformers have achieved nothing; therefore, I will lead an army against the Establishment. And don't underestimate me because I'm a soldier and I *will* spill blood.'

The danger lurking within Arthur's voice chills me more than ever before. I cannot bear to look at him, so I stand and withdraw from the room.

Perched on the edge of the bed, I'm defeated. Sad. Lost. There is one thing I know will lift my spirits. The time has come. I reach into my reticule and ease out Mr Westcott's gift.

The paper tears easily and slides away from the book. The leather cover feels warm and comforting in my hand. I run my fingers over the gold embossed lettering on the spine, then rest the book on my lap. As I open the front cover, my heart quickens. A folded piece of paper sits pressed against the flyleaf with my name written across it in flamboyant script. I lift the note between thumb and finger and stare at the elegant handwriting before replacing it and slamming the cover shut.

My heart pounds behind my ribs, beating out a tune of

infidelity. Sweat soaks my dress where the fabric rubs against my armpits. I concentrate on taking a few steadying breaths, then open the note and read.

Dear Mrs Thistlewood,

Forgive me for being so bold as to purchase this gift for you today. I assure you it's not my habit to buy a novel for a stranger, but there was something about you that compelled me to do so. I sensed a shadow lurking deep within your soul and I hope my gift will shine a light to shrink the darkness that stalks you.

Be assured that I am no predator. Mr Brown will vouch for me should you ever wish to know more about my person.

I pray it never befalls you, but if a day should come when you need assistance of a serious kind, I am, and always will be, your humble servant.

William Westcott

c/o The Magistrate's Office at Bow Street

London

I read the note a second time. And a third. The text is brief but fills me with hope.

I think back to Arthur's comment about leading an army against the Prince of Wales and the Cabinet. Did he mean it? Could he achieve such a thing? Does he intend to maim them... or take their lives?

'Oh!' My hands fly to my mouth to stifle my gasp. The note slips from my fingers and grazes the bed as it slips towards the bare floorboards. To murder a Cabinet member is to commit treason. The penalty for treason is death. If Arthur dies, I will live.

I bend forward and retrieve the note, my chest bubbling with possibilities. This gentleman, an officer of the law, has offered his professional help. Somehow, Mr Westcott will cut the ties that bind me to Arthur.

PART V
1818

CHAPTER 27

I MAKE myself swallow a spoonful of chicken broth, though I have no appetite. For weeks now, Arthur's attitude towards me has been as frosty as the ice that spreads across the interior of our windows.

Life has become more difficult. Food prices have risen, rent has soared and my wages cover the bills with nothing spare to replace worn-out clothes. Arthur has a trivial income, though the source is a secret, and pennies slip through his fingers like fine grains of sand, leaving no trace. It was a relief to me when Mrs Hooper introduced a uniform dress for work. So in front of customers at least, I am adequately attired.

'Arthur, you look troubled. What worries you?' Arthur's mood has grown sombre these past few weeks and I fear he's losing momentum for his campaign.

He considers me a while before answering. 'England needs decisive action but I'm alone trying to save our country and I don't know which way to turn.'

Disappointment floods my veins. An army of one man

cannot take on the Prince Regent and the Cabinet. 'What about the Spenceans? Has their support dwindled?'

'My friends believe the state of the country is improving. The beggars on the streets don't corroborate their claims, nor the hovels housing desperate families forced to share a room. Watson runs about on chicken legs fearing words will have him executed and interests have become selfish. He's no longer the best person to speak on behalf of the people.'

So Mr Watson has seen sense. I pray Arthur does not do the same.

'We demoted Watson from senior leadership of the Spenceans. The man's a coward and I want nothing more to do with him, but I fear his lily-liver might weaken the bold-ness of others.' Arthur finishes his broth before continuing. 'Sidmouth ignored my letters, no doubt laughing at me from behind closed doors. He'll know the drive for change is waning. But I'll show him. *My* courage is strengthening, not dwindling. He can't ignore me forever.'

'You've committed years to bringing about change so you mustn't give up now. What will make Sidmouth listen?'

Arthur smiles. 'I've challenged him to a duel.'

'You've what?' There's a flutter in my belly. My lips widen into a smile.

Arthur shrugs. 'It's the best way for two gentlemen to settle differences. Sidmouth's letting the country slide towards the gutter. And he refuses to reimburse me for my losses on the *Perseus* despite my 'not guilty' verdict and confirmation of wrongful arrest. If not for him, we'd be in America now.'

He's either confused or deluded. We planned to emigrate because Arthur was a fugitive and we were to use the oppor-tunity to start afresh. He incited violence, placed himself at the mercy of the law, and was lucky to get away with it.

'Arthur, I presume you're aware that duelling was outlawed a long time ago?'

'Your concern is touching, Susan, but you know nothing of the ways of gentlemen. It's a matter of honour. Sidmouth will be as eager as I to resolve the issues.'

'How did you make your challenge?'

'By letter.'

~

My legs tremble as I hurry along icy streets. When the building comes into view, I slow my pace. I haven't been here since Arthur's arrest. I take a moment to calm my nerves, admiring the grandeur of the architecture. A large lantern hangs from a portico entrance and columns stand sentry on either side, waiting for the undesirable characters who appear before the magistrates on an all too frequent basis.

Nerves get the better of me and I suspect my revelation would not be taken seriously. I scurry across the road towards the Covent Garden theatre and study a poster advertising *Zuma; or, The Tree of Health*. I haven't visited a theatre since I married Arthur. The last performance I attended was before I left my family home, a Boxing Day Harlequin pantomime, I think.

'Mrs Thistlewood, what a surprise to see you here. Are you considering purchasing a ticket?'

The gentleman's voice is familiar, and I worry my eyes will betray my joy.

'No,' I say a little too quickly. 'I was curious about upcoming performances.'

The exchange hangs between us, a brief little cloud of words frozen in time.

'There's nothing like the pleasure of a theatre performance to distract from the troubles that plague us day to day, wouldn't you agree?' Mr Westcott's voice is deep and mellow, authoritative yet kind.

'We had nothing as grand as this at home, but I always enjoyed a play.'

'*Zuma* is an amusing opera and well worth the price of a ticket.'

'Alas, my husband is not a man who appreciates the arts.'

'Perhaps you could go with a friend?'

Arthur would not allow me to attend an opera or play with anyone. He stopped me singing with Beckey's ladies after my attempt to move in with Anna, and my visits to Beckey are infrequent and clandestine because Arthur hasn't forgiven Samuel for evicting us.

I shake my head. 'My friends have commitments that spare them no time for such entertainment.'

Mr Westcott nods, sympathetic understanding shining in his eyes. 'My mother enjoys the theatre, and it's a regular pleasure for me to escort her. Perhaps you might join us?'

I would love to.

'With regret, I must decline. I work six days a week, and domestic chores fill the evenings.'

'A pity. Mother would have enjoyed your company.'

We gaze into each other's eyes. My heartbeat quickens and my pulse thrums in my ears. His grey irises sparkle with tiny streaks of silver like sun-dappled water.

'Some other time.'

'Perhaps,' I force myself to resume scrutiny of the poster.

'Forgive me for saying, but if you've no intention of seeing a performance, did some other purpose bring you here today?'

How do I put my concerns into words? The taste of blood tells me I've bitten a small chunk from the inside of my cheek. It's something I do whenever I'm troubled. No doubt I've been pulling a comical face while gnawing at my flesh.

Mr Westcott takes a step away from me. 'Please, it's cold out here. Let's go indoors and find a quiet office where we can speak in private.'

With his left arm he gestures we should move towards the Bow Street Magistrates' Court. I nod and take apprehensive steps across the slippery cobbles, relieved to have Mr Westcott by my side.

The office is cluttered with people and untidy desks, but we sit at a battered table in one corner and no one pays us any heed. Mr Westcott sits across from me and waits for me to speak.

Sweat moistens my palms. 'I have information about my husband.'

He stiffens. 'I see.'

'He plans to do something foolish, and you must be ready to arrest him.'

Mr Westcott says nothing. Silence stretches like a chasm between us.

'My husband challenged Lord Sidmouth to a duel.'

Mr Westcott remains impassive, his lack of reaction surprising.

'He means it, I know he does. If Lord Sidmouth refuses to meet his demands, Arthur will not shy away from murdering him with a bullet.'

'You're brave to share such news with me and you've taken a risk coming here with such an allegation.'

'I was careful. Mr Thistlewood is a wicked man and deserves to have the full weight of the law pressing on him. This current plan of his is but one of many, and others are more serious. Tell me, Mr Westcott, isn't attempted murder a

161

serious crime for which the perpetrator may be gaoled, or even hanged?'

Mr Westcott nods slowly. Something in his expression troubles me.

'Why aren't you concerned? I thought you'd want more details.'

'Alas, madam, this is old news. We are aware of your husband's countless efforts to engage the Home Secretary in correspondence. In fact, it was hard to miss because your husband had the letters published, including the challenge to Lord Sidmouth. I regret to say that Mr Thistlewood seems hell-bent on a course of self-destruction. No good will come of his actions.'

'The letters were published? In the newspapers?'

'I'm afraid so. It appears I've shocked you, Mrs Thistle-wood, and I apologise. Your husband's activities are of grave concern. I'm both grateful and relieved that you want no part in his dangerous games.'

'I confess to sharing his wish for a better England where children can expect nourishing food and a change of clothes, but I worry about how my husband intends to achieve it.'

'We have the same vision. There are appropriate ways of campaigning and there are illegal ways. Your husband has chosen a path that does not conform with that permissible within the boundaries of the law.'

'And that is why I came here.' I twist my wedding band around my finger. 'I must go. If Arthur returns home to find me absent, I will suffer for it.'

'You must go home, that's true. But Mr Thistlewood won't be there.'

'How do you know?'

'Because we have placed him under arrest.'

'I beg your pardon?'

'Mr Thistlewood is under arrest for high treason and for sending a challenge to our Noble Lord, the Home Secretary.'

A relieved giggle escapes my throat. I study Mr Westcott's face. His expression is serious, but kind. My thoughts drift to his handwritten note. He's a gentleman, an officer of Bow Street, with a clear understanding of right and wrong. He makes Arthur look a fool the way he lusts after violence and bloodshed. My choice of husband was a poor one. I'm sure he was a kind man once, but when I cast my mind back, I recall Arthur's controlling traits and eagerness to quash my opinions and sway them towards his own. I was naïve and made a grave mistake by marrying him. Arthur has evil gushing through his veins.

'His wrongdoings are his own,' I say. 'I had no involvement.'

'You're a respectable woman, Mrs Thistlewood, an upstanding citizen. Go about your life with confidence and a clear conscience. If you need help or advice while Mr Thistlewood is unavailable, please ask.'

As I step outside into the wintry February afternoon, I feel as if a burden has been lifted, for surely Arthur must be on his way to the gallows? With a lightness of step, I hurry home, eager to visit my dear friends and enjoy my first day of freedom.

CHAPTER 28

FRESH STRAWBERRY ICE cream calms my fevered mind. As each cold spoonful slithers down my throat, I feel a delightful cooling sensation behind my breastbone. It was too hot for travelling. The horses protested all the way to Horsham, and the journey seemed to take forever, but Beckey sat uncomplaining next to me while doing her best to lift my spirits.

Since dear Samuel's passing, I've spent every one of my days off with Beckey. Our friendship has blossomed once again and there's talk of reviving her musical gatherings. We've also used a few spare hours to help the needy, keeping my mind occupied and distracting me from the miserable diversion that is Arthur.

'You should hurry, Susan. Arthur's expecting you.'

I have no desire to see him. While he's been under lock and key, I have flourished.

'What will you do while I'm with Arthur?'

Beckey smiles. 'The town has plenty to keep visitors occupied. Don't worry about me. One or two shops have caught my eye, so I'll take my time looking at hats and trinkets, then return here for another pot of tea. Now, go.'

I lick the last traces of ice cream from my spoon and brace myself for the heat of summer. As I cross the road towards the gaol entrance, my pulse quickens. Sweat trickles down my back and my shift sticks to my damp skin. The weather is not entirely to blame for my discomfort. I'm here because Arthur sent for me. He may be behind bars, but with the help of his cronies he can still reach me.

At first glance, the gaol is imposing. A grand two-storey red-brick building stretches before me with wide steps approaching a central door. Conditions cannot be so bad if Arthur's cell is in a fine building such as this. My attention drifts to a small group of dishevelled women being herded through a high arched entrance on the left. Each woman has something in common with me – she's a felon's wife. I follow along behind them with my head bowed. I don't want to be here. One by one we approach a guard seated at a table. His facial expression lacks warmth and his eyes confirm he derives no pleasure from working here.

'Name?'

'Susan Thistlewood.'

He switches from one sheet of paper to another, running his fingertip over a column of names. 'Not on the list.' He flicks his hand towards the archway. It's my signal to leave. 'Next.'

'No, I'm Susan Thistlewood.'

He rolls his eyes.

'Here to see Arthur Thistlewood.'

He reverts to the previous sheet. 'No. Still not listed.'

'There must be a mistake.' I pull out Arthur's letter from my reticule. 'My husband wrote instructing me to come today.'

He takes the letter and disappears into an office. Irritable women shuffle in a short queue behind me and I sense I'm

165

depriving them of precious minutes with loved ones they long to see.

The guard ambles back and waves the letter beneath my nose. 'This is unusual practice,' he grumbles. 'Your visit's allowed. Special privilege from the Governor.'

I glance towards a deserted courtyard. 'May I ask where I'll find my husband?'

The guard smirks. 'First time, eh? Cross the courtyard, turn right, pass under an arch then turn left. You'll see an entrance straight ahead. Someone else will direct you from there. Next.'

I mumble my thanks, but it goes unheard as another visitor knocks against me, forcing me to move aside. I walk into the courtyard and am struck by the gravity of my surroundings. There's no shade apart from a thin strip of shadow running along one side of a very high wall which even the sun cannot penetrate. Maniacal shouts come from a nearby building. My eyes focus on the sign above the door. Infirmary. I wonder what torturous procedures take place within its walls. As instructed, I turn right and pass through a lower archway, then left into a small courtyard. The atmosphere is oppressive. Grunts and groans emerge from a long shed, the noises made by men struggling with hard labour. Not daring to look towards them, I scuttle across the courtyard towards a block of cells.

'I didn't think to bring food.' The man standing before me is a shadow of his former self. Skin hangs from his cheekbones and deep crevices line his face. Arthur is unrecognisable.

'I'd rather not have it,' he says sadly. 'It would be a painful reminder of what I'm missing at home, and I've too many months to endure before I leave here.'

'Nine,' I say.

Arthur approaches the bars and reaches for my hand. I make a show of gazing up and down the corridor, pretending not to notice.

'You're counting the days too. Why didn't you come sooner?'

A rat scuttles past my feet, brushing against the tip of my shoe. I shudder and watch it disappear into the cell next to Arthur's.

'It's difficult, Arthur. I'm working all hours and using every moment of spare time for housework and grocery shopping.'

'No time to yourself?'

'Not enough to travel this far.' The lie slides easily from my lips. 'Mrs Hooper granted me time off for this visit.'

'I hear there have been strikes since my arrest.'

'The spinners in Manchester. And riots, too. There's been talk of attempts to form a General Union of Trades. Lord Sidmouth insisted the magistrates put a stop to it, and they responded by making arrests. I can't see the strikes contin-uing much longer though. The workers and their children are hungry enough as it is. Arthur, newspapers report that desperate parents drag their children out of bed to walk to work before the sun is up. Children as young as six years old!'

Arthur sighs. 'Evidence we live in a cruel country.'

'Julian's doing well.'

'He's my son. He'll make a name for himself one day.'

Odd that Arthur thinks Julian will do well when he himself has achieved so little. But he's right. The signs suggest Julian will achieve great things. He's hard-working and determined.

The cell is claustrophobic and I can't imagine how Arthur tolerates it from one day to the next, but I suppose that's the idea. Part of the punishment package. 'Why are there two beds?'

Arthur grunts. 'It's a single-man cell but sometimes the gaol gets overcrowded and we have as many as three in here.'

The linen on the other bed is grimy and dishevelled.

'Are you sharing at the moment?'

'I am, but my companion's in the labour shed. You'll have left before he reappears.'

We fall silent, each minute dragging. The rank air of the gaol coats the inside of my nostrils and clings to my clothes. I must wash this dress before I wear it again. It's my favourite, crafted by Anna from remnants Mrs Hooper allowed me to buy for a single shilling.

'Tell me about your duties at work. It'll give me something to think about while I sit here staring at the walls.'

It cheers me to tell Arthur about Mrs Hooper and the young ladies at work. I smile as I describe the regular customers and Arthur chuckles at some of my stories.

A banging on a cell door further along the corridor announces it's time for visitors to leave. It's easy to abandon Arthur for another nine months in this mouse hole of a cell. He made my life miserable. It's what he deserves.

'Will you visit again?'

'I'll try, Arthur, but it's a struggle.'

His shoulders sag and he hangs his head.

'Goodbye, Arthur.'

I step into the passage, a long, dark corridor flanked on each side by a line of cell doors. A scrap of daylight beckons from the entrance.

'Wait!' The urgency in Arthur's voice causes me to spin round and stumble. He's clutching a bundle of letters. 'These are the reasons for asking you to visit. They're about the conditions here. No threats, I promise. I've written before, but the guards... well, I can't rely on them.'

I take the bundle and study the name scrawled across the top. Arthur's harassing the Home Secretary again. I'll burn the letters later.

Keen to leave Arthur to his small, damp, reeking cell, I stuff the letters into my reticule and stride away in search of Beckey.

CHAPTER 29

THIS IS the first time I've tasted blackberry trifle. The sharp undertones of the berries contrast with the sweet richness of creamy custard, and it's a struggle to resist the temptation to scrape my bowl clean with my spoon. Mrs Westcott must not think me uncouth.

'Time to leave,' says the elderly lady, her neat silver chignon bobbing up and down. Her faded blue eyes sparkle with delight. 'William tells me this will be your first experience of the theatre at Covent Garden.'

'Yes, and I'm so looking forward to it.'

An affectionate glance passes between mother and son. I stare at my lap, not wishing to intrude on the silent exchange. It has taken me the duration of the meal to relax because with each delicious mouthful I feared Mrs Westcott would ask about Arthur.

A maid places a shawl across the elderly lady's shoulders. Despite her age and thin frame, she cuts a striking pose. Her turquoise dress has silver buttons on the bodice, and the peach French-style shawl has an exquisite trim of embroidered silver leaves. For once, I feel at home with such elegance because Beckey insisted I wear one of her dresses for the occasion, and the graceful cut of the smoke-grey fabric is flattering to my ample shape.

When the coach stops outside the theatre entrance, a thousand butterflies beat their wings within my chest. William reaches for my hand to help me step down to the dusty pavement.

Four tall fluted columns welcome our happy threesome, encouraging us to step inside. My eyes rove around a large vestibule with a grand staircase set to one side. The inside of the building is more majestic than I imagined from admiring the grandeur of the exterior walls. Our progress up the stairs is slow. Mrs Westcott's limbs are no longer agile, and she leans on her son for support. I'm glad of the slow journey because it gives me time to admire my surroundings and the fashionable people of London in attendance this evening. The atmosphere is vibrant with men and women greeting each other and exchanging kind words. This joyful world is alien to me and it's a world I should very much like to visit again one day regardless of whether I enjoy the play.

An usher shows us to a box where Mrs Westcott greets friends of a comparable age. My limbs tense. I did not know we would socialise with others. As I brace myself for introductions, I hardly dare catch my breath.

'Oh, how rude of me,' exclaims Mrs Westcott. 'I must introduce you to Mrs Susan Thistlewood, a dear friend of the family.'

Mature women fuss over me like mother hens. My tension eases. I'm a welcome guest here.

'Any relation to—'

The ruddy-faced gentleman's question is halted by his wife tugging at his sleeve.

'Look, dear, Prince Regent is in the royal box.'

Mr Westcott and I exchange relieved glances. I swallow a nervous giggle and sit next to his mother. Conversations take place around me while I marvel at the theatre. There are three tiers of boxes and we are in the middle tier, not too far from the stage, and our seats are set at an angle so we may admire the full extent of the set. A heavy red curtain conceals the scenery and I try to imagine the spectacle beyond. A lofty arch frames the stage, and on each side there are ornate female figures holding laurel wreaths and trumpets. The ceiling is decorated in the image of a grand cupola, and the buzz of impatient members of the audience diffuses throughout the horseshoe-shaped room. The theatre is warm and comfortable, illuminated by an impressive chandelier hanging from the centre of the ceiling, and the acoustic design amplifies even the slightest tut or sniff.

A bell announces the imminent start of the performance. Those still standing take their seats, and to my surprise, Mr Westcott sits beside me. Scarlet velvet curtains twitch and glide open. The audience falls silent. The play begins.

I'm enthralled by the first act with its exquisite costumes, stunning scenery and lines that make my face ache with laughter. *The Clandestine Marriage* is a comical production. Never have I laughed so much. Funny though it is, the tale is superbly enacted.

'You can see why it's one of my favourites, can't you?' Mr Westcott leans so close that I can feel and hear his soft whisper.

'It has to be the most entertaining thing I've ever seen,' I reply, relieved the heat burning in my cheeks is invisible to him.

'Mother was thrilled you agreed to come with us this evening.'

It was a delightful shock to receive the formal invitation from his mother. How fortunate that Mrs Westcott should be a long-standing patron of Mrs Hooper's. We've enjoyed many lengthy conversations during her visits to the shop because of her tendency to arrive thirty minutes early for each appointment.

'You must join us again,' whispers Mrs Westcott in my other ear, during a pause for a change of scenery between acts. 'You've proven popular with my friends.'

'It's a joy to share this treat with you, Mrs Westcott, but you must let me pay for my ticket.'

She rests her bony hand across my wrist. 'Goodness, dear, no. It's good for us old folk to mingle with youngsters from time to time. Keeps us young at heart.'

I chuckle. 'I'm not a youngster.'

She pats my arm then removes her hand to whisper something to the friend seated to her other side. Seconds later, the action on stage resumes.

Mr Westcott adjusts the angle of his seat and our arms brush against one another. I should adjust my position to sever the contact, but something stops me. For the rest of the play, my skin tingles at his proximity.

After a brief interlude, we take our seats for an afterpiece, a short play entitled *Love, Law and Physick*. It's a farcical piece, although I don't understand the story because my attention is on the gentleman sitting beside me. Our forearms rest against each other and I sit still catching my breath in soft shallow gasps, reluctant to break the spell holding us together. For a brief moment, our eyes meet. When I look away, I'm confused by my feelings for him.

When the curtain closes for the last time, a shadow of sadness falls over me. I have enjoyed a wonderful few hours, an experience I am unlikely ever to repeat. With great reluctance, I step into the carriage and settle next to Mrs Westcott. She covers our legs with a blanket and squeezes my fingers before instructing her son to direct the coachman to my home.

'Please, don't go out of your way,' I say. 'It's no trouble to walk from your house.'

'I won't hear of such a thing,' replies Mrs Westcott. 'William, make sure the carriage goes to Stanhope Street first.'

'Please! There's no need.'

Mrs Westcott turns my face towards her. 'My dear, I will not sleep easy in my bed if I cannot be sure you arrive without incident to your home.'

'But the area is nothing compared to where you live.'

'One's neighbourhood should never be a cause for embarrassment. My husband may have provided well for me, but I started life in humble surroundings. Who knows what fate awaits any of us?'

'Who knows, indeed,' I mumble, settling back against the padded lining of the coach and ruing the day I met Arthur.

The journey passes in a flash. When the coachman opens the door, Mr Westcott steps out first and offers me his hand. It's all I can do not to cling to his fingers, and in my best impersonation of a lady, I step down from the coach.

'Thank you for a most wonderful evening,' I say, plucking up the courage to gaze into his eyes.

'The first of many, I hope.'

I sigh. 'I regret the future does not hold such luxuries for me. A few months from now, I will lose this freedom.'

'Have faith and keep courage. One day you'll find a path to happier times.' He places his hand on my upper arm and lowers his voice. 'You can always contact me via Bow Street.'

I murmur my thanks and walk to my front door. Once inside, I turn back towards the carriage to see Mrs Westcott smiling at me. She waves with a flutter of her fingers, then lets the curtain fall. I close the door and study my reflection in the hall mirror. I'm smiling.

This is a lifestyle I would enjoy.

CHAPTER 30

A GLASS of elderberry wine sits half-finished on the freshly scrubbed table top. It was a gift from Anna, and now I regret opening the bottle. The deep-red wine, balanced and mellow, caresses my throat with every mouthful, but I must not drink too much and say or do something inappropriate later. After chiding myself for lacking confidence, I replace the stopper in the bottle and set it on a high shelf. The glass taunts me while I wield the broom, sweeping the spotless kitchen floor. The webs between my fingers crack and bleed from scrubbing at imaginary stains that I feel the need to get rid of in case my visitor enters the kitchen. A streak of blood soaks into my skirt, diverting attention from my home to my appearance.

I hurry to the bedroom mirror and sigh at my reflection with its dull eyes, ruddy cheeks and lips darkened by the wine. I look as harried as a washerwoman after a day's work rather than the mistress of the house preparing for a social visit. After a quick prayer for the high colour in my face to subside to a rosy glow, I shed my bloodstained dress and ease into something more elegant. Employment at Mrs Hooper's has its perks. My dress collection has swelled to eight in recent months, with five distinct from work attire but just as well made.

I brush my hair until it shines, then encourage it into a chignon. I turn my head one way, then the other, and cannot help but think there's an elegance to the shape of my exposed neck. There's no scrawniness nor wrinkling despite the recent tough years, and I believe I'm more attractive now, in my early thirties, than I was in my twenties. A few stray locks frame my face and I leave them there to do as they please, adding a hint of playfulness to my rounded cheeks.

Because of the *Perseus* incident, I have neither jewellery nor perfume. Undeterred, I drape a scarf around my neck – an elegant strip of sheer pink fabric, embroidered with tiny white flowers.

A rap at the door catches me unawares. I dart to the parlour and check the time. He's early. I hesitate. Something tells me I'm about to make a mistake. Arthur's warning about our marriage vows echoes in my mind. *Forsaking all others, as long as we both shall live.* He may have someone watching me. The risk is considerable, I should ignore the door and allow the moment to pass. Another large gulp of wine. The decision is made. I will not answer.

Another rap. Louder this time. I stare ahead, challenging the door to do its worst. Holding my breath, I wait for the patter of receding footsteps. Nothing. I tiptoe closer. Still no sound. I steady my breathing and congratulate myself for seeing sense, then shape my lips into a smile.

But then comes a gentle tap. Before I can stop myself, my feet carry me forward and my hand pulls the door open. Mr Westcott stands on the doorstep with an expression that says he's delighted to see me – an expression I have read about in love stories and now I'm seeing it for real. The heat returns to my face, but my visitor does not laugh nor tease.

'Please, come inside.' My voice sounds timid.

'You have something...' His words trail away. He frowns and reaches towards my lips but stops before touching them.

I imagine how I appear to him, elegant in a special dress, with the coloured lips of a harlot. My tongue must be similarly tainted. I step aside so Mr Westcott may enter the hallway, but he does not move. My heart sinks. He has changed his mind. Perhaps for the best.

'A splendid day,' he says. 'I thought we might walk together.'

Arthur's threat forgotten, I snatch my pelisse and bonnet from the coat stand, and step across the threshold.

I do not know where we are, nor which route we took to get here, because I drifted along the streets as if carried by a dream. My gloved hand has slipped behind Mr Westcott's arm and rests on his sleeve. He looks into my eyes and smiles, a kind smile with no hint of mockery even though my lips will be stained for some time yet.

'I know what you need,' he says.

I tilt my head, brow furrowed, but say nothing because I suspect my tongue is more colourful than my lips.

Mr Westcott stops outside a confectionary shop and I remove my hand from his arm. He holds the door open for me to step inside. While I wait by the entrance, unnaturally interested in patterned sage-green floor tiles, he approaches the shopkeeper and makes a request. Moments later he links my arm with his and escorts me back outside.

'Beautiful,' he says.

I lift my head to see a small park surrounded by glorious daffodils fluttering in a gentle breeze. A thick carpet of perfect yellow. The colour is a welcome contrast to the grey grime of London. We settle on an elegant bench bathed in early spring sunshine, and Mr Westcott opens a package wrapped in linen.

'A segment of lemon?'

'Mother swears by it. Here.'

Mr Westcott tilts my chin and strokes the cut flesh of the lemon across my bottom lip. The gesture is intimate and sends a shiver through me. I wish it would last forever. He attends to my upper lip before removing his fingertips from beneath my chin.

'The juice removes staining from tongues too, but the bitterness is unpalatable for ladies.'

My heart flutters like the daffodils. 'I'm willing to try.'

He smiles, then produces another small package, this time wrapped in paper. I peer inside, then look at him in wonder.

'How did you know?'

His brow creases. 'Know what?'

'I'm fond of these.'

He laughs. 'I didn't. It's another of Mother's tricks to remove traces of red wine. Sugar plums are most effective, she says, because when you crunch them, the tiny pieces act as a mild abrasive and scrape the stains clean away.'

'A lucky coincidence,' I say, popping a pale blue one into my mouth. I offer them to him, and he is as eager as I am to eat one.

We sit in contented companionship, munching comfits, and watch daffodils dancing in the breeze. The sun slinks behind a cloud and the air temperature drops.

'Let us walk to warm ourselves.' Mr Westcott stands and offers me his arm.

We stroll along winding garden paths, passing other couples enjoying the pleasant weather. Conversation flows easily between us now my mouth and tongue are no longer deeply stained.

The breeze strengthens and the spring warmth fades, so we agree to leave the park. When we arrive at my front door, I'm desperate to extend this happy afternoon for a little longer.

'Please, Mr Westcott, come inside for a pot of tea. We're both chilled through.'

He considers my proposal for a moment. 'I'd enjoy that very much.'

There's no awkwardness between us while we sip steaming tea and laugh at my poor decision to taste the elderberry wine earlier in the day.

'Here, try it.' I giggle and pour a generous glassful.

'Only if you will.'

My home swells with laughter for the first time since I moved here. We immerse our lips in the dark red liquid, entertaining each other with the frightful consequences. We still have the lemon from earlier and help each other remove the traces of foolishness from our lips. Alas, the sugar plums have all gone so our tongues remain stained, but at least Mr Westcott can hold his head high when he strides along the street to hail a carriage.

I walk him to the door and fear my heart will break when we say farewell.

He touches my top lip with his index finger. 'You missed a patch.'

My insides lurch, and I resist the temptation to fling my arms around him. His face draws nearer to mine and our lips meet. A gentle brushing, as soft as an angel's breath. He pulls away and checks my reaction. I press my lips together, trying to trap the kiss forever, but then I part them a little and we kiss again.

Reluctantly, we pull apart.

'Forgive me, I'm a married woman and shouldn't behave this way.'

'I'm the one who should apologise,' he says. 'Not because I showed my feelings, but because you deserve so much more than your husband gives. If only circumstances were different.'

My eyes mist as I reach for Mr Westcott's hand. 'Arthur will never release me from marriage.'

I dread the day he comes home from prison. Life will be harder than before he went away.

'We'll make do with snatched moments and cherish every minute we spend together.'

My heart sings with joy. He intends to see me again.

'Goodbye, Mr Westcott. It was a wonderful afternoon.' I offer my lips as a parting gift and he accepts without hesitation.

When we release each other, he smiles. 'From now on, call me William.'

PART VI
1819

Mrs Hooper has a plate of French macarons for today's customers. The tantalising aroma of sweet almond sets my mouth watering. Willpower deserts me. As I walk past the counter towards the sewing room, I swipe a neat beige disc from the plate and pop it between my lips. It's a pity I must munch it rather than wait for it to dissolve upon my tongue, but I shouldn't be eating these delicious biscuits. I lower my eyelids for a few seconds, concentrating on the flavour, then swallow the evidence of my misdemeanour.

'Susan, are you unwell?' Anna has a concerned look in her eyes. 'I thought you might pass out.'

'Sit down, Mrs Thistlewood,' commands Mrs Hooper, dragging a chair from the customer waiting area. 'You're pale.'

'Please, don't fuss. I'm not ill, just… thinking, that's all.' Almond dust coats my tongue and I struggle to swallow. 'Perhaps a little sip of small beer, because my throat is dry.'

Mrs Hooper rushes to the counter and fills a glass. Her gaze sweeps over the plate of biscuits, then she glances towards me and frowns. Heat rises from my neck to my jaw

185

and I dash to the back room before Mrs Hooper sees my shame. I pass a message to Martha about an alteration required, then return to face my employer. She passes me the glass.

'I'm sorry, Mrs Hooper,' I say, my voice lowered so others cannot hear. 'My husband will come home soon, and I worry we are both much changed.'

'Your concern is understandable. Every married couple needs a period of readjustment after a prolonged separation. Try not to fret. No doubt Mr Thistlewood will be proud of you for coping so well during his absence. Everything will return to normal before long.'

That is what I'm afraid of.

Mrs Hooper attends to a customer, so I sit in a corner at a little sewing table. During quieter periods, I make basic repairs and alterations, or work on minor embroidery projects. I'm thrilled Mrs Hooper permits me to do such work as my needlework skills are much improved. While my eyes focus on the blue thread moving back and forth through the fabric, my thoughts drift to William. Several weeks have passed since our last encounter. He's in Basingstoke, working on an investigation. How I've missed his company. I don't know when he will return and dare not visit his mother to ask – nor will I enquire about him at Bow Street. Instead, I continue fortnightly visits to Paternoster Row and hope there will be a letter soon, as promised before he left.

～

'Pleasant day, Mrs Thistlewood.' Mr Brown holds the door open and greets me with a broad smile.

'Good day, Mr Brown. Is there a letter for me today?'

His smile evaporates, and he shakes his head. 'Perhaps next time.'

I stifle my disappointment and make straight for the shelf where the latest acquisition of novels is on display. From the corner of my eye, I glimpse his figure retreating to the store-room at the rear of the shop. I hope he'll return with a choice of new books because there's nothing appealing on the shelf today. Disappointment saps my energy. I migrate towards the poetry collections and choose one at random. Flicking through the pages, I find a poem about a love gained then lost. The words echo my fears.

'Read something on a cheerier theme.'

'William!'

I thrust the book back on to the shelf and throw my arms around William's neck. He holds me tight, pulling me close, and I bury my face into the angle of his neck, relishing the scent of his skin.

'You were away too long,' I say, in mock annoyance.

'I know, but I could do nothing to hasten my return.'

I glance over William's shoulder. Mr Brown smiles then averts his gaze. He peruses a ledger, allowing us a moment of privacy.

'There's somewhere I want to take you while it's still light.'

I nod and grin like a child who has just received a treat. Mr Brown opens the door and bids us farewell. William slips coins into his hand as recompense for his discretion. We pile into a hackney carriage with a gaggle of strangers and ride arm in arm like two young lovers before alighting from the carriage somewhere on the edge of the city near an area of woodland.

'Cover your eyes.'

I do as I'm told, and William rests his firm hands on my

shoulders, guiding me this way and that. When we come to a halt, he stands behind me, slides his hand around my waist and rests his chin on my shoulder. I could stand like this forever.

'Open your eyes.'

'Oh!' A vast sea of bluebells ripples between the trees and the sight brings tears to my eyes. 'I used to play in a wood like this, hiding from my brothers, darting from one tree to another.'

William's smile fades. 'I didn't mean to sadden you. Because you loved the daffodils so much, I thought this would please you too.'

'I'm not sad. Far from it. This brings back fond memories of moments I never want to forget.'

I turn to face him. He wipes tears from my cheeks and then draws me closer. As our lips meet, I yearn for something more intimate. I press myself to him and discover he wishes it too.

When I draw away, I take his hands in mine and we spend long seconds gazing into each other's eyes, sharing the pain of my circumstances. Tears drop to my shawl, spreading grief in damp circles.

'We should eat,' says William, with a husky voice. 'There's an inn nearby serving delicious roasted meats.'

~

'Susan?' A portly lady bustles over to our table. 'Susan Thistlewood? It is you! Oh, my dear, how are you?'

I search through my memories, trying to place this over-familiar woman. 'Very well, thank you. How are you? It's been so long.'

'It has. Beckey said you've too many commitments these days. It's understandable.'

A friend of Beckey's. I remember now. A pleasant woman from the musical evenings. Although they've started up again, I've either been too busy to attend because of altering dresses in the evenings or too exhausted after hectic days at work. I realise this woman knows about Arthur's circumstances. No doubt she wonders why I'm in the company of another gentleman.

'Forgive my rudeness. This is John Wilkinson. My brother.'

William stands and bows to the woman whose name I cannot recall. 'Always a pleasure to meet any friend of my sister's,' he says, casting a mocking glance as he returns to his seat.

'I was showing him the bluebell wood,' I say, feeling obliged to make conversation.

The woman claps her hands. 'We were there too. Delightful, isn't it? Ah, your food has arrived. I'll leave you in peace to savour it. Enjoy London, Mr Wilkinson.'

As her large frame recedes, William leans across the table. 'Your brother?' he teases.

I giggle. 'It was all I could think of.'

William's face drops. 'We must be more careful. I predict challenging times ahead, and you'll need an upstanding reputation to get through them. It might be prudent to forego time together until things settle.'

'No! It's knowing I'll spend time with you that gets me through each day. There must be a way.'

He reaches beneath the table and grasps my fingers. 'Be patient,' he says. 'I've no desire to put you in harm's way.'

CHAPTER 32

I WRINKLE my nose at the bitter taste of coffee. The aroma's pleasant, and the sweetness of the sugar suits my palate, but the flavour is something I've never enjoyed. Beckey's kitchen maid returns to the parlour with a fresh pot. I place a hand over my cup. I've already swallowed as much as I can bear.

'What will persuade you to join us next Saturday, Susan?'

'I'm sorry, Beckey, but I have a prior engagement.'

Beckey appears crestfallen. 'But you haven't heard Anna sing. She has the voice of a nightingale.'

Anna smiles, her complexion turning pink.

'I've heard Anna sing many a time,' I reply.

'When?' asks Anna.

'You often sing at work.'

'I do?'

'Yes. Beautiful songs that help us concentrate on our stitches. The words sound French and the tunes unfamiliar. Songs learned during childhood, perhaps?'

Anna shrugs. 'Maybe.'

Beckey dips a biscuit in her coffee. 'How are you enjoying the work, Susan?'

'Very much. Mrs Hooper's a joy to work for.'

Last month, I received a slight increase in wage. Mrs Hooper praised my skill for mending rips and leaving minimal traces of repair. She said the customers ask for me by name when their finest dresses need repairing. Recently, my services have been in high demand. As living costs rise, the women of London curb their spending, and alteration or remodelling of existing dresses is therefore in vogue. This economy drive will keep Mrs Hooper's business ticking over until the tide turns again and new dresses are back in demand.

The clock strikes the hour. George looks to Anna, expecting the instruction to put on his shoes, for he has learned that it's time to leave when the clock announces the fourth hour after midday.

'Stay longer,' pleads Beckey. 'The house is too quiet after guests have gone. Another half hour?'

I sense that Anna is about to agree, so answer on behalf of us both. 'Excuse us, Beckey, but we must go home. There's housework to finish before returning to work tomorrow.'

'Take me with you. And Margaret. She'll do anything you ask.'

Margaret is Beckey's newest housemaid, a skinny girl with a sallow complexion and quiet temperament who tends to Beckey as a personal maid and general house servant.

'Margaret deserves her Sunday afternoon of rest. It's best if I attend to my chores alone. They include nothing more exciting than a quick dust, sweeping floors and writing a letter or two.' The lies come easily and I'm making such a habit of this that I no longer blush at my subterfuge.

Beckey's no fool and has spotted Anna's frown. Anna knows I attended to those chores yesterday.

'Susan? What secrets are you keeping?'

I giggle. 'Secrets? Why would I keep secrets from my dearest friends?'

I know Beckey and Anna are trustworthy, but should I tell them? I chew on the inside of my cheek, wrestling with my dilemma.

'I wager it's a man,' whispers Anna.

Beckey's fingertips fly to her lips. 'Susan? Is it true?'

Anna grins. 'It eez, non?' Her French accent resurfaces with her excitement. 'Bien sûr! Only the love of a gentleman can 'ave that effect.'

'Dearest Susan, who is the lucky man?'

My palms are clammy, and I feel trapped into a confession. 'It would be inappropriate to become involved with another man while I'm married to Arthur.'

'Pah!' Beckey flicks her hand and grimaces. 'Arthur's dangerous. Samuel said he'd come to a sticky end. Pity Arthur can't rot in gaol until his dying day. Samuel always worried about you, Susan, and said if Arthur didn't get his own way for something, he'd take it out on you. Does he?'

I should contradict the accusation, but instead I nod in confirmation. My body has been free of bruises and grazes for twelve months now. I wonder how long Arthur will be home before fresh marks appear.

Beckey shakes her head. 'Get out of that marriage, Susan, before he goes too far.'

'How can I? He'll never consent to a divorce. I'm his until I die.'

'Or he does,' murmurs Anna.

My eyes widen. 'Are you suggesting—?'

'No she's not,' says Beckey. 'But his dream of revolution won't have died at Horsham. There's little else to do other than plan his next move. He'll soon be back in prison, mark my words.'

We fall silent for what feels like several minutes.

Beckey strokes my arm. 'If the Lord sees fit to offer you a second chance, Susan, Heaven knows you should take it.'

I wring my hands. 'But if Arthur found out, he'd kill me.'

'Then promise to take care. You deserve a gentleman who respects and cherishes you. Don't pass on an opportunity for true love. The Lord moves in mysterious ways. If He offers you happiness, don't question Him. Accept that this gentleman is in your life for a reason... and for pity's sake, tell us who he is!'

I smile. 'His name is William, and he's an officer from the magistrates' court at Bow Street.'

My friends beam at me, urging me to continue.

'He's the most charming person I've ever met, and he's collecting me at five because I'm having supper with him and his mother.'

'Then leave at once!' Beckey jumps to her feet and wraps my shawl around my shoulders. 'Tell me more when I see you next.'

By the time I return home, it's late in the evening. William insists on escorting me to my door, but I cannot leave him standing on the doorstep while we say goodbye. Laughing, I grasp the lapels of his coat and pull him inside, kicking the door shut behind him. We know our secret meetings will be rare after Arthur's return. As a result, the farewells take longer and longer.

We caress each other's faces and the flame of desire intensifies within me. The fire grows, burning at my core, and my lust reflects in the black pools of William's pupils. I take a step backwards until I'm pressed against the wall. William leans against me and his hardness teases against my groin. His fingertips graze the top of my bodice and travel across the exposed mounds of my breasts. I shudder and gasp, tilting my pelvis forward so it presses against him. How I long for his flesh to move against mine and to experience tender lovemaking in the arms of a man who adores me. Thoughts of Arthur cast grey clouds over my joy, holding my actions in check. William plants feather-light kisses on my neck. I draw his face back towards mine and close my eyes, savouring the softness of his lips. How I yearn to peel off my clothes and lie with him! But I can't.

Not yet.

CHAPTER 33

IT'S EARLY for sipping gin, but I need something to dull my senses. Today is the day of Arthur's release. There was a problem securing sureties, but somehow these difficulties were overcome. I wish we'd encountered more problems, but fate was not on my side.

My stomach is churning. Arthur is at the door.

'I expected to see you outside the gaol, Susan. Were you not eager to celebrate my freedom?'

'Forgive me, Arthur, but I had to work this morning, although Mrs Hooper was gracious enough to allow me the afternoon off to spend a few hours with you.'

'No matter. The journey would have wasted your well-earned coins. We'll need every spare penny in the coming months.'

'We will?'

'I'll need a few weeks to sort my finances – what little remains of them. It's up to you to feed and clothe us from now on.' He moves closer and grips my upper arms. 'There are things I must do, Susan. The country's in decline. I didn't think it could get any worse, but I was wrong.'

'I'm relieved you've kept your fighting spirit.'

Arthur laughs. 'Someday we'll put the country right. Fear not, Susan, plans are afoot and we'll be more careful this time.'

I smile, praying for him to return to gaol as soon as possible.

'You're thin, Arthur. Are you unwell?'

'Prison food is not up to your standard of cooking.' He sniffs the air. 'Nothing roasting yet?'

'I wasn't confident of your arrival time. And I thought it best to keep meals simple at first to allow your stomach a chance to readjust.'

He smiles. 'And there I was, worried your affection might subside while I was away. I'm pleased you still care.'

I cringe as his bony fingers stroke my face. When they slide towards my shoulders, I shudder with disgust.

He feels my muscles twitch. 'Come, let us enjoy a sweet reunion.'

'But, Arthur, it's mid-afternoon.'

He places his fingertip under my chin and tilts my face towards him. 'Is there somewhere you need to be?'

'No.'

'Expecting a visitor?'

'No.'

'Then what's the problem? You trembled. You want this as much as I. Don't be prudish, Susan. Come upstairs.'

I need more gin, but an entire bottle could not numb me from this dreadful situation.

When Arthur removes his clothes, I'm appalled by his skeletal appearance. Only his manhood was unaffected by incarceration. Meanwhile, I have gained more weight than he has lost. I have a full figure, like Titian's Venus, and Arthur explores my body, mauling every ample curve and nuzzling against my flesh.

I bite down hard on my lower lip, desperate to keep tears from spilling and soaking my cheeks with regret. How often must I endure such humiliation?

'What's wrong?' Arthur's on his hands and knees, hovering over me, a grim expression on his face. 'Why do you not respond to my attention?'

I force myself to smile. 'Arthur, it's been so long since we were last intimate, and it will be... difficult... at first.'

His lips curl upwards at the corners and his eyes sparkle. 'It'll get easier with time.'

He lowers his body onto mine. I grit my teeth. As Arthur forces himself into me, I think of William and how his delicate kisses set my skin alight. If only he were the one thrusting into me now.

It takes an age for Arthur to sate himself, and there is no pleasure in it for me. Instead, I experience a sense of detachment. My soul leaves my body and floats above, watching Arthur use me as if I'm nothing more than a workman's tool.

I loathe him.

Out of gaol for less than a week, Arthur's already attending rallies. I'm both anxious and relieved. For my safety, I must convince him of my support, but it's been a long time since my opinions echoed his.

The shop was quiet this afternoon, so I left early in return for taking a small pile of mending to attend to at home. An ideal opportunity to visit Paternoster Row.

When the bell rings above the door to Mr Brown's bookshop, two pairs of eyes turn towards me. My broad smile reflects my joy – William is here. Mr Brown dips his head in greeting and hurries towards me. I'm surprised to see him scurry past and turn the sign in the window from 'Open' to 'Closed'. Then he mumbles something about paperwork, retreats to his office and closes the door.

William grasps my fingers and guides me to a narrow aisle between two bookcases. Our silent reunion takes several minutes. We haven't seen each other for six weeks and have both suffered for it.

'How am I to cope with seeing you so infrequently?' I say, regretting the whine in my voice.

'It'll not be forever.' William holds me tight against his chest.

'You don't know that!'

He looks deep into my eyes. 'I'm sure of it. It's only a matter of time before a solution to our problem becomes clear. We must be patient. How long can you spare this afternoon?'

'Not long. Arthur's out of town for a rally. He's been away two nights already and is likely to return home today.'

'Then we'll go to my mother's. She's visiting her sister so we'll have the parlour to ourselves for an hour before I must leave to interview a witness. We'll take bread and cheese, and you can tell me how things are at home.'

I nod meekly. One hour with William is simply not enough.

CHAPTER 34

'William will be here soon.'

I choke on a morsel of fatty sausage.

'A hard-working fellow who suffered at the hands of the government, and now an asset to the Spenceans.'

Not my William, thank goodness. 'Why is he coming here? Are you to hold meetings at home now?'

'No. He offered to fix the warped door on the clothes press. I don't like it hanging open all the time. Looks untidy and I keep walking into it. William owes me a favour and said it would be an easy fix. We'll head off to a meeting afterwards.'

The press door has been a problem for years and I wonder why Arthur's bothering about it now. Perhaps because there's no cost involved.

Arthur glances at his pocket watch. 'Tidy this away, Susan. We don't want our guest to think we're reduced to paupers' rations.'

A greasy sheen shimmers on my plate beside remnants of my meal. It was embarrassing asking a Clare Market butcher for this dreadful meat. Arthur insists on taking my earnings and gives back too little with which to buy decent food. Fortunately, he's unaware of my exact wage. I didn't declare the correct total from the outset and I'm building a small kitty to prepare for a future without him.

Men's voices drift from the hallway. I finish stacking clean dishes before emerging from the kitchen to greet our visitor. Arthur and his guest have moved to the bedroom by the time I complete my chores.

As I step through the doorway, I'm confronted by a man on his knees, fiddling with the lowest hinge of the press door. He turns his head towards me and flashes a gleaming smile.

'Mrs Thistlewood.' He scrambles to his feet, takes my hand in his and raises it to his lips. 'William Davidson at your service – literally.'

'A pleasure to meet you, Mr Davidson.'

I smile at his smooth charm. His eyes sparkle with humour as he looks me up and down. Mr Davidson is handsome with a prominent forehead, dark brown eyes, black curly hair and chiselled cheek bones. His outfit is smart considering the task at hand, and he appears untroubled by wood dust clinging to his coat. The chestnut hue of his skin gives him an exotic appearance.

Mr Davidson faces Arthur and grins. 'Your wife's pretty. Why didn't you warn me? How am I to concentrate while Cleopatra watches me work?'

'Fetch a jug of ale, Susan,' snaps Arthur. 'The dust dries our throats.'

Mr Davidson turns back to me and gives an exaggerated shrug. This is a ladies' man.

When I return with the ale, the job is complete.

'Now you may shut the door on your clothes,' announces Mr Davidson, showing the ease with which the door now moves.

'It was generous of you to repair it for us,' I say.

'It was a simple task.'

Arthur looks agitated. 'We'll have drinks now and leave in half an hour.'

I follow the men into the parlour and top up their cups. I'm about to retreat when Mr Davidson says, 'Mrs Thistlewood, don't go. Business can wait. Grace us with your charm for a few minutes.'

Arthur's curt nod tells me to sit on a hard-backed chair at the table while he and Mr Davidson enjoy the comfort of the armchairs.

'You have an unusual accent, Mr Davidson. Are you from outside London?'

'Well spotted, Mrs Thistlewood. I was born in Jamaica, but my mother sent me to school in Edinburgh. After that I moved to Liverpool, interspersed with unpleasant episodes at sea. A few years ago, I moved to London. My accent is a mix of breeds, much like myself.'

'Forgive me, I didn't mean to pry.'

'Oh, I'm not offended. I used to teach at Sunday school and am accustomed to curious enquiries from children, including my own. It's refreshing for an adult to show interest.'

'How many children do you have?'

'Six. My wife already had four when we married. Children put sunlight into each day, don't you think?'

The very thought of Julian brightens my day.

'They do. Arthur's son knows how to cheer me whenever I'm out of sorts.'

Arthur scowls. 'Enough small talk. We should leave now, William, and discuss the rally planned for Manchester next week. It should draw a sizeable crowd and I'm inclined to attend.'

We all stand. Arthur bids me a curt farewell whereas Mr Davidson's is as warm as his greeting. I'm still smiling when I close the door, relishing the prospect of an evening to myself. It would have been an opportunity to see my William, but an investigation has him working all hours, so I content myself with a few chapters of *Emma*. A treasured reminder of when we first met.

∼

'You seem different.'

'How so?'

Arthur's reflection glowers from the mirror.

'More confident.'

I swivel to face him. 'Arthur, that should come as no surprise. Left to support myself for over twelve months, I had to become assertive and attend to matters you used to address. A timid woman can't fend for herself in a city such as London. I couldn't risk appearing vulnerable.'

'There's something else. You've become flirtatious and too relaxed in the company of men.'

'Whatever do you mean?'

Arthur rises from the bed and strides towards me. He beckons me to stand. I do as he commands and hold his gaze.

'You were disrespectful today.' His bottom lip trembles. Muscles twitch at his temples – a sign he's clenching his jaw.

I divert my gaze to a thin rectangle of faded carpet on the bedroom floor.

'You flaunted yourself in front of Davidson.'

'No, Arthur. You're mistaken. Mr Davidson was friendly and charming, but I did nothing to encourage his attention.'

My eyes flick back to Arthur. He interprets this simple reflexive action as a challenge and slaps me hard across the cheek. I stumble backwards, knocking over a chair and crashing down on top of it. The wood makes a sickening crack as a leg breaks off, thrusting a sharp shard into the back of my thigh. Whimpering, I stagger to my feet, but my fighting spirit enrages Arthur. He clenches a fist and thrusts it into my belly, knocking the air from my lungs. Falling to my knees, I raise my hands and plead with him to stop, but my voice is silent, buried beneath a thick blanket of pain.

'You've become a whore. That was clear today. You wanted that man to bed you, I could tell.'

'No.'

Arthur's foot connects with my chest, kicking away my denial.

Tears blind me. I can't imagine what has angered him like this. I curl into a ball, bracing for the next blow. It doesn't come.

'Take my hand,' says Arthur, before heaving me upright.

I would have preferred to stay put. The act of standing pulls hard on my bruised body, preventing me from straightening up. My chest aches with every breath as if I'm suffocating.

'Lie down.'

I sit on the edge of the bed, light-headed and nauseous. Arthur lifts my legs onto the mattress, twisting me round, forcing me to fall back against the pillows. My eyelids stick together as if glued. I refuse to look at him.

'Open your eyes.'

I taste bile, and my stomach clenches. Please, God, don't let me be sick. Not now.

'I said, open your eyes.'

'I'm trying, but I don't feel well.'

Arthur slaps my cheek and the stinging pulses like an echo of his violence. I force my eyelids open. He leers and grasps my shift in both hands, renting it apart to expose my nakedness. Then he peels off his own nightshirt, revealing his lust in its engorged ugliness.

'This is how a man treats a whore.'

Arthur holds my neck with one hand and uses the other to force my thighs apart. I try to think of William but can't associate his image with such defilement, so I erase him from my mind and focus on surviving.

At last, Arthur rolls off me with a smug smile. 'Get up.' There's a sinister edge to his voice. 'Clean up the mess.'

I struggle into a sitting position. The gash in my leg has bled onto the sheets. My thigh is throbbing, and I must attend to it soon or it will heal with an ugly scar.

'Never flaunt yourself again,' says Arthur.

I look into his eyes. 'I promise I will only ever flaunt myself to the man I love.'

CHAPTER 35

'Susan?' Confusion flickers across Mrs Westcott's face. 'Forgive me, my dear, I wasn't expecting you.'

The curious eyes of William's ancestors stare from portraits on the hallway walls. Their scrutiny is unsettling.

'My apologies for interrupting your afternoon, but I must speak with William. I went to Bow Street, but they said he was attending to a personal matter.'

Mrs Westcott gives me a pitying look. 'He's gone away for a few days. But, dear Susan, it's delightful to see you. You know you're welcome anytime. Come and join us. Share the joyful news.'

'Oh, no! I mustn't intrude.'

She links her arm through mine and grasps a walking stick in her other hand before leading me towards her parlour. 'No objections. I want you to share this special occasion. William would insist.'

It's my turn to look confused. Three elegant ladies replace teacups on saucers and rise in unison to greet me.

'This is our dear friend, Mrs Susan Thistlewood,' says Mrs Westcott, beaming at me.

The youngest of the ladies steps forward and reaches for my hands. 'Mrs Thistlewood, a pleasure to make your acquaintance. I'm Miss Jane Hurst. This is my mother, Mrs Margaret Hurst, and my sister, Mrs Charlotte Harris. Louisa has told us all about you. I understand your embroidery is exquisite.'

'The best in the city,' declares Mrs Westcott. Turning to me, 'Make yourself comfortable, my dear, and take tea with us.'

I stifle a grimace as I lower myself into a plush armchair. The soft cushion pad is no match for the scars of Arthur's brutality. My eyes drift back towards Miss Hurst. Her oval face radiates beauty from a clear complexion, and her silver-grey eyes twinkle with joy. Her rosebud mouth crinkles at the corners as it widens into a warm smile, and her fashionable dress sits well on her elegant figure.

Mrs Westcott pours a cup of tea and passes it to me. My hand trembles, causing the fine bone china cup to rattle in the saucer. I steady it with my other hand, hoping the ladies present are oblivious to my discomfort.

'Susan, you've become a dear friend, and so it's my pleasure to share the most delicious news with you. Miss Hurst is to become Mrs Westcott. Isn't that wonderful?'

The cup and saucer fall from my hands, filling my lap with a puddle of hot tea. The heat is a welcome distraction from my pain. Mrs Westcott opens the parlour door to call for her maid, while Mrs Hurst dabs at my soaked skirt with a square of lace-edged linen.

'Forgive me,' I say to no one in particular. 'I didn't mean to distract from your news.'

A few minutes pass while the maid squeezes dry cloths against my dress to absorb the dampness. Then she brings another tray with a fresh brew and a clean cup and saucer for me. Serenity returns to Mrs Westcott's parlour, and we all concentrate on sipping our tea.

I force myself to take an interest in the forthcoming wedding. 'Have you fixed a date?'

Miss Hurst and her mother exchange satisfied smiles.

'Next spring,' replies Miss Hurst, fixing her friendly gaze on me. 'Mrs Thistlewood, you must embroider my gown! With your reputation for your needlework skills, it will be the envy of my friends, and others will want your expertise when it's their turn to wed.' Her face drops. 'Forgive me. That was inappropriate. Here you are, a friend of the family, and I'm treating you as a maid. Thoughtless of me.'

I can't help but warm to Miss Hurst. She has dashed my hopes for a future coloured with happiness, but she is friendly and sensitive. She will make a more delightful daughter-in-law for Mrs Westcott than I ever could. The rest of my visit passes in a blur, my thoughts too distracted to follow conversations. At last, a suitable moment arrives to take my leave.

Mrs Westcott bustles into the hallway, her stick tapping on the cream painted floorboards. 'Susan, I didn't ask why you wanted to see William. Is there a message for him?'

'It can wait,' I reply, forcing cheer into my voice. 'Congratulations on the thrilling news. Miss Hurst is a delight.'

'She is, isn't she? It's always a concern who one's heir will choose for his wife. I confess, it's a relief that my wayward son is settling at all, and has chosen a charming young lady.'

I wouldn't describe William as wayward, but it seems I don't know him as well as I thought. The front door stands open, inviting a draught into the hallway. I secure my bonnet with a new pin, then step outside into a world filled with pain and uncertainty.

~

The Thames gushes and swirls beneath London Bridge, gathering flotsam and churning it with mud before rushing towards the sea. The river is busy today, congested with boats of various shapes and sizes. Some carry freight while others ferry passengers from one riverbank to the other. I'm fascinated by one craft in particular. An oarsman pulls against the tide, trying to hold position, while two other men struggle to haul a large object from the water. A body, perhaps. A lost soul, much like myself, whose last chance of happiness vanished like a snuffed candle flame.

The current moves faster where the bridge piles reach through the surface – a trick of science beyond my comprehension. A seagull makes a precarious landing on the water, jabs its beak into the murk and pulls out a chunk of discarded meat. The current sweeps the distracted bird through a rapid arc and spits it into a fast-moving stream of water. When the seagull recovers its senses, it chooses not to continue towards the sea but beats its wings, struggling to escape the river's grasp. The victorious creature circles above me, riding the breeze, screeching a warning to other gulls.

I wonder, if I jumped into the river, would I be dashed against the solid supports, my head split open and ruined like a dropped ripe apricot? Or would the current spit me into a slower stream, only for three well-meaning men to drag me into a small wooden rescue boat?

I perch on the balustrade and swing my legs over. My feet dangle high above the water. The river is calling to me, beckoning me to succumb to its embrace. The ripples are mesmerising, and I study patterns created by waves rushing out from the pilings, separating into ever-increasing concentric circles. Rebellious undercurrents lap at the bridge supports, as if licking an ice cream, eroding it away.

The carcass of an animal swirls beneath me. I lean forward to see what it is. A dog? Too small. A fox? Maybe. It doesn't matter because it's dead. I wonder if anyone will grieve for me? Not Arthur. He wasted no time recovering from the loss of his first wife and soon turned his attention towards me. William? He has Miss Hurst now. Julian would pity me for having to choose between Arthur and the river. And my demise would sadden my parents, but they'd recover soon enough.

I cannot think what purpose I have served in this life. Whatever it was, it's over. The grey-brown water looks cold but will burn my lungs when it fills them with water. Dear God, have mercy. Let my drowning be quick.

'Susan?'

I'm ready. I edge a little further forward, wincing when the balustrade presses on a bruise. A warm trickle of blood escapes from the gash on my thigh. How did that break open? Something else that no longer matters.

'Susan!'

I've made my decision. My right shoe slides from my foot and plummets to the murky river. 'One… two… three…' More seconds pass. There's no sign of the shoe. Good. If I'm held beneath the surface of the river, my ending will be quick. 'Eleven… twelve…' I squint at the water downstream, in case the shoe resurfaces there. No trace. I slip off the other shoe to be certain. Again, the river swallows it, refusing to spit it out anywhere within my line of view.

I rest my stockinged heels on the edge of the bridge, toes protruding into empty air. A pale sun creeps out from behind a black cloud and warms my cheeks. It's God, preparing to welcome me to the afterlife, whatever that may be. I tilt my face towards Him and tell Him I'm on my way.

My eyelids close and my hands separate from the balustrade. I tilt forward. I'm at peace and ready to fly.

Something wraps around my midriff, squeezing me tight. My eyelids snap open.

'Susan!' A sob this time. 'Whatever saddens you, don't do this. You have friends who love you.'

My heart lurches. It's Anna. She must have followed me.

My hands grapple for the balustrade and my feet seek firm ground. Hot tears drip from my cheeks into the river, lost in a pool of cold hostility. Anna whispers in my ear, her words loving and kind as only a true friend's can be.

I'm on the safe side of the balustrade now. Strangers withdraw to the bridge alcoves, sheltering from drops of summer rain. A blurred image of Beckey hurtles towards me. Soon I'm enveloped by my two dearest friends.

'Thank the Lord you're still with us. As soon as I received word from Anna, I had to come and fetch you. Dear Susan, what were you thinking?'

Beckey helps me into a hansom cab and Anna sits next to me, her arms wrapped around my trembling body.

'How did you know I was here?'

Anna presses her cheek to mine. 'You weren't yourself at work today and when you left early, I knew something was wrong. I called at your house on my way home, but there was no answer. Then I saw you hesitate at the end of your street. You looked sad, Susan. Distracted. I was concerned and called out, but you turned and hurried away. Something compelled me to follow you. I kept my distance so as not to intrude, but when I realised you were heading for the bridge, I panicked and paid a coachman to fetch Beckey.'

'It's as well you were in no hurry to jump,' says Beckey.

'Please, don't tell Arthur.'

Beckey snorts. 'He's the last person we'd tell. You'll stay with me tonight, and we'll talk about whatever has saddened you so.'

'Arthur will insist I go home.'

'He'll have no choice. Anna will tell him you were with me when you succumbed to a sudden bout of vomiting. She'll say you're not well enough to travel. You may return tomorrow, provided you're up to it.'

Anna kisses my cheek. 'Don't let a foolish husband drive you to despair, Susan. No man is worth that. The pain you feel, whatever the cause, will ease in time.'

Despite being widows, Beckey and Anna live fulfilling lives, and Anna has worked her way out of poverty while raising a child. My friends are intelligent, courageous women. Fate has given me an opportunity to reinvent myself. I will follow their example.

Beckey opens a twist of paper and offers it to me. I take a barley sugar and post it between my lips. The sweetness is a balm to my damaged soul. I suck on the boiled sweet and force a smile for my friends. I haven't lost my feeling of despair, but with Beckey and Anna by my side, I can survive anything.

There's a pricking in my left foot and I bend forward to determine the cause. A sharp stone has ripped through my stocking and sits embedded in the thickened skin of my heel. I dig it out with my fingernail, surprised I felt nothing while walking across the cobbles to the cab.

'My shoes!' I picture them tossed to the riverbank by the ungrateful Thames, waiting for a scavenger to free them from the mud.

'Our feet are similar in size,' says Beckey. 'I have grey

jacquard boots I've worn only twice. You're welcome to them.'

I smile my gratitude, too exhausted to protest. And anyway, I have no spares of my own. The thought of seeing Arthur again fills me with foreboding and I worry about how I will explain the change of footwear.

I must not allow my fear of Arthur to taint my optimism for the future. His punches and kicks will not continue forever, and one day the scars will disappear. I misplaced my faith in William, but I'll not let an error of judgement ruin my dream of a happy future.

From this day forward, I will strive for happiness. It may take a while to find the future I deserve, but while I work towards it, I will be courageous.

CHAPTER 36

A FAT BLACK housefly perches on the edge of my plate and drinks from a puddle of strawberry jam. Any other time I'd swat it away. Today I don't care. There are worse problems in the world than a fly sharing my food. And anyway, I've eaten enough jam for now. My teeth feel furry against my tongue, and a tooth is twingeing.

Arthur went out early this morning. Mrs Hooper's shop is closed for three days, undergoing a radical refit thanks to her rising fame in the dressmaking and repair business. I used most of the first day of my unexpected holiday to scrub our modest home from top to bottom. The kitchen table is glowing from a generous application of beeswax, and the parlour is bright and welcoming now that grime no longer obstructs the passage of sunlight through the windows. It's time to let out my dresses, for they have grown tight of late.

I push my armchair across the bare floorboards and wince at the loud scraping sounds. Positioning it next to the window, I sit and watch the street below. An amorous young man escorts his blushing companion towards the nearby park, both of them glowing in the evening's warmth. Despite two years at this address, I don't recognise them. Our neighbours from either side greet us well enough, but we never step across one another's thresholds. Nor do I wish that situation to change. They throw me pitying glances the morning after a violent night with Arthur, and I could not bear deeper scrutiny.

I pull a dress from the top of my mending basket and unpick the stitches at the seams. Why am I becoming so bulky? I'm not with child, and I'm gaining weight all over. My thighs are large, my ankles thick and my face rounded. I know I'm not sickening for something. In fact, I enjoy the best of health considering the life I endure. A sudden craving drives me to the kitchen. My appetite for jam has returned and I devour two heaped spoonfuls before returning to my seat to continue contemplation.

'Susan?' Arthur bursts into the parlour, flushed with excitement. 'Susan? Did the news reach you?'

I replace my work on top of the basket and rise from my chair. 'No, Arthur. I haven't left the house today.'

Arthur rushes across the room and grasps my hands. A broad smile illuminates his face and I see traces of the charm that once attracted me.

'England is turning.' His eyes are wide. He presses my fingers to his lips. 'The government will listen now.'

'What's happened? Was there a protest?'

'There was. Henry Hunt drew fifty thousand men and women to St Peter's Field.'

'Fifty thousand?' I can't imagine a crowd of that size gathered in one place. My surprise fuels Arthur's enthusiasm.

'What did you expect? Deprive workers of a decent standard of living and they will revolt. Ruled by a corrupt parliament, unable to vote and cast aside like rubbish by those who were elected, it's not surprising the workers take to the streets and support those who make their interests a priority. This is a momentous day, Susan. The people have had enough. Now they're interested in what we say and will do what we ask. I knew this day was coming. I will have my revolution.'

Arthur pulls me to him and kisses me hard on the mouth. His lips move to my neck and his hands reach for my skirts, screwing them up in his fists, raising them to my thighs. My body goes rigid.

'Arthur, stop.' I push him away, scratching around in my mind for justification for my reaction. 'I can't. Not today.'

'Why not?' There's an edge to his voice.

I can't think of an excuse. My pulse is loud in my ears. If I don't think of something soon, I will pay for my reluctance. Sweat coats my palms, and my legs tremble. Arthur glares, daring me to uphold my refusal. I look towards the window, hoping for inspiration, and see my sewing basket.

Arthur follows my gaze.

'I've been altering my dresses,' I say, tiptoeing towards a dangerous lie.

His expression softens. 'How far along?'

'Hard to say.' I bite the inside of my cheek.

'Dearest Susan.' Arthur strokes my face with unfamiliar tenderness. 'Perhaps this time…'

The unfinished sentence hangs between us like a dare, neither one of us wishing to complete it. May God forgive my lie, but I need a break from Arthur, and this is the only way I can be certain he'll leave me alone.

'Take things easy for a while. A maid's out of the question, but attend to only the essential chores.' His brow furrows. 'Can you work a few more months?'

It's no surprise to hear that question because I'm the only

reliable source of income. I nod. The lines on his forehead fade.

'Sit by the window,' he says. 'Enjoy the last hour of daylight. Shall I fetch a book?'

I shake my head. It's been a while since I visited Paternoster Row, so I have nothing new to enjoy. 'No. There's plenty of needlework to keep me busy.'

He rests a palm on my belly and smiles. 'May God protect this child of ours. I'm going out. I'm meeting a fellow by the name of George Edwards. Don't wait up.'

A few days have passed since the meeting at St Peter's Field. The newspapers are fat with details and describe the event as a massacre. I stare at the pages through misted eyes. So absorbed am I in making sense of the atrocity, I don't hear Arthur enter the kitchen.

He places a proprietorial hand on my shoulder, sending an icy chill through my spine.

Arthur scoops up the papers and places them to one side. 'Imagine the scene,' he says. 'Bands playing, banners flying, Hunt standing on the hustings, and loud cheers echoing for miles. They knew he intended to put their suffering into words and make their feelings known. The cheering lasted so long, he couldn't begin his speech before the cavalry charged. Hunt was a hero, and the people applauded him for it.'

'Many died.'

Arthur grunts. 'Casualties of war.'

'Children, Arthur!' I dig my fingernails into my palms. I must not make him angry. 'And hundreds of adults injured.'

He shrugs. 'The magistrates made an error sending in the yeomanry. Would have passed off peacefully enough if army officers and their middle-class buffoons hadn't sabotaged the meeting.'

'But Arthur, women and children?'

'Sacrifices for the cause. The government backed that slaughter but refuses to take responsibility for the deaths. More people could die before the wheels of change turn. I intend to seek support for more such meetings.'

'More slaughter including innocent children who know nothing of politics?'

His lips slide into a mean, calculating smile. 'We'll do whatever it takes. Our streets may have to turn red several times over before we get the result we want. I will raise an army unafraid to spill blood. We will force change on the government of England.'

He speaks of human sacrifice as if it's as simple as butchering an animal. God willing, it will get him into the trouble I dream of. But at what price?

May something good come out of this. Something of benefit to the masses. Don't let those lives be sacrificed in vain!

My tooth is throbbing, the pain intense, like something gnawing through the bone of my jaw. It will have to be pulled.

CHAPTER 37

WITH TREMBLING HANDS, I slice into a pineapple. A frivolous expense, but it's Arthur's favourite fruit. God knows he will need sweetening when I break the news. I pray the rally went well today and Arthur returns home in high spirits. The better his mood, the less likely he is to punish me for the crushing blow I must deliver.

The front door creaks as Arthur forces it open. A prolonged bout of damp weather caused the wood to swell and we have to shove it away from the jamb. Another favour to ask of charming William Davidson.

Arthur looks tired.

'Did the rally go well?'

Arthur sits at the kitchen table and lets out a sigh. 'Well enough. The yeomanry attended, but it was peaceful. The speakers weren't interrupted, and members of the crowd expressed opinions without the fear of sword tips being pressed against their necks.'

'Were your words well received?' A few days ago, and much to my surprise, I learned that Arthur has been a principal speaker at many meetings.

'I think so.'

'Then why do you appear unhappy?'

'There are signs the economy's improving. As a result, the workers are less inclined to revolt.'

'A better economy is what England needs, is it not?'

Unwelcome news for me if it quells Arthur's lust for a revolution.

Arthur glares. 'An improvement in the economy is preferable but doesn't change the fact that the selfish fools who govern won't flinch when it declines again – and believe me, it will. The battle will happen, but not yet because my soldiers are deserting, Susan. The weavers have withdrawn support and other trades will follow. I cannot fight without troops.'

His tone confirms his lust for bloodshed is waning. Innocent lives will not be taken, but my dream of happiness is ruined.

He sniffs the contents of the glass bowl I've set before him. 'Pineapple,' he says with a glimmer of a smile.

'A bargain from the market. The season's ending and they're no longer at their best. This one had a large bruise.' It's almost the truth. Much to Beckey's amusement, I won a small discount after persistent haggling. But the damage occurred after I paid for it.

Arthur skewers a chunk on his fork and closes his eyes, relishing the sweetness. I've already eaten my share and a piece or two of Arthur's while waiting for him to return home. Beckey counselled me against sweets and other such treats when insisting I lose weight. She fears I may succumb to a diseased heart or lose more teeth. She said Samuel often ranted about the perils of overeating. I'm substituting fruit for the treats I enjoy, but I'm always hungry. I've no choice but to follow Beckey's advice because there's not enough spare fabric to let out dresses again.

With the dishes cleared away, Arthur beckons me to join him at the table.

'I'll be out late tonight. There will be a spate of evening meetings as important matters have arisen that are difficult to resolve.'

'Where do you meet at such a late hour?'

'Does it matter?'

I reach for his hand and my skin crawls at the contact. 'I fear for your safety. It sets my mind at ease if I know where you are.'

Arthur raises his eyebrows at my uncharacteristic concern. I'm trying to gauge how long I will have to enjoy myself alone at home before I must resume the pretence of being a dutiful wife.

'It's better you don't know,' he says. 'If the authorities discover the locations of the meetings, there'll be repercussions. This way, if they question you of my whereabouts, you can honestly say you do not know.'

His reply has an ominous undertone. My heart lifts. 'Arthur, what are you plotting?'

'We're exploring options,' he says, wearing a thin smile. 'It's growing ever more unlikely that we'll start a revolution in London, but we expect our friends in the North to be more obliging.'

I'm relieved the flame of revolution still flickers.

Arthur toys with the lid of his snuff box before plucking out a pinch of powder and snorting. 'Time to get going.'

'Arthur, I have disappointing news.'

'What?'

'The baby.' I pause, preparing to release the rest of the lie. 'It wasn't to be.'

Arthur stands and catches the chair with his legs, tipping it backwards. He returns the chair to its feet, then strides towards the door. He pauses and turns. 'We can't afford another mouth to feed, so it's no loss. Don't wait up.'

~

Less than a minute after Arthur leaves the house, there's a loud rapping at the door.

'Letter, miss.' A boy stands on the step offering me a folded piece of paper. He's young, about ten years old, and scruffy. Thick green mucus creeps from his left nostril. He sweeps it away with the heel of his hand, leaving a shiny streak on his grimy cheek.

'Who sent you?'

The boy shrugs. 'Dunno, but he paid me to bring it you.'

I glance up and down the street. 'Is he here?'

The boy shakes his head and waves the letter. When I take it from him, he scampers away and soon disappears from view. I unfold the paper to find the signature of the sender, but as soon as I see the handwriting I freeze. Gathering my senses, I check the street for Arthur. My mouth is dry, and I'm dizzy. I close the door and lean against it, gasping for air. The letter is from William.

Dearest Susan,

Mr Brown said you've deserted him as a customer and that's why you did not receive my notes. Is all well, dearest? I worry. Please reply to this letter, or better still, visit Mother and reassure us both that there's no cause for concern.

Not a day passes without me thinking of you. Mother thought you looked peaky the day she shared news of the wedding. Did you not find Jane charming? At first, I was glad you made her acquaintance. Now I worry her presence has affected our relationship.

I'm at risk of rambling. Your husband is a dangerous man. I beg you to put our minds at rest.

I long for your company. Without you, I am incomplete.

Forever yours,

William

How dare he! I hold the letter to a candle flame and watch it burn to nothing. His promises of being together were as empty as Arthur's heart. Did he think because I'm trapped in a loveless marriage, I would bless his union with the delightful Miss Hurst and continue to meet in secret? There was a time when I imagined becoming his wife. I didn't realise he wanted me as a concubine. The tone of his letter confirms enduring feelings, but can a man love two women at the same time? Is it possible Miss Hurst knows of his affection and is unbothered?

May God forgive me for falling in love with William. So many nights have passed when I have dreamed of uniting my body with his. From this day forward, I will push him from my mind. Forever.

CHAPTER 38

THE AROMA of baked apples fills the room. It reminds me of carefree autumn days spent in my mother's kitchen rolling pastry, stewing fruits and making preserves. Mother was planning to visit this month but has succumbed to a malady of her chest so it would be unwise for her to inhale the filthy air of London. And anyway, my father needs her. He recovered well from his apoplexy two years ago but has become forgetful.

'Baked apples again?'

Arthur looks like he's swallowed a wasp. The recent change to our eating habits has affected him adversely. While I relish the slackening of clothes against my shrinking flesh, Arthur is gaunt and short-tempered.

'I don't earn enough to provide us with hearty desserts,' I reply. 'Most of my wages go into the coffers for the cause.'

Arthur huffs and puffs but tucks into his dish of two baked apples, making approving grunts with every mouthful. 'You've done something different.'

It's unusual for him to notice.

'I replaced the sugar with honey. We were each given a pot after our performance yesterday.'

He scowls at this. The concert was part of a fundraising event organised by the wife of a government minister.

'It was for a good cause, Arthur. You can't hold a man's wife responsible for the foolish ways of her husband.'

'I suppose not.'

'How was your meeting last night? Do you see a way forward?'

To an outsider, it will appear as if Arthur has my full backing for every one of his decisions, but I loathe the man he has become and will do whatever it takes to part from him. I believe the only way to end my marital misery is to play the role of dutiful wife and encourage behaviour that will lead him back to gaol. I can only be free when Arthur is behind bars.

Arthur shakes his head and lets out an exasperated sigh. 'London is awash with lily-livers. There's no prospect of starting a revolution here.'

'So what will you do?'

'The rebellion will start in Northern England. I would have preferred it to be in London, but the North's more viable. We've a new fellow working with us, and he's as eager as I to instigate change. He has the energy and passion required to persuade the other leaders to pursue a new direction. We'll see how things go at tonight's meeting.'

A loud knock has Arthur rushing from the table towards the front door. 'That'll be him now. I told him to come here first. I have some ideas to run by him before I present them at the meeting.'

A thin, pale-faced gentleman steps into our hallway. Arthur introduces him as Mr George Edwards. He's of short stature, perhaps an inch or two shorter than me, and has a straight nose and grey eyes that give him a weasel-like appearance. Arthur escorts him to the parlour and makes a point of closing the door to prevent me from joining them.

'How much money do you have?' Arthur's face is florid. The skin at his temples flickers in tiny waves, betraying his repressed anger. 'Empty your reticule.'

I do as I'm bid and tip the contents onto the table – a simple tortoiseshell comb; a lace fan with a slight tear at the centre; a folded square of linen; and a handful of coins.

Arthur sweeps the coins towards him. 'Three shillings and sixpence. Is that it? Any money stashed in a hiding place?'

'No, Arthur. You know we use my wages for your campaign leaving barely enough to cover the cost of food, candles and coal.'

His eyes darken. I clamp my lips together, afraid I'll say something inappropriate. Sometimes he gives me coins for an extra sack of coal, but I know nothing about the source of Arthur's income. I suspect he's reliant on his wits at gaming tables. Arthur storms out of the kitchen and his feet thud upstairs to our bedroom. I hear drawers being ripped open and cupboard doors banging. I hurry to join him.

'Arthur, what are you doing?'

'There must be money somewhere.'

'Have you checked your pockets?'

His glare suffices for an answer. He grasps the bedroom rug and heaves it to one side, throwing up a cloud of dust. My heart quickens as he studies the floorboards, then drops to his hands and knees.

'Old houses like this often have hiding places beneath the

boards.' He removes a small dagger from somewhere inside his jacket. I've never seen this weapon before and wonder if he carries it all the time. Hairs rise on the back of my neck.

He inserts the blade between two boards and manoeuvres it back and forth. 'I knew it,' he exclaims as one board lifts.

My dress clings to my damp armpits and my palms turn clammy. I can't recall whether I removed all my treasures from their hiding place or if I took only a few to conceal them in the yard. Arthur pulls out a small cloth bag. He turns it inside out and buttons tumble to the exposed floorboards. They resemble silver filigree but are mere imitations, remnants from a dress Mrs Hooper asked me to finish. I didn't think she'd mind if I held on to a few spares.

Arthur throws the buttons aside, scattering them in all directions. 'Waste of time hoarding those.'

'I think they're pretty,' I say, crawling to retrieve them, speaking in a tone that suggests I've not seen them before.

Arthur sits back on his haunches. 'Anything hidden in the kitchen?'

I shake my head.

'Let us double-check. A bag of coins may have been stashed on a shelf for safekeeping and forgotten about.'

With hesitant steps, I follow him back down the stairs.

Arthur's about to sweep a row of jars from a shelf when I reach out and grasp his arm to stop him. 'No, Arthur! I can't afford to replace the contents if you knock these to the floor. They'll smash on the flagstones. Allow me.'

My chest tightens as I lift down pots and jars. Arthur watches wide-eyed, unblinking, like a hunter stalking his prey.

When every shelf is bare, Arthur staggers towards the table, his chin wobbling.

'Tell me, Arthur, why such desperate behaviour?'

Arthur slumps into a chair. 'I need money to travel to Manchester. I thought the others would contribute, but between us we can't raise sufficient funds. If we don't go north and speak to our followers, their support will wane like everyone else's.'

I leave him to ruminate in silence while I clean the shelves and reload them with the pots and jars. At last, Arthur drags himself to his feet and shuffles into the hall. After putting on his winter coat, he leaves the house, slamming the door behind him.

With slow deep breaths, I count to fifty, then hurry to look through the parlour window. The street is deserted. Satisfied Arthur's not about to come back through the door, I dash to the kitchen and reach for the largest storage jar. I plunge my hand deep into the flour and retrieve a muslin bag. The weight of it confirms my savings are intact. For now.

CHAPTER 39

THE SOUP IS watery and disappointing. I begrudge the time spent boiling the carcass, skimming fat, and picking out the best bits of weary vegetables.

Arthur has been subdued for days.

'You mustn't give up, Arthur, not after investing so many years trying to improve the plight of our people. You'll think of an alternative way forward, I'm sure of it.'

A newspaper lies folded on the table, and Arthur stares into the distance. His brow crinkles, but he says nothing.

'Your mission's important, and the real workers of this country need you. Someone has to overthrow our corrupt and selfish government, and that someone is you.'

We spend the rest of the evening in silence. I sit and read, struggling to concentrate, fearful Arthur will abandon his cause. With no focus for his violent mind, what will become of me?

Arthur fidgets in the armchair nearest the hearth. He takes out his snuffbox and flips the lid open, then snaps it shut and thrusts it back into his pocket.

The fire dies. The temperature of the room plummets. Reluctantly, I close my book. It's time for bed.

As I turn the handle of the parlour door, Arthur says, 'You were right, Susan.'

'About what?'

'The solution has become obvious. Now I know what to do.' There's a pause, then Arthur says, 'I can't think why I didn't consider it before. There's only one option.' His smile is joyous and genuine.

'Tell me,' I say, reflecting his good humour.

'Revolution's not the answer. I must target members of the Cabinet.'

'Target them for what?'

'Assassination,' he replies with a grin.

CHAPTER 40

A STREET VENDOR offers me a pear. I admire its perfect form and golden hue, then hand over a coin without a second thought. I didn't intend to eat it right away, but as I navigate the dirty city streets, I clamp my teeth against the crisp autumn flesh. The pear is disappointing, the promise of juice unfulfilled and the fruit bland and lacking in sweetness. Things are not always as they seem.

An elderly woman is kneeling on a street corner by Leicester Square and extends a clawed hand to every passer-by. Her face is dotted with scabs, her front teeth missing. I wonder what misfortune reduced her to such a pitiful plight and offer her the pear. She shakes her head and points to swollen gums before giving me a toothless smile. I'm ashamed of my thoughtlessness and hand over the last of my change, hoping she will find something warm to eat on this bitter December night.

I finish the pear and drop the core into the gutter, adding it to a pile of detritus. The old woman has unsettled me. Anyone could end up in reduced circumstances. If Arthur went to prison, my wages would be adequate unless I became incapable of work.

I cover my chin with my scarf, wishing I owned a thicker winter coat. I have enough money to buy one, but I'm not prepared to use the bulk of my savings. And how would I explain the extravagance without revealing my secret hoard?

Arthur isn't coming home this evening. These days, his meetings continue through the night and he stays out until morning, preferring not to risk catching the eye of a night patrolman. I consider a detour to Paternoster Row. I haven't been there for so long, but it would add at least forty minutes to my walk, and I have no money for a coach. A flurry of snowflakes forces my decision and I head for home.

There's an eerie glow as darkness falls. The icy air stings my face, but the promise of a warm fire propels me forward. This evening, I will start reading *Emma* for the second time.

A small stone works its way into my shoe. It's sharp against my skin and I have no choice but to stop and remove it to prevent staining the grey fabric with blood. I have no other decent pair. Winter bites at my toes, my stockings offering no protection. The tiny jagged rock falls to the pavement. A pretty thing, grey and white with streaks of silver. It's a wonder something so small can cause such discomfort. As I slide my foot back into the shoe, a horse and cart rumbles past, steam puffing out in clouds from the horse's nostrils. His shoes clang against the cobbles at a tempo that encourages me to quicken my pace. I can't keep up with the horse and am disappointed when it turns a corner, disappearing from view.

When I reach Drury Lane, I stop dead. An echo repeats one… two… three times. My heartbeat quickens and I glance up and down the street. Even the prostitutes prefer to remain indoors tonight. A customer emerges from a gin shop and collides with me. He apologises then scuttles away, huddled over his purchase. I try to keep pace with him, noting his foot-steps create no echo. He enters a dilapidated building, leaving me alone once more. I break into a run and turn into Prince's Street, my skirts wrapping around my legs, threatening to tip me over. At last, Stanhope Street appears, and I gasp for breath at my front door. I turn the key in the lock and stand on the threshold, pausing before entering my home. A man turns the corner and stops. He holds my gaze until I withdraw from view. Whoever he was, he'll not see me again tonight.

Walking home alone for the third day in a row, I long for Anna's companionship. George tumbled partway down a flight of stairs at the weekend and has been getting nasty headaches.

A toy-trader has a wheeled horse on offer at a reduced price. There's a tiny chip on one of the back legs, but it's been rubbed smooth so as not to hurt a child. George will like it, so I spare a halfpenny hoping the toy will distract him from his suffering. The horse has a russet body with a golden mane and a white patch on its face. The wheels turn smoothly and there's a length of string tied about the horse's head, like a set of reins, so a child can pull it along.

With the gift wrapped in brown paper, I continue on my way home. Anna lives three streets to the east of mine, so I ignore the turning for Stanhope Street. The neighbourhood is busy tonight, and I sense I'm being followed again. I take a sharp left then right and flatten myself against a brick wall. Beads of perspiration bubble on my brow. I count to twenty, wondering what to do if the stalker should appear before me.

Nerves get the better of me and I scuttle towards Anna's home. I glance over my shoulder and recognise the man behind me – the same one who followed me before. At the entrance to Anna's building, I gasp with relief. The door is ajar. I dash inside and slam it shut, my heart hammering against my chest. Tears cascade down my cheeks. There's a small boy playing in the doorway to his tenement and he looks up at me with wide eyes. I force a smile, then climb the stairs to Anna's.

Mrs Hooper senses something is amiss, but I keep my anguish to myself. When she sends me home an hour early, I step out of the shop and scour the street for anyone who might follow me. Ladies gather at shop windows admiring goods on display, while others pass by in stylish carriages, homeward bound with purchases. Few men walk the pavements, and none have a sinister air. I turn onto Leicester Square to find it bustling with visitors. Noise spills from the open door of a coffee shop where husbands pass the time in cheerful debate while waiting for their wives. This time, I stroll along the pavement, listening for the slightest sounds. I deviate from my usual route home and wander through Covent Garden, reassured by the hubbub that increases in volume as I draw near to the centre. I stop by a table of gloves displayed beneath a shop window. A choice of colours, all cut from fine quality leather, but alas I must resist the lure of owning a pair. From the corner of my eye, I see an ominous figure withdraw to a shadowy side street. I straighten my posture and thrust out my chin, then walk towards the spot where I saw him. He's no longer there, but I know he's close. And watching me.

I look around, contemplating my next move. If the man wishes to hurt me, I'm defenceless. I could flee, but he knows where I live.

My temples throb, my fingers tremble. Arthur dismissed my claims of being followed, declaring me of no interest to anyone. My imagination runs wild. What if the stranger derives pleasure from hurting women? I know such men exist.

There is one person who can set my mind at ease, and he is a mere stone's throw away in Bow Street.

'Susan!' William scrambles to his feet and dismisses the clerk who escorted me to his office.

William strides forward, extending his arms to draw me into an embrace, but I step back and stand rigid.

'Susan? What's wrong? You're as white as milk.'

'Someone's following me.' The words gush from my lips, and I fall to my knees.

'Dearest, please, don't distress yourself.' He tries again to embrace me, but I resist. He holds out a hand to raise me to my feet. 'Come. Have a seat. Tell me what troubles you so.'

I dry my tears and stare across the desk, uncertain of where to begin.

'I've missed you,' he says. 'Why didn't you answer my letter?'

'There was no point. Not while other pressing matters beg your attention.'

His brow furrows. 'What do you mean?'

'Miss Hurst.' I cringe at the petulance in my tone.

'Miss Hurst?'

'For pity's sake, your betrothed!'

His frown evaporates, and he chuckles. 'Whatever gave you that idea?'

His mirth fuels my anger. 'I've met her, remember?'

He shakes his head.

'The beautiful Miss Jane Hurst, at least fifteen years my junior, so it's no wonder you prefer her to me. I trust the wedding plans are progressing well?'

'They are. But they're not my plans.'

'The bride-to-be and her mother always take control of such matters.'

William tilts his head to one side. 'No, you don't understand, I'm not involved at all.'

I have no wish to consider the matter further and stare at my hands, wondering how to introduce the topic I came to discuss.

'Jane's not my betrothed.'

I lift my head to look at him. 'Why not? Did you break off the engagement?'

'No. Miss Hurst is my brother's fiancée.'

I catch my breath. 'You have a brother.'

William nods. 'Edward, and he's chosen to settle at last.'

We both fall silent. I'm processing his revelation while he must wonder at my misunderstanding.

Eventually I break the silence. 'I didn't know you have a brother.'

'Edward's older than me. An officer in the Royal Navy. He's put his wayward life behind him and become a gentleman of business instead. He's much older than Miss Hurst but his boyish charm won her over, and probably his fortune too.'

I hide my flaming face behind my fingers. 'I've been such a fool. Please forgive me.'

William smiles. 'A little misunderstanding, nothing more.'

I rise from the chair, my legs unsteady. William stands at the same time and comes around the desk towards me. Then we enjoy a fond reunion, clinging to one another as if our lives depend upon it.

'Tell me, Susan, why did you come here today?'

I release myself from his embrace and burden him with my troubles. He does not seem surprised that someone has been tailing me.

'You've nothing to fear. From the description, I know who's been watching you. He works for the magistrates. I'll instruct him to intimidate you no more. And anyway, it's not you who is of interest, it's your husband.'

'William, there's something you should know.' I look towards the door to check it's still closed. 'Arthur intends to murder members of the Cabinet.'

William sighs. 'We know.'

A breath catches in my throat. 'You do?'

William pulls me to him. 'Dear Susan, believe me when I say it won't be long before we can be together.'

I nuzzle against his shoulder, relishing the comfort of his protective embrace. 'How can you be sure?'

'We know of Arthur's plans. But, Susan, you mustn't tell anyone else what you've heard, or things may not turn out as we hope.'

'I don't understand, William, how did you learn about Arthur's intentions?'

William holds me at arm's length, and his lips part into a loving smile. 'Because one of his closest allies is a spy.'

CHAPTER 41

MRS WESTCOTT'S cook baked a delicious cherry pie. The sweet-sour taste of preserved cherries is balanced by a generous quantity of sugar. The pastry is light and crumbly, and the syrupy juice laced with a hint of brandy. It's by far the tastiest pie I have ever eaten, and I wonder if it would be disrespectful to request a second helping.

'I'm thrilled you agreed to work on Jane's dress.' Mrs Westcott blots her mouth with a corner of the tablecloth. 'There's no finer needlewoman than you.'

I smile at Jane before sipping tea from an elegant china cup. Something about the delicate floral pattern reminds me of the sugar bowl given to me by my mother.

'What is it, dear? You look sad.'

I force a smile. 'I had a piece of china similar to this. Forget-me-nots rather than cornflowers, and it was only a sugar bowl but of great sentimental value.'

'What happened to it?' asks Jane.

I hesitate, wondering how best to reply. 'We were ready to emigrate to America, but things didn't go according to plan. We boarded a ship, but because of unforeseen circumstances had to disembark and leave all our possessions in the cabin. My husband tried to get them back, but to no avail.'

Jane's eyes widen. 'The ship sailed with your things still on board?'

Mrs Westcott senses my discomfort. 'A most unfortunate situation. Jane, dear, play a tune on the piano. Susan has a delightful singing voice; your mother and I would enjoy listening to you both perform.'

Jane raises an enquiring eye. I smile. Singing will provide a welcome distraction from thoughts of Arthur's antics.

As Jane brings the last tune to a close, Mrs Westcott and Mrs Hurst applaud enthusiastically. A third pair of hands joins in, and my eyes dart towards the door. William meets my gaze with an intensity that sends a shiver through me.

'Bravo,' he says. 'Best performance ever.'

Mrs Hurst is all of a twitter. 'Mrs Thistlewood, you must sing at Jane's wedding.'

Heat flares in my cheeks. 'Oh, I don't think so. I'm not a soloist. I'm more used to singing in a group.'

William grins. 'Mrs Thistlewood has friends who sing too. Perhaps a trio?'

'Consider it,' presses Mrs Hurst. 'It would add an elegant touch to the celebration.'

I wonder what I would wear for such a fine occasion. 'I'll speak to Beckey and Anna and ask if they're willing.'

Mrs Hurst claps her hands. 'That's settled then.' She is obviously a woman accustomed to getting her own way.

'I must go,' I say, reaching for my reticule. 'It's been a pleasure to spend the afternoon with you. I'll work on the embroidery over the next few weeks and send a message when I've finished. Then we'll plan the final alterations.'

'I hope to see you long before then, my dear,' replies Mrs Westcott. 'William will walk you home. It'll be dark soon.'

'Thank you, but it's not far. I'm happy to go alone.'

'Certainly not.' Mrs Westcott is as indignant as I thought she would be.

A ripple of amusement crosses William's face. He knows I would love nothing more than to return home with him as my escort.

'I'll be out a while, Mother. I have to call at Bow Street to finish a report for the court session tomorrow morning.'

A maid helps me into my scarf and coat. When the front door opens, a bitter chill engulfs us. I step outside into the icy grip of winter, warmed by William's presence. As soon as we turn the corner, he offers me his arm.

'Is your husband home?'

'I'm not sure. He keeps irregular hours and doesn't always tell me his plans. We should part at Drury Lane in case someone recognises me.'

William sighs. 'I crave a few minutes alone with you.'

'We can't take the risk.'

William stops and turns to me. 'Come to Bow Street. If asked, I'll say I'm interviewing you as a witness to a case, then we can enjoy privacy in an empty office upstairs. There won't be any magistrates in today, and very few officers with it being a Sunday.'

I squeeze his arm, then pull up my hood, then tilt my head forward to hide my face. I'm treading a dangerous path by associating with William, but my heart will not allow me to dismiss him from my life a second time.

The officer at the main desk ignores us when we enter the building. I suppose he's used to officers coming and going with all manner of companions. We climb the staircase and hurry to an office at the end of the corridor. Once inside, William kicks the door shut and pulls me close. In William's arms, I feel safe.

Heavy footsteps pound along bare wooden floorboards. We draw apart and scurry to the chairs placed on opposite sides of the table. I sit with my back towards the door.

'Oh, it's you,' says a deep voice.

William gives a curt nod. 'I'm interviewing.'

'Do you have to do it here? Can't you go downstairs? I've reports to write.'

'The case in question is of a rather delicate nature and strictly confidential. There are other offices you can use.'

'I like this one,' comes the gruff reply. 'Get fewer interruptions this far along the corridor.'

'Precisely,' says William, fixing the unwelcome visitor with a hard stare.

'Understood. I'll leave you to it.'

The door closes with a click. We both exhale.

William waits for the sound of receding footsteps. 'How are things at home, Susan?'

With reluctance, I turn my mind to formal matters. 'Much the same. Arthur is as volatile as ever. But I'm no longer being followed, thanks to your intervention.'

'Does Arthur still hurt you?'

I grip the fabric of my coat and crush it against my palms. A silence falls between us and I'm compelled to look at William. I can tell from his expression he knows what remains unsaid. Tears threaten. I close my eyes, blinking them away.

'I don't know how much longer I can pretend to be supportive. He repulses me.'

'Dearest, you must be strong. Arthur will do something wrong and we'll catch him. We know his plans are evolving and he intends to set something in motion soon. When we know the details, and have evidence, he'll be arrested and tried, and you will be free.' William's gaze is full of love. 'Trust me, I will see that Arthur gets what he deserves.'

'Can I help?'

William tilts his head. 'There is something you could do.' He hesitates. 'No. I shouldn't ask it of you.'

'Tell me.' I wince at my petulance.

A shake of the head.

'William, please! Every day, it gets harder to endure Arthur's attention.'

'Well...' He leans forward and neatens the edges of a pile of paper on the desk. 'No, I can't ask you. You're in enough danger, and we have spies.'

William has piqued my interest and I'm determined to hear his proposal.

'Tell me! If there's some way I can rid myself of my despicable husband, don't I deserve to know?'

William looks me in the eyes. There's a sharpness I don't recognise in his expression, an attitude he must reserve only for official matters.

'The informants have done well to date, but none are close to Arthur. Not like you. As his wife, there are certain... moments when you might persuade him to confide ideas before he shares them with anyone else.'

My cheeks flush, and I stare at my lap. I can't believe what William is asking of me.

'But you have men watching and listening at all of his meetings.'

'Trouble is, he attends so many and we can't be confident of having a spy at all of them. What if they're absent the day he makes a crucial decision? If you can seduce him into talking, we'll know his intentions sooner than we would otherwise and have more time to prepare for making an arrest.'

'I'd have to convince Arthur of my devotion to him and his cause, and I'm not confident I can keep up the pretence.'

William sits back in his chair. 'It was a foolish idea, and wrong of me to suggest it. Forgive me.'

There's a pressure building behind my eyes. 'I can try,' I say, in little more than a whisper. 'Every time I lie with him, a part of me dies.'

'Then don't, Susan.'

'It's my duty and I have no choice. I may as well turn an unpleasant situation into something useful. I'll do as you ask.'

'Dearest, you don't have to, but I believe you have the courage to see it through.'

'William, if I succeed at getting Arthur to confide in me, you can't let them arrest me as a traitor. Protect me, please, because any support I offer Arthur is only for gathering information. Lives are at risk, and not by my choosing.'

'I'll protect you.'

'When Arthur's caught, what happens to us?'

William rises from his chair and comes to my side of the desk. He takes my hands in his. 'When you're free of all ties to Arthur, the future will be ours for the taking.'

'I can't imagine growing old without you.'

William raises my hands to his lips. 'Nor I without you.'

He helps me stand, and we say our farewells before leaving the office. I reach for the door handle, but William places his hand over mine.

'I have a present for you,' he says, withdrawing a package from inside his jacket. The brown paper and lilac ribbon tell me the gift is from Paternoster Row. 'Open it.'

I untie the ribbon and pull off the paper. '*Northanger Abbey*!'

'Published only last year.'

I stroke the blue-green marble pattern of the cover, then

open it to peer inside. 'The first volume of *Northanger Abbey: and Persuasion*.'

William's expression radiates happiness. 'Considering our conversation, *Persuasion* seems apt.'

For a fleeting moment, I wonder if William brought me here intending to recruit me to extract information from Arthur. I dismiss the idea and dust his cheek with delicate kisses.

'I purchased all four volumes. You may have the next whenever you like, but do not risk Arthur's suspicion by taking them all at once.'

He's right. If I arrive home with all four, Arthur will demand to know how I can afford such self-indulgence.

William walks me to the corner of Russell Street and Drury Lane. The streets are quiet tonight. After scrutinising those who are braving the cold, we shelter in a doorway and press our lips together.

'Susan,' he says, cupping my face in his hands, 'I love you.'

'And I love you,' I reply, warmed by the truth within my words.

Our declarations of love linger in little white clouds, captured in time for a few brief moments.

CHAPTER 42

MR EDWARDS SITS OPPOSITE me at the table. Veal shrivels on the side of his plate. I'm half-tempted to reach over and spear the untouched meat with my fork. I can't bear to see it go to waste.

'Fetch the Madeira, Susan.'

Arthur's gravelly voice drags me back to the role of wife and hostess. Mr Edwards is staring at me and appears deep in contemplation. For a second or two, I wonder if he's a spy in Arthur's network, but then dismiss the idea as a foolish notion. Mr Edwards has been flinging around proposals with the zeal of a fanatic and even advocated the use of violence. A spy wouldn't suggest such radical ideas, would they?

'Susan, the Madeira?' Arthur's tone betrays frustration.

'Sorry, my mind was elsewhere.'

'What important matter takes your attention from your husband and guest?'

'I was reflecting on your conversation about how best to turn the government for the benefit of the people.'

'Is that so? And what do you conclude?'

I stare at Arthur's mean face. 'You're not there yet. The ideal solution remains elusive.'

He acknowledges my reply with a grunt. Mr Edwards conceals a smile behind his fingers. I look back at Arthur and raise my eyebrows just a fraction. He knows the Madeira bottle holds only a glassful for each man and gives the slightest hint of a nod to acknowledge my concerns. As I rise from the table, the gentlemen stand, and Arthur proposes they move to the armchairs by the fire. This is a clever ruse because while I pour the Madeira, I will have my back towards Mr Edwards, concealing the fact we have little available to share. I hope Arthur has a plan to avoid a request for a refill.

I select two small glasses and drain the bottle into them. When I turn to carry the glasses to Arthur and Mr Edwards, I become rooted to the floor. Mr Edwards has a large knife in his hand. Arthur's eyes sparkle as he takes the weapon and turns it one way then the other, running his fingers over the smooth surface of the blade. Mr Edwards looks at me and smiles. There's no warmth in his expression, but it's enough to prompt me to pass him a wine glass. Arthur gestures for his to go on a small side table.

'Well?' says Mr Edwards.

'Needs sharpening.'

Mr Edwards pulls a small block from his bag. 'Use this.'

Arthur runs the cutting edge of the knife against the stone, first pressing with one side of the metal, then the other. The shrill scraping sets me on edge. Arthur holds the knife near the candle and squints at it. Mr Edwards leans forward, eager for Arthur's approval. Arthur smiles, then turns his eyes on me. Two things leave me cold. First, he's aroused by the prospect of plunging the knife into another man. Second, I detect a darkness in his soul, more evil than anything I've seen before. I have an overwhelming urge to run away from home but must resist and make myself useful to William and the magistrates of Bow Street.

'Ready?' Arthur drains his glass and slams it on the table as a statement to Mr Edwards that the time for drinking wine has passed.

Mr Edwards gives his empty glass to me.

'We'd better hurry,' says Arthur. 'Tonight, we appoint a special executive committee and swear in George as one of the five members.'

'An executive committee. Plans must be progressing if you need such formal appointments.'

Arthur makes a show of kissing me on my cheek. 'Thanks to George and his connections, we're ready to arm our soldiers.'

Mr Edwards appears uncomfortable at this revelation. 'Come, Arthur. They'll be waiting at the White Lion. First round of drinks is on me.'

I wait over thirty minutes before dragging on my coat and heading out into the frosty night. When I arrive at Bow Street, I pull up my hood and cover my mouth with my scarf, then enter the warm building and approach the duty officer. I give him the note with William's name written on the outer surface and an old-fashioned wax seal to deter curious eyes from peering at the contents.

'I'll put it on his desk ready for tomorrow morning,' the officer says with a kind smile.

I curse the fact William's not working late tonight. If someone overheard Arthur and his men discussing their plans, there might be sufficient grounds for arrest. I mumble my thanks and hurry back into the chill night air. I consider calling at William's mother's house, but then I might stay too long. After watching Arthur with the knife and seeing the effect it had on him, I suspect he won't stay out late tonight. And I need to see Anna before I return home.

I push my fingertips into Arthur's knotted shoulder muscles.

'Did all go well at the meeting?' My voice sounds casual yet caring.

'Reasonably. We have fresh ideas that are a vast improvement on previous ones. Now it's a matter of getting the timing right.'

'What do you propose to do?'

Arthur doesn't reply. His muscles tighten beneath my fingertips, and I know I must act fast if I'm to learn the details. I clench my jaw and glance at the clock. Eight minutes until the clock strikes ten.

'Arthur, I'm proud of you,' I say, sliding onto his lap.

I register his surprise as I drape my right arm across the back of his shoulders and trace the line of his jaw with my left index finger. I adjust my position, moving my face close to his so we breathe the same air. His pupils widen, opening windows into the black depths of his soul. I force myself to stay there, feigning love and lust. This is for William. For England. For me.

'I've always admired your commitment, but the recent steps you've taken show incredible determination. I'm in awe and believe you to be General of the most important army ever created. When I watched you with that knife in your hand, I saw a warrior within you. It's an honour to be your wife.'

My words have the required effect and his arousal throbs against my thigh.

I stand and lift my skirts to straddle him. As I settle astride his lap, Arthur gasps. I close my eyes, unable to look at him as our lips touch.

I rub my cheek against his. 'So, tell me, General, what will you command your army to do?'

Arthur nuzzles my neck. 'First, we'll get the attention of members of the Cabinet by attacking Coutts bank. Second, we'll set fire to a few buildings, although we've yet to decide which ones.'

I play with the buttons on his pantaloons, pressing my palm against the straining flesh beneath the fabric. 'Targets that affect the ministers personally. Clever thinking.'

Arthur catches his breath.

'Then what?' I shift position, rubbing myself against him, teasing him with the promise of more.

'Then we seize the Tower.'

'Will you succeed this time?'

'With better planning, I'm sure we will.'

I raise myself a little so he can free himself from the confines of his clothing, then lean forward until our noses touch. 'I sense something great will happen.'

Arthur places his hands on my hips, but I keep my stance. I want him to think his grand ideas stimulate me as much as they arouse him.

'Tell me more,' I mouth, before clenching my top teeth against my bottom lip.

The clock strikes the hour. I hold my breath.

He smiles. 'When ministers gather for a formal dinner, we'll storm the building and assassinate them.'

He studies my face for a reaction. My insides are churning and I'm trying to shut out images of mutilated bodies, but I feign surprise while concealing my abhorrence of such a plan. His grip on my hips tightens and my leg muscles ache from resisting his pull. One minute after ten.

'And then?' My voice is thick with fear. Arthur interprets it as encouragement.

'Then you'll become the wife of a key member of a provisional government.'

'Goodness.'

The ticking of the clock marks out my hesitation. My legs tremble. I have no choice but to lower myself on to him.

Frantic knocking at the front door.

'Ignore it,' says Arthur, grasping my wrist. His fingernails dig deep and tear my skin.

More knocking. Loud. Persistent.

'We should see who it is.' I press my fist hard into his belly, winding him. 'They sound desperate.'

'Come back here,' he snarls. 'Finish what you started.'

'Arthur, it might be someone for you. Perhaps there's a problem with one of your soldiers, or maybe your plans have reached the wrong ears.'

'No!' He springs to his feet and adjusts his clothing. I get to the door first and fling it open.

'Mrs Thistlewood?' A man stands on the doorstep, twisting a cap in his hands. He has a serious frown. 'Anna sent me. Please come with me. It's an emergency, and Anna said you'd know what to do.'

I turn towards Arthur. He won't refuse such a request in front of another man.

'Probably little George,' I say. 'His breathing has deteriorated of late.'

Arthur pretends charm for our surprise caller. 'Hurry! Go! Anna's a dear friend.'

I reach for my cloak and leave Arthur standing in the

doorway while I hurry along the road with Anna's neighbour. I allow myself an indulgent smile. Now I know the basis of Arthur's plot.

Anna was as good as her word, and the plan worked.

PART VII
1820

CHAPTER 43

THE STENCH of burnt cabbage destroys my concentration. After placing a ribbon to mark my place, I close the cover on *Northanger Abbey: and Persuasion* volume two. Acrid smoke curls from the rim of the cooking pot and makes my eyes water. I leap up from the chair and regret it instantly. At work, I spent most of the day standing, and now my feet are paying for it.

Grasping a cloth, I lift the pot away from the fire. The blackened remains cling to the bottom, forming a thick rim around a hole in the base. How could I have not noticed it was burning? I throw open a window, inviting frosty air into the kitchen. All is quiet in the shared back yard, the air temperature plummeting towards freezing. I hobble outside to draw water and grimace as my palm sticks to the icy metal handle of the pump.

I set a second pot of water over the heat and wait for it to come to a boil, then add the remaining cabbage which I'd saved for tomorrow. An ice-cold draught creeps through the kitchen. I can't afford the temperature of our home to drop too far or it will take many hours to rewarm. With a heavy sigh, I shut the window.

'Susan?'

I secure a stray lock of hair beneath my cap and rush into the hall to greet Arthur. My stomach clenches. Mr Edwards is with him.

'Why didn't you mention you were bringing a guest?' I help Arthur out of his winter coat and hang it on the stand.

'We have reason to celebrate,' says Mr Edwards, presenting me with a large flagon of porter.

'Is that so?' I accept Mr Edwards' gift with my free hand. 'And what's the occasion?'

'I'll tell you over dinner,' says Arthur. 'Is it ready?'

'Almost.'

'Then we'll wait in the parlour and continue our discussion.'

'Very well. The food is nothing elaborate.'

'We haven't eaten for eight hours, so I'll be grateful for anything,' says Mr Edwards.

I withdraw to the kitchen to stare at near-empty shelves and the meagre offerings in the pot and on the table. The men will have to make do with ham, yesterday's bread and boiled cabbage. I will have nothing.

'What's this?' Arthur wrinkles his nose as I deliver the plates to the table.

'I worked an extra couple of hours for Mrs Hooper and could find nothing fresh so late in the day.' I turn towards Mr Edwards. 'Please accept my apologies, but this is the best I can offer.'

'Fine by me. A glass of porter or two to wash it down and my belly will be full.'

Something about his acceptance of the situation endears

me to him a little. I pour three glasses of porter and take my seat at the table.

'You're not eating,' observes Arthur, before taking a large bite from a hunk of bread.

'I've no appetite.' My stomach makes a soft gurgling sound and I pray they cannot hear it. 'I'll eat later. Tell me the news, Arthur.'

'Time passes too fast, Susan. We're already in a new year and have yet to wound the government. But today, we took a great step forward.'

Mr Edwards looks smug, and I address my next question to him. 'And what have you achieved?'

'The time to act is almost here. We'll target each Cabinet minister in a coordinated strike, taking them by surprise in their homes.'

Arthur stretches across the table to reach for the flagon. His jacket falls open, revealing the smooth wooden handle of his knife. It's a shocking reminder that these men are not playing at being soldiers. They intend to kill.

'Do you know where the ministers live?'

Arthur nods. 'They make no secret of their addresses.'

'But what of their families?' Images of blood-soaked bodies pour through my imagination.

Arthur gives a reassuring smile. 'We don't want to kill any wives or children, but it's inevitable one or two innocent family members will get caught up in the affray. Be comforted knowing they will not lose their lives in vain.'

I want to yell at him, chastise him for his nonsense, but I dare not. 'And when will this occur?'

Mr Edwards answers. 'Soon. We haven't decided on a specific date. We need the right foot soldiers for a coordinated attack. And more weapons, although I have that in hand.'

'And afterwards? What then?'

'Do you recall a fellow by the name of Watson? We were in court together.'

'Vaguely.'

'We visited Dr Watson today. The circumstances of our meeting were difficult, because a prison's not the best location to discuss plans. But we've prepared a proclamation and drawn it up with Watson's help. As soon as the deed is done, we'll appoint a provisional government and summon a meeting of representatives.'

I meet Arthur's gaze. 'You're sure this will work? And serious about seeing it through?'

Arthur takes a swig of porter, then wipes his mouth on his sleeve. 'Deadly serious.'

After another busy day at Mrs Hooper's, I hobble home with Anna by my side, the pair of us cursing the early start of this year's London season. I hoped to have finished the embroidery on Miss Hurst's dress by now, but progress is slow because I'm tired in the evenings and straining my eyes with fatigue and poor candlelight.

'I spoke to Beckey about singing at the wedding,' says Anna, as if reading my thoughts. 'She's keen to perform.'

My heart sinks. 'How can I refuse when you two are so willing to oblige?'

'Susan, it's an opportunity to get involved with something positive and happy. Winter is a miserable season. An early spring wedding is just what we need to lift our spirits.'

I let out a frustrated groan. 'I'm so far behind with the embroidery.'

'Let me help. We can work together.'

'You don't mind?'

'It will be a pleasure. Mary King can take care of George while I help you. He's developed a surprising fondness for her.'

'Remarkable, how much she's changed.'

'Isn't it? I can't imagine how I'd cope without her now. Shall we meet for a few hours on Sunday, to work on the dress?'

'That will be perfect. Thank you, Anna.'

'It's a pleasure. You'd do the same for me. Ask Beckey to join us. I'm sure she'd do a little dusting while we sew. We could practise a song or two while we work.'

I turn to look at my friend, and she beams at me, her brown eyes twinkling.

'I'll ask,' I say, laughing.

We link arms and quicken our pace as a flurry of snowflakes flutters around us.

CHAPTER 44

'THE KING'S DEAD! Died last night.'

I pause, a small cube of sugar-coated raspberry jelly pinched between my thumb and forefinger. I stare at the butcher's boy. His eyes are wide, his shirt spotted with blood. There's an air of excitement about him, and I imagine him running from one shop to another, spreading the news like a contagion. I pop the sweetmeat into my mouth, taking care not to chew it.

'God rest his soul.' Mrs Hooper crosses herself, then reaches for the appointment book. 'Susan, I'll need your diplomacy for this. Postpone as many appointments as you can. For the next few days we must focus on mourning dresses for the courtiers who bless us with their patronage.'

News of King George's passing comes as no surprise. It's common knowledge he was unwell in body and mind, hence his son ruling as Prince Regent for nine years. I expect our new king will notice no difference when he transforms from regent to king, although he'll demand a lavish coronation. He's renowned for self-indulgence and extravagance. I replenish the dish of jellies, then turn my attention to the appointments book and begin writing polite notes of cancellation in my neatest hand.

The shop is all of a flutter. King George's funeral will be a state occasion, and our workload will more than double. Anna gives us each a length of black lace to wear as an armband, then organises an assault on near-finished pieces to ensure they're completed to the usual high standard. Mrs Hooper leaves the shop in a hurry to buy as much black fabric as she can find before other drapers and dressmakers hear the news. Meanwhile, the rest of us rearrange furniture, clean worktops and tidy shelves.

Mrs Hooper knows her clientele well. By midday, eight ladies wait their turn to place orders.

Arthur is in a celebratory mood. 'The king's death couldn't have happened at a more convenient time.'

It troubles me he's full of glee discussing a death. 'How does it help you, Arthur?'

'With the funeral arrangements in place and a general election looming, there will be official dinners bringing Cabinet ministers together, and some venues will be easy to infiltrate.'

'Yesterday's newspaper said the economy's strengthening again. Is action still appropriate?' I yearn for freedom and don't want Arthur's plan to lose momentum.

Arthur's eyes narrow to slits. 'It is. The situation is improving, but for the working classes life is still a struggle. Their lives are governed by men with deep pockets and no comprehension of the plight of the common man. Come, Susan, you know this.'

'I do, Arthur. I was making sure you've not lost sight of

the reasons for the fight. Isn't it important to review plans and question motives to ensure we make the best decisions?'

Arthur puts his arms around my waist. 'There was a time when I doubted your loyalty, Susan. It pleases me to have your full support. You're right; we should always consider the repercussions of every decision taken. The last thing we need on our consciences is a list of poor choices.'

It takes all my courage to keep my face impassive and stop my body from tensing. 'I couldn't agree more. Sometimes I've encountered situations I wouldn't usually countenance, but after careful consideration I've known them to be right for me.'

'For example?'

My blossoming relationship with William, for one.

'Planning to emigrate to America. It would have been a wonderful fresh start for us, and such a pity it wasn't to be. My decision to work for Mrs Hooper is another example. You're a gentleman, Arthur, and might have considered it unseemly for your wife to work, but I didn't want us to fall into debt and did what I thought was right. I don't regret my decision to work. In fact, I've flourished. I've dared to dream that one day you'll allow me to open a dress shop of my own.'

'We'll wait and see about that. If plans unfold as we hope, I'll be organising a new government and won't have time for your foolish fancies. And anyway, owning a business is very different to working in someone else's. What makes you think you could make it a success?'

'Mrs Hooper established her business from nothing. I'm not afraid of hard work. I believe I could do the same.'

Arthur snorts as he releases me. A rapping at the door brings a welcome distraction.

'It's probably for you,' I say. 'I'll be in the kitchen.'

A visit from Mr Edwards restores Arthur's good humour. Mr Edwards has become a frequent guest, inciting Arthur's bloodthirsty ambition and proposing violent ideas. I cannot help but like the man, for at every visit, he treats me with respect. And despite the theme of their conversations, Arthur remains in an agreeable mood for many hours afterwards.

I purchased four ounces of tea this morning and it gives me pleasure to prepare a tray with new cups and saucers. Mother sent a note to say she fell in love with this delicate chinaware and thought I might appreciate a few pieces for myself.

'A refreshing change from wine and ale,' says Mr Edwards, with a kind smile.

'I know it's not the usual choice for a gentleman,' I reply, 'but I thought you'd want something warming after being in the snow.'

Mr Edwards nods his approval and watches me pour. I feel a flush of pride because I suspect he's admiring my physical attributes. I still carry plenty of flesh but having reduced the frequency of my sweet treats and preferring to load my dinner plate with vegetables these days, I know I have become more appealing to the eye. William said so.

Arthur's engrossed in an item in today's *New Times*.

'Arthur? What are you reading?'

'A notice,' he replies. 'Lord Harrowby's hosting a dinner. Look at this.'

Arthur turns the newspaper so Mr Edwards and I may read. Printed on the second page is an announcement in bold print declaring a grand Cabinet dinner planned for tomorrow at Grosvenor Square. I have often wondered about this practice of publishing social events involving high-level political figures, for it informs discontented individuals of the whereabouts of those who have aggrieved them. But now, I'm grateful for it.

'We must find the other committee members.' There's a glint in Arthur's eyes. 'Drink your tea, George. We have work to do.'

CHAPTER 45

A DISH of candied walnuts sits untouched on the counter. My appetite is poor today.

I struggled to sleep last night. The hours passed in a haze of anxiety as I tossed and turned, my night chemise sticking to my skin. Now, my mind will not attend to any one thing in particular, and I cannot tell a soul what troubles me. If Arthur persists with his plans, I will soon become a murderer's wife.

'Susan, are you sickening for something?' Mrs Hooper considers me with her large honey-brown eyes.

'Sorry, Mrs Hooper. I'm not myself today.'

'Would you prefer to work in the sewing room, away from public view?'

'No, thank you. I'd rather spend time with the customers. Conversation is a welcome distraction.'

A tinkling sound from above the shop door signals the first patron of the day. Mrs Ridlington, an elderly lady of considerable charm and many a tale. I could not wish for a more talkative individual to keep me engaged for an hour or two. Mrs Hooper and I exchange smiles, and I step forward to welcome my favourite customer.

While Mrs Ridlington chatters about her grandchildren, I wonder if William received my message that Arthur's assault on the ministers is going ahead this evening. The day drags towards closing time. I have an ache deep behind my eyes and crave the comfort of sleep, but after work I excuse myself from walking home with Anna, using the pretext of a personal errand. My loyal friend does not pester for details but gives my hand a reassuring squeeze and urges me to be careful.

Dirt and rubbish swirl at my feet and a biting wind whips at my inadequate coat. The air is thick with dust from coal fires, and my chest tightens as I scurry through the smog towards Mrs Westcott's house. My eyes rove the murky streets, seeking any man, woman or child who might recognise me and report me to Arthur. While Arthur risks his life for his ideal, I risk mine as a Bow Street officer's informant.

When the house comes into view, I shrink towards the shadows of a narrow alley and check the street in both directions. A coach rattles by, the coachman's eyes fixed on the road ahead while the occupants remain hidden behind a curtain. After what feels like several minutes, I run across the cobbles and knock twice on Mrs Westcott's front door.

'Please, come in,' says a liveried butler, a recent addition to the household staff. 'Mrs Westcott is expecting you.'

I hesitate by the parlour door, but Mrs Westcott is quick to welcome me.

'Susan, you're here at last.' Her smile fades and her expression turns grave. 'William mentioned something serious might happen today and hoped you'd come here with information rather than risk being seen at Bow Street. He's due home any time now.'

I nod. A fluttering in my chest makes me nauseous. I try to ignore it.

'Come, dear. Sit by the fire. You look as though you might freeze to death. Let us take tea. It will warm you.'

Many hours have passed since I ate or drank, and I hope a cup of tea will ease my headache. I watch golden-brown liquid fall from the spout, then relish the fragrant steam rising from my cup. Mrs Westcott makes a soft, satisfied sigh, and we sit in companionable silence. A long-case clock announces the end of every quarter hour. Mrs Westcott does not push for conversation. Instead, she concentrates on a book and leaves me alone with my thoughts.

When the clock strikes seven, my jaw muscles clench and my breathing quickens. 'I should go.' There's a tremor in my voice. 'If Arthur arrives home and I'm not there...'

Mrs Westcott nods. 'William will be sorry he missed you.'

I drag myself to my feet, reluctant to leave.

'You're welcome here any time, dear, you know that don't you?'

'Yes. Thank you.' I reach inside my reticule and pull out the folded sheet of paper intended for William. 'Does it bother you that I have feelings for William when I'm married to another man?'

Mrs Westcott shakes her head. 'Not at all. William has said enough about Mr Thistlewood for me to understand he isn't a fit husband. No wife should have to endure a loveless marriage. I pray that, one day, women can petition for divorce from the monsters who masquerade as charming men. My son derives great pleasure from your company, my dear. I cannot ask more of any woman.'

I pass the piece of paper to her. 'If they don't capture my husband tonight, it's likely he'll seek refuge at White Street in Moorfields. This is the address. Burn it when William has seen it. I can't risk anyone discovering it was me who betrayed Arthur and his men, or that you were party to the information.'

Mrs Westcott tucks the paper into the bodice of her dress. 'Understood. My carriage will take you home.'

'No! I mustn't do anything unusual. I'll walk.'

'Then it will drop you at Drury Lane. Don't wander the streets alone, my dear. Not tonight.'

I wonder how much she knows.

Despite exhaustion, sleep eludes me for a second night. Arthur's space in the bed stays cold while I fidget, wondering what has become of him. The street outside is eerily silent. There are no shouts of shocking news, no banging at the front door from officers seeking Arthur. Did he abandon the mission? It's the not knowing that's hard to cope with. Please God, let Arthur be dead. Or, at least, a wanted man.

I stare at my reflection in the mirror. A gaunt image stares back, violet-grey shadows highlighting tired red eyes. My face looks narrow and pinched, my hair flat. I consider returning to bed, but my loyalty to my employer prevents me from doing so, and Anna will be here at any moment.

At a quarter after eight, I open my front door. Anna is standing there, as I knew she would be, but she's not alone. A tall gentleman stands next to her and strikes a confident pose in a double-breasted jacket and hunting boots. I recognise him from Bow Street. William once addressed him as Fernside.

'Mrs Thistlewood,' he says, his face solemn.

'I will make your excuses to Mrs Hooper,' offers Anna. 'She'll understand.' Anna gives a sympathetic smile before bidding us both a farewell and resuming her walk to work.

'Is Mr Thistlewood home?'

I shake my head. 'Haven't seen him since yesterday morning.' Curious onlookers stand in the street, gawking. 'Come in.'

Officer Fernside steps through the door and I close it behind him. We stay in the hallway, facing one another.

'Were you not concerned by his failure to return home? Is it usual for your husband to stay out all night?'

'It's not unusual. He enjoys the company of like-minded men and they often discuss politics late into the night.' I choose my words carefully. William does not want his fellow officers to know of my informant role.

'Do you know what happened last night?'

'No. Is my husband injured?' I swallow hard, bracing myself for the news he is about to share.

'Arthur Thistlewood killed a man.'

The news falls like a blow to my stomach, and I stumble backwards. At last he's in serious trouble, but it cost someone their life.

'There's a warrant for his arrest, and the magistrates have dispatched a group of officers to pick him up.'

My breaths are fast and shallow. The walls ripple and blur. 'A group?'

'Your husband fled the scene of a murder. Others are on the wanted list too, but your husband dealt the fatal blow.'

'You're sure it was Arthur?'

'There were witnesses.'

I lean back against the wall and press my palms against the striped paper. The hallway seems to tilt. I'm giddy with relief. 'Who did he...?' My voice fades. I'm loath to acknowledge the true cost of my happiness.

'A young fellow by the name of Smithers. He didn't deserve to die. Murdered by your husband's sword.'

A mother and father have been robbed of their son and I'm saddened by this.

'My husband did what he thought best for the country. I'm sure he didn't intend for Mr Smithers to die.' My words lack conviction, but I must play my part of loyal wife.

'So, you support his actions?'

'Not at all. But I share his dreams of an honest government and improved rights for the common man.' An image of a stricken officer enters my thoughts. I see Arthur run him through with a long sharp blade and the man collapses in a pool of blood. 'A life should not have ended.'

I thank God only one life was taken when many more murders were planned.

The officer gives me a hard stare. 'We have to search these premises.'

I straighten my posture and look him in the eye. 'Now?'

'Later. First, you're wanted at Bow Street for questioning.'

'As you wish.'

Steeling myself for a gruelling day, I open the front door. The officer steps outside and extends his hand for my door key. He must worry I'll return to conceal evidence. We walk side by side. Every now and again I break into a trot to keep pace with his long strides. I hear Bow Street before I see it. A large crowd is assembling in front of the magistrates' offices, and the mood is angry, women as vocal as men. It's hard to make out their words but I hear Arthur's name several times. A coach arrives at the far end of the street and the mob surges towards it. Several officers swarm from the building, creating a divide in the throng of protesters. One officer opens the door to the coach and the shape of a man emerges. For a moment, I pity that man. He looks old, withered and shabby. He removes his hat and waves it in the air as if celebrating good news. Then I realise it's Arthur.

'Murderer,' screeches a woman.

'Hang the villain,' shouts a man.

The crowd echoes the protests, chanting them over and over. They press forward, each individual trying to get near to Arthur and shove him or spit in his face. Four Runners move in to surround him, while others clear a path towards the court house.

'Come,' says Officer Fernside, slipping in behind Arthur's escort and dragging me by my sleeve.

Once inside, they lead Arthur to an anteroom next to the courtroom, kicking the door shut to deny him the chance to see me. I'm taken to a small office upstairs and instructed to stay put until another officer is available to question me.

I relish a few minutes alone, reliving the magnificent spectacle of Arthur under arrest. He cannot hurt me now.

CHAPTER 46

LAST NIGHT, I slept well, but whether because of fatigue or relief that Arthur is no longer a danger to me is hard to say. It may have been for both reasons. Thank goodness Mrs Hooper was generous enough to grant a leave of absence for a few days while I adjust to my new circumstances. Plenty of other employers would have dismissed a killer's wife, but she refused to hold me responsible for the actions of my violent husband.

A steaming bowl of oatmeal sits on the table, taunting me. A large knob of butter rests on top, melting into a glorious, unctuous yellow liquid that will add richness to my breakfast when I stir it in. I've indulged in adding a spoonful of my best leaves to the teapot, and steam climbs from the teacup in delicate fragrant curls. When I raise the cup to my mouth, a fierce hammering at the door destroys my peace.

'Stand aside.' A hefty Bow Street Officer steps across my threshold, beckoning three others to follow.

William is among their group. Our eyes meet and he makes a subtle gesture to reassure me all will be well. My house has already had a preliminary search, and a constable returned my key. No doubt they intend a more thorough job this time, and they're welcome to it. I've already checked that Arthur had neither blades nor shot hidden here.

The four officers turn out chests and drawers. Determined to maintain my composure, I return to the kitchen, hoping my oatmeal has not yet gone cold. A puddle of butter waits to be mixed in, and I sit at the table to give it the attention it needs. I'm relieved to see it's William who searches the kitchen. He stifles a chuckle at my reluctance to let wonderful food go to waste and watches me load the spoon and raise it to my lips.

'I'm sorry to have to do this,' he says in a quiet voice, removing a lid from a pan and sending it clattering across the flagstones.

I shrug and continue eating. 'It's your duty.'

Heavy footsteps thud across the ceiling, followed by the sound of floorboards being ripped from their fixings. I take a sip of tea and wonder about my future. I have no wish to stay in this house. It reeks of Arthur. The smell will fade with time, but the rooms echo with unpleasant memories. Later I'll discuss it with Anna. Perhaps we might share lodgings in a better location away from the slums. Somewhere safe to raise George. The thought makes me smile.

William reaches for the canister of flour and my smile fades.

'Must you look in there?'

William pauses.

'Find anything?' asks the burly officer in charge of this operation. He takes the canister from William and wrenches off the lid. 'What's this?' he asks, withdrawing a flour-coated hand clutching my precious cloth parcel.

'Savings,' I reply, keeping my voice steady.

'Money for weapons, more like.'

He's trying to goad me. I must stay calm. 'My wages don't stretch far, but I try to put a little aside each week. I doubt it would be possible to buy arms of any significance with that paltry stash.'

'Anything else hidden?'

I shake my head. My treasured possessions are all on display in the parlour where I can enjoy them.

'You're very calm, Mrs Thistlewood.'

I press my fingertips together and tilt my head to the side. 'Because I've done nothing wrong. I agreed with my husband that action was needed to improve the running of this country, but taking innocent lives would never achieve it.'

'So, you knew about the plan?'

William gives a quick shake of his head.

'Not until yesterday after my husband's arrest.'

The officer glares, then storms into the yard to continue his search.

William moves towards the hallway. As he draws level with me, he whispers, 'Keep heart, my love, this will soon be over, and we'll continue from where we left off.'

I smile. 'I long for that day.'

His hand brushes against my shoulder. 'Until then, resume our routine at Paternoster Row. No one must suspect a thing between us, for both our sakes.'

I nod and he leaves me alone with my cold breakfast. Fat globules sit on the surface of the oatmeal, and my appetite evaporates.

Last night I had a dream that Arthur was back at home and beating me for not visiting him in gaol. The nightmare left a flicker of doubt in my mind, and I must protect myself in case he is ever freed.

Arthur's in the Bloody Tower guarded by yeoman gaolers. To keep the façade of a devoted wife, I visit in the afternoon.

'This way.'

A guard ushers me into a small waiting room. It's cold and smells of mildew. A middle-aged woman bustles in after me, closing the door behind her. I smile, thinking her to be the wife of another conspirator.

'Remove your hat.'

Assuming she is used to this routine, I do as she instructs.

'And cap.'

She probes my hair with her fingers, leaving me dishevelled and embarrassed.

'What are you doing?' I say, struggling to keep my poise.

'Checking for small metal objects that might pick a lock.'

I realise she's no visitor and is acting on orders to search me.

'Take off your coat and dress.'

Her eyes are lined and deep pockmarks scar her sallow skin. It's clear she'll take no nonsense. I remove my dress and shiver.

'Stays.'

'Surely not!'

The woman glares.

I reach behind my back and pull at the lace to loosen it. Clothed only in my shift, I stand erect and feign confidence while the woman pats up and down my legs and across my body. This humiliation should infuriate me, but Arthur is charged with murder and high treason, and I accept she must be thorough.

'Put your clothes back on.'

The woman flings the door wide open, permitting two

yeoman guards to see me in a state of undress. I ignore their chuckles and do as instructed.

～

'This was Walter Raleigh's room,' says Arthur, preening.

'Then you're in good company, but no doubt he enjoyed a few more home comforts.'

Arthur's prison is a sizeable room with two small mullioned windows. A fireplace occupies one corner with cold ashes lingering in the grate. Bread and water sit untouched on a rickety old table, while discoloured plaster peels from the walls. There are tiny droppings on the floor confirming Arthur is not alone in this prison. There's a basic wooden chair which Arthur pushes towards me. He leans against a wall, his sweat-stained shirt fluttering in a brisk draught from a gap at the side of the window frame.

'Aren't you cold?'

'Sometimes. But when I consider what lies ahead, I forget about it.'

'How long will you stay here?'

Arthur shrugs. 'Depends on the trial date. They'll move me to Newgate before it starts – sooner rather than later, I hope. I want to get this over with.'

'Arthur, what happened?'

He turns towards me. In three days, he has turned from a neat, upright man with a soldier's bearing to a thin and grubby felon.

'A group of us assembled at Cato Street to collect weapons. We were due to go to Lord Harrowby's house for nine o'clock, by which time the Cabinet ministers would have been sitting together in the dining room, making them easy pickings. But the Runners knew our plans.' He pauses. 'Remember Davidson?'

I nod, recalling the charming gentleman with excellent carpentry skills.

'He was downstairs keeping watch. Two officers grabbed him. Others came up the ladder to a small hayloft where we were checking weapons. It was chaos. I snuffed the candles for a chance at a getaway, but it made things worse and someone gave the order for the Runners to kill us. One drew a sword, so I dealt with him before he used it.' Arthur smiles. 'It was his life or mine.'

The rest of the visit drags and I'm eager to leave. At last, Arthur grows weary and lies on a lumpy mattress on the cold flagstone floor. When his throat rumbles with the first sign of sleep, I knock on the door for the guard to let me out.

I begin the long walk home, my mood subdued. If Arthur's found guilty at trial, my actions will have contributed to condemning him to a traitor's death. I too will have blood on my hands. But I recall the dread of sharing his bed, the beatings, the violations of my body, and his fingers pressing against my neck. It would only be a matter of time before he went too far.

I did what I had to do. It was his life, or mine.

CHAPTER 47

THE WEDDING IS A MERRY OCCASION, and I'm glad Anna and Beckey persuaded me to accept the invitation for the three of us to sing. Jane looks radiant in her gown, and the embroidered forget-me-nots weaving around anchors have created a stir among the ladies. In return for our needlework skills and angelic voices, we feast on heaped bowls of lemon syllabub. If I'm ever blessed with the chance to remarry, I will have it served to my guests as part of the wedding breakfast.

All too soon, it's time to take our leave. First, we stop at Beckey's and recall the highlights of the day over a glass of wine or two. Then, as the spring evening brings a fall in temperature, Anna and I pull our shawls about our shoulders and head for our homes.

Our mood is buoyant as we scurry along the street. Coal fires are no longer needed to chase away the cold, and most of the smog has cleared. I gaze up at a clear blue sky, and for a few delicious moments I believe anything is possible.

'Anna, would you consider moving home?'

Anna smiles. 'I would love to, Susan, but I don't have enough money.'

'What if we moved in together? Between us, we could pay the rent for a respectable home, and I'd enjoy sharing with you.'

'And George? He can be boisterous, you know.'

'Of course, with George. I'd love to have a child in my life. I'm unlikely to have one of my own, and I miss Julian. He's almost a man now, and I don't see him as often as I'd like. Please take your time, but at least consider it. George could attend lessons during the daytime if we find a home with a school nearby.'

Anna looks at me through shining eyes. 'I dream of a better neighbourhood and an education for George. But it's a lot to ask of you.'

'It would be a joy.'

'Then I'll give it serious consideration.'

At the corner of Stanhope Street, we part company and I quicken my pace. When my home comes into view, I'm returned to the reality of my life and my happiness evaporates. Arthur's trial begins tomorrow. When I open the door, I find two notes jammed underneath, one written in an elegant script, the other an untidy scrawl. I study the elegant handwriting first. It's an instruction to attend a meeting for friends and family of the accused conspirators. Many of the families have fallen upon hard times with their husbands no longer able to provide for them, so we are to meet with Mr Harmer, solicitor to all the accused. He will appeal on behalf of us all for support from the nation during our time of hardship. A meeting has been scheduled for seven o'clock at Mr Harmer's office, so I must rush to make it on time.

I run upstairs to fetch a warmer pelisse, clutching the scrawled note. As I reach into the clothes press, I squint at the scruffy handwriting. The words chill me to my core:

One of us must be an informer. How else would our husbands have been caught so easily? Watch the wives and help us trap the traitor. We will administer the punishment she deserves.

Sarah Davidson and Celia Ings

Even though Arthur is secure behind bars, I am still in danger.

~

A large crowd has gathered outside Newgate Gaol. Julian grasps my hand and pulls me through the throng and into the Sessions House, where we take our places and sit in silence. Julian's relationship with Arthur is as complicated as mine, and no doubt he has mixed feelings about his father. The large hand on a wall clock flicks into place. Ten o'clock. Time for the trial to begin.

The accused men file into the courtroom, with Arthur in the lead. He hangs his head, his pale face a striking contrast to his black woollen coat. When he raises his right hand and swears his name, his voice is hollow and unrecognisable.

Asked how he pleads to the charges of murder and high treason, Arthur looks towards the judge and replies 'Not guilty.'

'How would you be tried?' asks an official.

'By God and my country,' says Arthur.

Each man takes a turn. The charges are read out, followed by an announcement that Arthur's trial will begin on Monday. Then the prisoners are led away.

Julian and I part company with the promise of meeting early on Monday morning so we may sit together. Today is Saturday. If I hurry, I might arrive at Mr Brown's for half an hour of browsing before closing time.

Mr Brown is quick to greet me. He knows precisely who I am. Thistlewood is an uncommon name, and the newspapers are full of reports about Arthur. But Mr Brown is a true gentleman and I'm a long-standing customer. We are loyal to each other.

'I hope you are well, Mrs Thistlewood?' His left eyebrow rises in genuine concern.

I glance around the shop. No other customers are present. 'I am, thank you, considering the circumstances.'

'A troublesome time,' he murmurs. 'But I have something to lift your spirits.'

He turns his back towards me and switches the sign on the door to "Closed". He reaches behind the counter for his coat, then presses the door key into my hand. 'I must attend an appointment. Lock the door behind me and you'll not be disturbed for thirty minutes.'

He leaves the shop, giving me no time to protest. Turning the key in the lock, I relish the opportunity to indulge myself in any book I fancy. I'm in the mood for poetry and select an anthology of modern poems from a display on the counter. Mr Brown's office has a well-worn chair which will be a comfortable place to sit, so turning to the first page, I read as I walk into the room at the rear of the store.

'I thought I'd find you here.'

I spin around, and there is dear, sweet William standing behind the door. After dropping the book onto a small table, I fling my arms around him and bury my face against his neck.

He holds me at arm's length. 'How are you?'

I sigh. 'With Arthur as the ringleader for the conspiracy, the widows look to me to head petitions for all those standing accused. I thought life would be easier with him behind bars, but it's harder.'

'Be strong, dear Susan. It'll be worth it.'

'I'm frightened, William.'

'Don't be.'

I realise he's unaware of the note. I pull it from my reticule.

William's face drops. 'Take care, my love. The danger should fade when the judge passes sentence but do protect yourself in the meantime.'

A sob escapes from my throat. Tears flow.

'Come to me.' William holds me tight while I soak his shirt with distress. I silently chastise myself for wasting these snatched precious moments.

'How long must we continue this deception?'

'Hard to say. For now, we can pass letters via Mr Brown, but should keep our distance otherwise. Your husband's case draws a lot of attention, and I fear the repercussions if the wrong person were to see us together.'

We spend several minutes enjoying being close to one another before a tapping at the door announces Mr Brown's return. I pass the key to William and he strides across the shop floor, then slips outside as Mr Brown enters.

Mr Brown sees the poetry book in my hand. 'Keep it, with my compliments. You've bought several books over the years. Consider it a reward for your patronage.'

I haven't bought as many as he's suggesting, and certainly not as many as I'd have liked. 'You're very kind, Mr Brown. I'm in your debt.'

'Nonsense. Would you like it wrapped?'

I shake my head. 'I'll take it as it is. Thank you.'

He hands me the book and opens the door, releasing me to an uncertain world.

CHAPTER 48

I SHARE a handful of dried apple slices with Julian while waiting for Arthur's trial to begin. Neither of us could face breakfast, but now we are both hungry. The viewing area of the courtroom is noisy with family members and curious onlookers. We are so tightly wedged on the benches that it's difficult to move without irritating the person seated on either side.

After initial formalities, we watch with interest as the wise men of law spout words and phrases we don't understand. Arthur's permitted to sit, because they expect proceedings to extend beyond the day.

The first witness is called at the start of the afternoon session. My buttocks are numb, my concentration waning, but I do my best to follow all that he says. He makes all kinds of allegations against Arthur, some of them barely credible while others are uncomfortable truths.

The trial enters a second day, and more witnesses take the stand. I daydream about life twelve months from now. Anna, George and I will have long since settled into new lodgings, and this case will have faded to smudged print on discarded newspapers. Mr George Edwards is called as a witness, and suddenly I'm alert. I watch the door, eager to see who walks in, but no witness appears, and the wise men of the law make no fuss about his absence. Could the elusive George Edwards be the gentleman who visited my home? The man who stoked the fire in Arthur's belly and fuelled his appetite for violence? I don't understand why there's no reaction to the witness failing to respond to his summons. Arthur's confused too. His puzzlement turns to anger, and he makes a poor effort at hiding it. His eyes seek mine, and I read disappointment in his expression. Now it makes sense. Mr Edwards was a spy.

The rest of the day passes in a blur and we return for a third day of Arthur's trial. It pleases me that his counsel makes an issue of the elusive Mr Edwards, as I too am curious about his absence. The court becomes rowdy. The wives howl their discontent. I join in with them, for fear they still hunt their own traitor.

The court returns to order. Reliable testimonies are revisited, showing how Arthur led an army hell-bent on carrying out the most heinous of crimes. The jury withdraws to another room to consider four separate counts of Arthur's alleged high treason. Their absence is brief. Before fifteen minutes have elapsed, they file back to their benches.

The court falls silent, preparing for the verdict.

'On the third count of the indictment, where the prisoner is charged with conspiring to levy war, we find the accused guilty. On the fourth count of the indictment, where the prisoner is charged with the actual levying of war against the king, we find the accused guilty.'

The verdicts come as no surprise. The courtroom remains silent as guards escort Arthur away. Julian slumps beside me. Relief or disappointment, I cannot tell. The presiding judge, Lord Chief Justice Abbot, adjourns the court, and the room fills with the noise of men and women shuffling to their feet, eager to stretch their legs and step outdoors.

Julian and I walk home in silence. We struggle through a simple meal of bread and ham, and when his sad figure walks away from the house my heart aches for him.

Mortals judged Arthur, and now the day has come for God to take His turn. It's early in the morning and a large crowd has assembled. Julian forces a path through the heaving mass until we reach the front, pressed against a barrier. He insisted on coming with me today. A mature seventeen-year-old, he dismissed my protests with a flick of his hand so reminiscent of one of Arthur's mannerisms. All vantage points are occupied. Residents hire out balconies as viewing decks, young men cling to lamp posts, and two youths perch on top of the main Newgate water pump. A man inspects the gallows while another scatters sawdust across the scaffold platform. The crowd cheers.

I've never been one for executions, but I'm eager to watch Arthur leave this life. Today, he releases me from my marriage vows. Today, he sets me free.

Soldiers stand guard in neat formation opposite the entrance to Newgate gaol while onlookers wait in silence for events to unfold. A hangman comes out. A man who has executed at least one hundred and seventy men. Coffins lie in a neat row on the scaffold platform. They too have sawdust thrown into them.

Arthur is the first convicted man to emerge from the cells. He tilts his face towards the sky and speaks to his guardians, although I cannot hear his words. When his shackles are removed, he stands still and waits for his accomplices to join him. He shakes hands with the next condemned man to arrive, and they hold a brief conversation.

Five conspirators stand in a row, but not all are as composed as Arthur. Arthur has an orange in his hand. He steps forward and surveys the crowd. I wonder if he is looking for me. Julian waves. My arms stay rigid by my sides.

'God Almighty bless you,' cries someone in the crowd.

Arthur bites into his orange, and one of his companions bursts into song. The hangman ties ropes around their necks, fumbling with the knots, making me doubt his suitability for the role. Arthur refuses the offer of a hood and then his accomplices follow his lead.

The spectators fall silent while the chaplain stands with the condemned. When he walks away, there's a loud crash as the trapdoors fall open. I stare without blinking until my eyes ache. I want to witness the moment of Arthur's death. His legs jerk several times then hang lifeless, the rope swaying back and forth, the creak just audible above a deafening silence.

A single tear slides down Julian's cheek. I wipe it away with my fingertip and we both turn our eyes back towards the scaffold. Minutes pass while the dead bodies are arranged like floppy dolls on the stage, ready for the last stage of punishment. A masked headsman approaches Arthur, a small knife in one hand. He places the blade against Arthur's neck and the crowd roars as the sharp edge connects with his skin. He hacks at Arthur with less care than a novice butcher dissembling a carcass. The headsman holds Arthur's head by the hair and passes it to the hangman's assistant.

'This is the head of Arthur Thistlewood, the traitor.'

The crowd roars. I breathe in and out, slowly. Arthur's

body is hauled into a coffin and his head is dropped in afterwards. Then the headsman moves along to the next man.

'Come,' I say to Julian. 'We've seen enough.'

We make our way to Fleet Street. I have agreed to meet with other wives, to write a letter to petition for the bodies of our husbands. I will deliver it by hand tomorrow morning. Success or failure is of no consequence to me, but my pretence of loyal wife must continue a while longer. If our request is refused, I'll direct a second petition to the Privy Council, marked for the attention of His Highness, the King. The widows must not have any reason to suspect my contribution to the downfall of our men.

CHAPTER 49

THE WIDOWS ARE A NUISANCE, and I begrudge them the slices of pound cake that I pass among them. I thought I'd done enough with my petitions for the bodies, but still they expect more from me. It was no surprise the authorities declined my requests. They buried the bodies on the evening of the execution, mere feet away from where they drew their last breaths. I assume the graves were filled with lime because I was told they could not return the remains under any circumstances. There's probably nothing left.

Today, we each signed a bill of indictment against George Edwards. I don't expect it to achieve much. I hope not, for I've no wish to see these other women again. They mean well, but we've discussed the betrayal of our husbands umpteen times and I'm eager to move on.

Mrs Davidson is the last to step outside. As she walks away, the tension leaves my muscles and I let out a lengthy sigh. I'm about to close the front door when Anna comes into view with George skipping along beside her. My mood lifts and I welcome them home.

George doesn't wait for an invitation to take a slice of

cake. Eyes wide with anticipation, he takes a large bite and closes his eyes, savouring every crumb. A lusty four-year-old, he has a vigour for life that needs feeding at least four times a day. It's a joy to have Anna and George as my new family.

'How was his visit?'

Anna settles in the armchair that used to be Arthur's. 'Successful. In fact, Beckey said George played so well with her grandson, she'll have him every day.'

'No doubt she made a big fuss of him.'

'She did. And asked him to call her "Aunt", so he feels like a member of the family.'

'That's wonderful.' George rests sticky hands on my skirt. I smile and ruffle his hair. 'Darling boy, I'd love for you to consider me as your aunt, too.'

After a bitter winter, we endure a wet summer. Anna and I hurry home, arm in arm, giggling like children. As we dodge deep puddles, she teases me about the evening ahead. Mrs Westcott is to host a special family dinner and invited me to join them. At Leicester Square, we come upon noisy groups of early evening revellers, and it takes all our concentration to avoid stepping into the path of a carriage. It's a relief to turn into a street where the pavements are quieter. A short distance ahead, a scruffy young boy snatches a lady's reticule and runs towards us, clutching it to his chest. Not looking where he's going, he collides with me and Anna pulls his jacket, forcing him to stop.

'Return the reticule at once,' says Anna.

The boy refuses and wriggles from our clutches. In one deft movement, Anna pulls the reticule from the boy's hand. She steps away to return it to its rightful owner, but the boy's face turns crimson and he pummels at Anna's arm. From the corner of my eye, I see a man rushing to our aid, but he's not fast enough. The boy charges at Anna. I grasp his collar and try to pull him away, but he lifts both legs and thrusts his feet at her, shoving her towards the road. Her foot slips off the edge of the kerb and she sprawls sideways, striking her head on cobbles.

Someone bellows a warning, but it comes too late. A carriage approaches at speed and the horse tramples over Anna's legs, followed by the wheels. The distraught coachman pulls the horse to a halt and hurries back to join us, his gentleman passenger in close pursuit. A scream rings in my ears, piercing and persistent. I realise I am the source and clamp my hands to my mouth. The boy runs away with his bounty.

I rush to Anna's side and join the gentleman kneeling in the filth. The gentleman places his ear above her mouth, then presses the side of her neck. His expression is grave. He removes his jacket and spreads it across Anna's upper body.

'No!'

The gentleman stops me from pulling the jacket away. 'She's alive,' he says. 'But we must act fast.'

I nod, shedding tears in big drops which merge with damp cobbles.

'My friend is a gifted surgeon. I'll take her to him.'

'Thank you,' I say between gulping sobs. 'She has a son.' After that, I can say no more.

'I'll pay the surgeon's fees,' he says. 'It's the least I can do. A tragic accident. I'm so very sorry.'

He helps his coachman lift Anna's limp body into the carriage, and I follow them inside. It's opulent, but I pay little attention. All I can think about is Anna.

After a ten-minute journey, we come to a halt. The

gentleman pats my hand. The gesture is kind, reassuring, but sets tears flowing again.

'Is there someone who can comfort you? You shouldn't be alone after an incident like this.'

I mumble Beckey's address and reach for Anna's cold, limp hand. After pleading with God to save her, I sit back and wait for two orderlies to lift her onto a stretcher and carry her towards the hospital entrance. The gentleman instructs the coachman to take me to Beckey's, then hurries after the orderlies. There's a large pool of blood in the carriage, and I wonder if Anna has enough left to survive.

George sits curled on my lap, his thumb in his mouth. He doesn't understand what has happened to Anna because twice he asked when his maman will come downstairs. Both times I explained that she's not at home, and both times we sobbed together. Now we sit in silence and I stroke his forehead hoping he'll fall asleep.

His head is drifting when a loud knock returns him to full wakefulness. 'Maman?' he asks with a smile.

'Not this time,' I say.

We hurry along the corridor, hand in hand, to see who is disturbing us at this late hour.

I open the door to find William standing on the doorstep.

Tears prick at my eyes. 'William, forgive me, the dinner slipped my mind.'

His brow furrows. 'Susan, has something happened?' He looks from me to George then back to me again.

I nod and beckon him to enter. We return to the parlour and I settle in my chair with George snuggled against me. William sits opposite and waits for me to speak.

George slumps in his sleep, and I tell William in brief whispers about Anna's dreadful injuries. He listens attentively, then takes George from my lap, instructing me not to move while he puts George to bed. When he returns, he pulls his chair near to mine and we sit facing one another, holding hands.

'What am I to do?' I exclaim between sobs.

'Concentrate on the boy for now. Anna's strong. She'll pull through.'

'But she'll never walk again. She can't come home because of the steps to the front door and kitchen. She'd be a prisoner here, stuck in one room.'

William gives an encouraging smile. 'I have an idea. It'll take time to organise but should be ready before Anna leaves hospital.'

'This changes everything, doesn't it? For us, I mean.'

William wrinkles his brow. 'How so?'

'Anna will need someone to care for her. She won't be capable of work.'

'Will she be able to embroider and sew?'

I know Anna well. She has a determined nature and will want to earn a wage if she can. 'I suppose so. But she'll need help to wash and dress and prepare her meals, and I won't abandon her.'

'I should hope not,' says William, a sad smile settling on his lips.

'Go home,' I say. 'Send my apologies to your mother. She'll be wondering what has happened.'

'She'll understand.'

William kisses me lightly on the cheek before saying goodbye. When he turns his back towards me and walks away, I wonder if I'll ever see him again.

CHAPTER 50

GEORGE LOOKS adorable in sky-blue trousers and matching jacket. He stands on a chair, peering through the window.

'Is the coach here?'

He shakes his head and clambers down from the chair. 'Maman's not here either.'

I move across to him and scoop him up in my arms. 'No, George. Maman isn't here. Maman is still in hospital, but she's getting better and should be home soon.'

We hear the distant clatter of wheels. George wriggles from my arms and runs to the window.

'It's here,' he cries. He rushes back to me and grasps my hand. 'Aunt Susan, hurry!'

I scurry to the door as eagerly as George. Ten weeks have passed since I last saw William, so it was a surprise to receive an invitation to join Mrs Westcott for the afternoon. I'm apprehensive about seeing William again, but I'm resolved to my change of fate and enjoying caring for George until Anna resumes mothering him again.

It's the first time George has visited Mrs Westcott's home

and his eyes confirm he's overwhelmed by the attention. Jane makes a particular fuss of him, and I suspect it's because of the child growing in her swollen belly. Once upon a time I might have envied her. Not any more, with George in my life.

'Time for the surprise,' says Mrs Westcott, clapping her hands and beaming.

William sidles from the parlour and an expectant hush settles while we wait for his return. When he re-enters, he's pushing a large wheeled contraption covered with a thin sheet. He parks it in the centre of the room, then removes the sheet with a flourish. There is Anna, resplendent in a new blue dress, sitting in an invalid chair. Her cheeks are flushed, and she's smiling.

I can't believe what I'm seeing. My gaze switches from her to William. William smiles.

George rushes to his mother's side, and Anna tousles his hair.

'Soon you'll be able to sit on my lap and ride around with me,' she says with a chuckle.

George grins and nestles against her arm.

My smile fades.

'What is it, my love?' says William, perching on the arm of my chair.

'What you did for Anna is remarkable, and I'm sure she's grateful, but our home is too small for the chair. We can move furniture to make space for her to move about, but I fear the novelty of being trapped in one room will soon wear off and she'll feel like a prisoner in her own home.'

William fidgets beside me. After a brief pause he says, 'Susan, may we speak in private?'

I have been dreading this. His letters at Paternoster Row became less frequent, and although the dust has settled since

Arthur's departure, William has made many excuses for being unable to spend time with me. I drag myself to my feet and catch Mrs Westcott looking at me as we are about to leave the room. She averts her gaze and beckons to George.

William and I cross the hallway and step into a room I've not seen before. It's a large study and I'm struck by the masculinity of it. The striped curtains are crimson and cream, the desk a rich mahogany polished to a high sheen. Bookcases line the walls with four long shelves devoted to matters of law. A stack of papers sits on the desktop next to a quill and half-full bottle of ink. This room is well-used.

'Is this your office?' I ask, wondering if William lives in his mother's house. I'd assumed we met here for the sake of propriety.

He nods. 'I'm not ashamed to say that, although in my thirties, I still live with my mother. As a bachelor, it was more convenient than living on my own.'

'Oh, I see.'

'No, I don't think you do. There's something I wish to tell you.'

I take a deep breath and chew my top lip, bracing myself for disappointing news. Whatever he says, I must stay strong for Anna's sake.

'I resigned from Bow Street to pursue a career in law. I've been studying texts for over two years now and recently secured a junior position within a law firm.'

'When do you start?'

'Next month. It will involve long working days and I must study in the evenings and during days off.'

'You sound determined.'

'I am.'

He's letting me down gently and I appreciate that.

'There's something else.'

I brace myself for confirmation of our parting.

'The position's not in London.'

I stare at the opposite wall, trying to focus on the geometric pattern of the paper. The lines soften and swirl as my vision blurs. 'So you'll not have many opportunities to visit?'

'I'm afraid not. Susan, I have money and plenty of it, thanks to my father's sound investments before he died, so I've bought a house. It's not a large property, but it's attractive with plenty of rooms for family and visitors.'

'I'm thrilled for you.'

William places a finger beneath my chin. His eyes are sparkling, his lips parted in a smile. 'You haven't heard the best of it yet.'

I force myself to meet his gaze but say nothing.

'The house comes with two smaller buildings in its grounds. One would make an ideal venue for workrooms and a small shop. It's close enough to the town to attract customers, but far enough away to provide plenty of outdoor space for George.'

'Why do you mention George?' His words float around me, making no sense.

'The other building is a single storey. I've had workmen convert it to a home. It's modest but will accommodate Anna's new chair. Anna is a dear friend to you, and I believe she will make an excellent business partner.'

'I don't understand.' I'm confused by talk of workrooms, Anna and George.

'Ask where the house is,' he teases.

'Where is it?'

'Lincoln,' he says, grinning.

'Why there? You have no association with Lincoln.'

'Ah, but dearest Susan, I do. It's near Horncastle, and I made it my business to make your father's acquaintance. We got along well, and he both approved and blessed my proposals.'

'William, what are you saying?'

'My love, I want you to move with me. I promise to always love and respect you, and I will never hurt you. Susan, I want you to become my wife.'

I don't know what to say. I replay his words over and over in my mind, and each time they mean the same. 'You're asking me to marry you?'

'I am. Will you?'

I was Arthur's second Mrs Thistlewood. If I accept, I will become William's first Mrs Westcott and the thought fills me with joy.

'There's nothing I would love more than to spend the rest of my life with you, William. I accept.'

We seal the arrangement with a tight embrace before William draws himself away. 'I nearly forgot.' He opens the top drawer of the desk. 'I have a gift for you.'

He gives me a cream-coloured package secured with a shimmering golden bow. I place it on the desk and untie the ribbon before removing the paper. Inside is an exquisite box, the size of my palm. The lid is smooth with vibrant yellow daffodils painted on enamel and a plain gold trim around the edge.

'It's wonderful. Thank you.'

'Open it,' he says, grinning.

I lift the lid and gasp. A delicate brooch twinkles at me with tiny topaz bluebells catching the light. Stems are fashioned from tiny emeralds and the delicate posy is surrounded with a silver metal ribbon embossed with diamonds. William removes the brooch and fastens it to the bodice of my dress. I study the remaining contents of the box, and I know this man truly loves me.

Sugar plums.

AFTERWORD

Thank you for reading this book. If you enjoyed the story, please help other readers discover it by leaving an honest review on Amazon, Goodreads, or your favourite bookstore's website.

You might also enjoy my other novels:
Running With The Wind
The Winter Years

Have you joined the Allium Books Readers Club?

Members receive a monthly newsletter, advance notification of my new releases, and a FREE downloadable short story. If you'd like to know more about this club, visit my website at www.dionnehaynes.com.

SELECT BIBLIOGRAPHY

If you'd like to read about the Georgian and Regency eras or the Cato Street Conspiracy, these are the books I particularly enjoyed while researching this novel:

Behind Closed Doors, At Home In Georgian England – Amanda Vickery

Eavesdropping On Jane Austen's England – Roy & Lesley Adkins

Georgian London, Into The Streets – Lucy Inglis

Fashion In The Time Of Jane Austen – Sarah Jane Downing

The Georgians In 100 Facts – Mike Rendell

Enemies Of The State, The Cato Street Conspiracy – M. J. Trow

An Authentic History Of The Cato Street Conspiracy; With The Trials At Large Of The Conspirators – George Theodore Wilkinson, Esq.

ACKNOWLEDGMENTS

I'm grateful to my husband, Paul, for encouraging my love of writing, for listening to my ramblings about characters and scenes, for reading early drafts (even though there are no Romans featured in any of my plots) and for putting the sunshine into every day.

Charlie, my son, is a constant source of moral support. I couldn't ask for a better motivator when days are less productive than I'd like them to be. Thank goodness for mobile phones and FaceTime.

Next, huge gratitude to my mum. Not only does she read and reread early drafts, but she copes with lengthy conversations about my writing progress and acts as a sounding board when I'm wrestling with a plot. My mum was critically ill while I was writing the first draft of this novel, but her bravery and confidence were inspiring during that difficult time. Thankfully, she enjoys good health again now, and I hope I've learned to face uncertainty with similar fierce determination!

When writing a novel, the author can get too close to the story and stop seeing the flaws. I'd therefore like to thank

Louise Walters for her superb editorial input and guiding me towards a sturdier story structure. Susan would have been a lesser character without Louise's input.

An important word of thanks goes to Beverley Sykes from superscriptproofreading.co.uk for providing a top quality final buff and polish to the text of this story. Any remaining errors are mine, and mine alone!

My fellow writers at the Plymouth Writers Group deserve a mention. Each month we work on assignments and their reactions and feedback are so helpful. Special thanks goes to Veronica Bright and John Ashby for reading and critiquing this story before I approached the final edit.

The museum at No. 1 Royal Crescent, Bath, England, inspired settings and scenes within this story. The property encapsulates the splendour of Georgian life for the wealthy and was a template for Beckey and Samuel's home. I visited No. 1 on a sodden spring day, expecting my visit to last an hour or two. The volunteers were so knowledgeable and enthusiastic that I spent four hours in the house writing notes, taking photos and enjoying the stories and anecdotes. (https://no1royalcrescent.org.uk/explore/ has wonderful images of the rooms.)

Book cover designer, Robin Vuchnich, has created a magnificent image, sure to catch the eye of readers. Sincere thanks to her for capturing the essence of this tale in her creation.

And thanks to you for reading this story. May it inspire you to overcome difficult situations and remain hopeful in the face of adversity.

Made in the USA
Coppell, TX
28 March 2022

75684637R00184